The Prince and the Arc

THE PRINCE AND THE ARCHER

Book 8 in the Lord Edward's Archer series

By Griff Hosker

The Prince and the Archer

Published by Sword Books Ltd 2024

Copyright ©Griff Hosker First Edition

The author has asserted their moral right under the Copyright, Designs and Patents Act, 1988, to be identified as the author of this work.

All Rights reserved. No part of this publication may be reproduced, copied, stored in a retrieval system, or transmitted, in any form or by any means, without the prior written consent of the copyright holder, nor be otherwise circulated in any form of binding or cover other than that in which it is published and without a similar condition being imposed on the subsequent purchaser.

A CIP catalogue record for this title is available from the British Library.

Contents

Prologue	7
Chapter 1	9
Chapter 2	23
Chapter 3	37
Chapter 4	47
Chapter 5	56
Chapter 6	65
Chapter 7	73
Chapter 8	85
Chapter 9	94
Chapter 10	106
Chapter 11	115
Chapter 12	127
Chapter 13	135
Chapter 14	148
Chapter 15	156
Chapter 16	166
Chapter 17	178
Chapter 18	189
Epilogue	197
Glossary	204
Historical Note	206
Other books by Griff Hosker	208

The Prince and the Archer

Real characters who are mentioned in the novel.

King Edward - King of England and Lord of Aquitaine and Gascony
Queen Margaret of England
Edward of Caernarfon - Prince of Wales
Edmund Crouchback - 1st Earl of Lancaster and King Edward's brother
Thomas 2nd Earl of Lancaster - son of Edmund Crouchback
Henry Lacy - Earl of Lincoln and Constable of Chester
William de Beauchamp - 9th Earl of Warwick
Walter Langton - Bishop of Coventry and Lincoln and the King's Treasurer
Robert de Brus - 6th Lord of Annandale and Earl of Carrick and latterly King Robert 1st of Scotland
John Balliol - Lord of Galloway and Barnard Castle and, latterly, King of Scotland
John (Red) Comyn - claimant to the Scottish throne, supporter of Balliol and enemy to de Brus
Antony Bek - Bishop of Durham
Sir John de Warenne - 6th Earl of Surrey and John Balliol's father-in-law
Andrew Murray (Moray) - one of the Scottish leaders of the rebellion against King Edward
William Wallace - one of the Scottish leaders of the rebellion against King Edward
William Heselrigg - Sheriff of Lanark
Henry Percy - 1st Baron Percy
Henry de Beaumont - French Mercenary
Sir John Stewart - Commander of the Scottish bowmen at the Battle of Falkirk
Sir John de Graham - Wallace's second in command at the Battle of Falkirk
Sir John Menteith of Ruskie and Knapdale - Sheriff of Lennox
Arnaud de Gabaston - the father of Piers Gaveston
Piers Gaveston - a favourite of Prince Edward
Aymer de Valence - Earl of Pembroke
Robert de Clifford - Lord Warden of the Marches
Roger Mortimer, 3rd Baron Mortimer of Wigmore, 1st Earl of March
Roger Mortimer, 1st Baron Mortimer of Chirk, the uncle of Roger Mortimer
Lady Hawise ferch Owain ap Gruffudd ap Gwenwynwyn - heir to Powys and known as Hawise the Hardy
Griffith de la Pole - heir to Powys Wenwynwyn and elder brother of Lady Hawise

The Prince and the Archer

Dedication

To Linda: you are a brave lady. Be strong.

England in 1300

The Prince and the Archer

Prologue

It had taken me a long time, longer than either King Edward or I intended, but William Wallace had finally been captured. The Scottish symbol of independence had asked for a chance to die by combat, I think to give him a warrior's death, but it had not worked and my strength had disarmed him and my sword wounded him. My duty done I took him prisoner and delivered him to Berwick. Others would claim the credit for his capture but I did not mind. I had suffered enough notoriety in my life and now, as I grew older, I hoped for a quieter life. King Edward was getting old and, I sensed, weary.

As I sat in the castle at Berwick I contemplated my future. Now it was over and I could go back to my home in Yarpole. I had done that which had been asked of me. I had been the archer King Edward had used since I had been a young man who had been wanted for murder. I could have been hanged as a common criminal but the young prince had saved me and our lives had been tied ever since. I could not refuse a command for blood and war bound us. I was still the king's man and I would remain so until the end.

Instead of being allowed to travel home I was thwarted, for instead of heading directly to Yarpole I was asked to escort Wallace to Guisborough. It was one of the manors owned by the de Brus family. I would be travelling south and it was on the way home so it was an easy order to obey. The trouble was that travelling with just my men I could have reached home far more quickly.

The longer journey meant I was with Wallace for a longer time than I had intended. He seemed to like me and that was perverse for I had hunted and captured him. He felt betrayed by those he had trusted and by other Scotsmen. I was English and an enemy but he seemed to think that I had treated him fairly. John de Menteith would get the credit for his capture and he was Scottish. It was one of Wallace's own men, Jack Short, who betrayed Wallace. Wallace had killed his brother and it was his vengeance. The result was that William Wallace would not speak to any other on the way to Guisborough except to me. We reached the River Tees and I thought that my duty was over. I could regain my life after my years hunting the giant Scotsman.

The Prince and the Archer

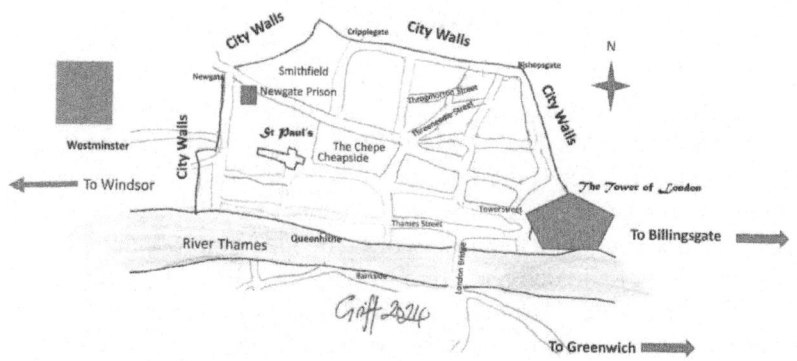

The Prince and the Archer

Chapter 1

August 1305

I did not manage to reach my home after we fulfilled the task appointed by the king. We left Wallace at Guisborough and headed for Lincoln for that was the easiest and quickest way home. I did not relish a ride over the high moors that were the spine of England. It would be quicker to go to Lincoln and then head west. We had much to talk about on the road. We had captured the elusive William Wallace and the long hunt was over. None of us felt good about it. As Dick said, "All that he was doing, my lord, was fighting for his land. He did not attack England, at least not in the last years. He was an enemy but you do not execute your enemies when they have surrendered."

I nodded, "I agree with you but this is not about right and wrong. Wallace is a symbol. The people respect him far more than Comyn, Balliol and even de Brus. While he lives the Scots will never submit to English rule and King Edward wants an end to this troublesome thorn. I think that Wallace knew that and wished me to kill him in combat."

Harry said, "I can't see why they want the place. It is full of midges and the people who live there are too poor to tax. Now, defending Gascony and Aquitaine I can understand. They are rich places and worth fighting for, but Scotland? None of us filled our purses and the armour that we found was only fit for melting down to make horseshoes."

My man at arms was right. Our soldiers were paid for their service and wars and battles normally meant profit for them. My men were good. They never lost and were skilled at avoiding any wounds or hurts. War to them was a necessary business. I was not a warlord and did not take my men to raid for profit. When we warred it was for England and the king or to protect our homes.

We took the easier road west from Lincoln, through Nottingham and Derby. There was still high ground but there were more castles and places for us to stay. The castles were good and my name alone would give us comfortable accommodation. We enjoyed a fine meal at Conisborough Castle as we broke our journey. John de Warenne was descended from a long line of warriors. He was a young lord and yet to be knighted. He spent the whole meal asking me about the wars in which I had fought as well as the leaders I had met. His questions meant that we did not enjoy an early night of sleep and we rose later than I wished. The rider who came from London was happy to have found me still within the walls of that mighty castle.

The Prince and the Archer

"I was told at Lincoln that you had headed west, Sir Gerald, and I have ridden hard to catch up with you." I nodded. "My lord, King Edward seeks your attendance in London at Westminster Palace. He wishes you to attend the trial of the traitor, William Wallace."

I groaned inwardly. I had no wish to see a mockery of a trial but I could not afford to upset King Edward. "Wallace is still in the north. The trial cannot take place yet. I have time to go to Yarpole, have I not?" I could see that the pursuivant was torn. The king had given him a command but he was talking to an old dog of war who had a tendency to snap and growl. I made it easy for him, "I have no fine clothes with me and the king will wish to see me attired well for such a trial. Yarpole will add just three days to the journey and Wallace will not be travelling quickly. You may return to the king and tell him that his faithful archer will be in London before the trial begins."

Defeated he said, "Yes, my lord."

We rode hard and covered the one hundred and ten miles that remained in less than two days. I was exhausted and my rump felt like a well-beaten piece of beef but it meant I could spend a night at home with my wife. I also got to see Jack's recently born son, John. Hamo had returned to his home so the meal I enjoyed with my wife, foster son and his family was cosy.

I told them of the command and my wife rolled her eyes. She and Queen Eleanor had been close, "The queen would have chided the king for his demands. Your presence is unnecessary." She squeezed my hand, "I had hoped to have you at home for a little while."

I sighed, "I was the man who captured Wallace. I can understand the reason for my summons but I agree, the king is being unreasonable." My home was somewhere I could speak openly and honestly. "The king has a son who disappoints. Perhaps he might change but…the king trusts me and I am flattered that he often seeks my opinion on matters of import. He likes to think of me as his common touchstone. He may not like all my answers but he knows they are truthful. My presence at the execution is an excuse, he wants to speak to me. I will go."

Jack nodded, he was eating one handed for he had been wounded in the hunt for Wallace, "And I will come with you."

I snorted, "I have no time to look after a one-armed warrior. Stay here and let Robert tend to you. Enjoy the time with your son. I will take Harry. He is experienced and might enjoy a few days in London."

Harry had not taken a wife and I knew the taverns and whorehouses around the palace of Westminster would be a lure for him. Yarpole was a small place and Harry was too much of a gentleman to sully a maid.

The Prince and the Archer

He and I got on well. There would be no unnecessary words and we could ride hard. He would be the perfect companion.

My wife went to pack a bag for me and I sat and enjoyed some wine. My body ached from the hard ride and another three days of hard riding lay ahead. My body did not recover quickly from such exertions these days. I had seen more than sixty summers. My father had been murdered when he had seen barely fifty. By rights, I should have died many times already. Something always kept me alive. All that I really wanted was to enjoy my old age, but so long as King Edward lived I knew that I would have to follow my fate. The king was a little older than I was and had been luckier than me. The assassin in the Holy Land had almost ended his life and he had survived many close encounters in battle. He did not shirk combat. Our lives were so intertwined that I knew I could not escape my destiny.

We took a good sumpter with us to carry my clothes and all that I would need. Time was I would have been happy to use any horse but times had changed and I now had a stable of good horses including coursers and war horses. My stable master chose one that had not endured the northern campaign and was fresh. He picked one that could carry me and my weight easily. Neither of us was mailed but we took our swords. We left as the sun rose. August meant days that were very long and we used every moment to hasten to London. We stopped regularly to rest horses and buttocks and we had to sleep wherever we could be accommodated. Fine castles such as Conisborough were not so readily available.

We reached Westminster on the 15th of August. The horses had been well chosen and managed the journey well. Wallace had yet to arrive. I was given a room in the palace and I let Harry find an inn in the city. I would not need him and he told me he would send word to me when he had found one. After changing from my travelling clothes and using the water provided to bathe for I stank as badly as my horse, I went to the Great Hall. King Edward was in a small room off the main court and I joined those who were seeking an audience with the king. They hung around the court for hours, some waited for days, in the hope of having the opportunity to present a petition to the king. Until Wallace was tried they would have little hope. I found a niche away from the would-be petitioners. I waved over a servant and said, "Wine, if you would be so kind."

The steward at the door, Edmund, must have told him who I was for he said, "Yes, Sir Gerald."

My sour face ensured that none of the petitioners came over to attempt to speak to the grizzled old, and almost deformed, man. I was an archer and they would dismiss me as a man who was of no importance.

When Sir Richard of Craven, the former pursuivant entered, they were like seagulls that see a morsel to devour. They flocked around him. I smiled for he looked noble and was dressed well. Even my best clothes hung on me awkwardly as though they were ashamed to be on my body. He suited the fine raiments he wore. He spied me and brushed aside the petitioners, "Sir Gerald, I wondered if you would be here."

The servant brought the wine and I nodded at Sir Richard, "And one for Sir Richard, if you would be so kind."

"Yes, my lord."

"I was summoned, Richard, and you?"

"The king also asked me to come but I know not why. It was you and Sir John who captured Wallace."

I had little time for the opportunist John de Mentieth and I snorted, "Sir John was present, aye, but I saw little action from him. Will Wallace be housed here?"

He nodded as the servant brought his wine, "He will and when he is found guilty he will be taken to the Tower."

"Better to simply slit his throat and be done with him. He does not deserve that but a mockery of a trial is also wrong."

"The king wants to show London his power. There will be a trial and a public humiliation." Sir Richard had been a pursuivant and understood politics and the nature of people far better than I did. I was a warrior.

I shook my head, "You are too young to remember, Sir Richard, but when we fought de Montfort at Lewes, it was the fickle Londoners who drew The Lord Edward away. I neither trust nor like them."

He laughed, "It is refreshing to speak to you, Sir Gerald, for you are both blunt and honest. You tell the truth and care not who is offended."

I shrugged and downed the wine, holding my goblet up for a refill, "It is the only way to be. Why hide behind a false face and words that belie their meaning?" I smiled at the young knight, "And do you still serve the king?"

"No, Sir Gerald. He has rewarded me. The Romille family has died out and Skipton Castle needs a firm hand. Sir Robert de Clifford needs to be in Carlisle Castle and I am appointed Constable of Skipton. I will watch Bowland and Craven. It is close to where I was born and I am content. It feels as though I am returning home."

"A fine castle."

"It is but I still hope to be rewarded with a manor. Now that the war is over men will be punished and the king may have a manor to give to deserving knights." He waved his goblet around the crowded room, "It is why there are so many men here now."

I was a cynic, "It is a pity they were not in the north to fight the Scots. Had they been they might deserve a reward." I saw Bishop Langton and a clerk emerge from the room used by the king. There was a buzz around the room as men discussed who was next to visit with the king.

It was as the servant brought our wine that the pursuivant who had come to Conisborough approached us, "Sir Gerald, Sir Richard, the king seeks your company. If you would follow me."

I took the freshly poured wine and downed it in one. The servant's mouth dropped open.

King Edward was in a small chamber just off the main hall. There were two bodyguards with him. They knew me and I nodded back at their smiling greetings. As long as King Edward's infamous archer was in the room then the king would be safe.

He looked up and I thought he looked a little gaunt. I had known him since he was a young man and I had watched time take its toll. His eyes, however, were just as sharp and I knew his mind would be too.

He growled, "Sit, I cannot crane my head to look up at you and I know that Warbow wants a seat."

"Thank you, King Edward, thoughtful as ever."

He gave me a searching look as though wondering if I was being sarcastic. We sat.

"Firstly, I wish to thank you, Warbow, for bringing in the traitor. That was well done. When I was told of the capture I knew that it was you and not de Menteith who achieved it." I nodded. "Craven, I will not keep you long. I want you to visit Wallace." He handed him a parchment, "Here is a pass. I would have him make this trial easy. Take parchment with you and have him write a confession for all his misdeeds."

Sir Richard took the parchment but frowned, "Will he do that, King Edward?"

"If we do not ask then we shall never know. The trial is set for the twenty-fifth of this month. Let him know that and tell him that if he agrees I will allow a confessor into his cell." He waved a dismissive hand. Sir Richard rose and backed out of the chamber. "You two, wait without."

The two bodyguards snapped to attention and left us. I noticed that there was no scribe or clerk in the room and that was unusual. Kings like records of conversations. We were alone and whatever passed between us would be secret.

The Prince and the Archer

The king seemed to relax once they had gone. He nodded to the small table, "Pour us some wine. I need to speak to you."

I did so. I would sip this wine. I had guzzled the other wine too quickly. It would not do to become drunk for there lay the danger of unprompted words or thoughts spoken by a drink-befuddled mind.

We sat in silence and he studied me. "We are old you and I. Others have died yet we live. My cousin, Henry of Almain, was a more devout man and yet he was murdered whilst still a young man. What might he have achieved? My poor wife was taken before her time. Yet you and I survive. Has God a purpose for us? Is the taking of Scotland intended?"

I did not think for one moment that God wished us to burden Scotland with an English overlord but I prudently remained silent.

"If so," he continued, "I fear that it will be my son who finishes the task I have begun." I could not disguise my face. It was not in my character. He chuckled, "Your face, Warbow, is as a book where men can read your thoughts. You do not think much of my son."

"I did not say that but he is young and has little experience in war."

"I was younger than he when I was winning victories." He paused and looked up at me, "but then I had you at my side." He drank some wine and then fixed me with his hawk-like stare, "I wish you to be a mentor for my son."

I shook my head, "I do not think he likes me, my lord. You ask me to be a mentor. I can only advise if one is willing to listen. I am too old to learn new ways, my lord, and Prince Edward is a man grown. I cannot shape a mind that is already formed."

"You are a good father, Warbow. Hamo is well thought of and that boy, Jack, you took under your wing has impressed many older knights. You moulded them. Do the same with Edward."

"They were my family, my lord, and I began to train them when they were still unmoulded clay. Your son is almost fixed in his ways."

"You are right, he may not like you, but he must respect your skill. I will ask him to take you to war as his captain of archers when we next go to war."

"But now you have Wallace, my lord, the Scots are cowed. Balliol is no more and Comyn is not a threat." I paused, "De Brus, it seems to me, is the one to fear. He bows the knee but I think he is ambitious."

"You are a clever man and see things as I do. Men who take you for a simple archer from common stock underestimate you." He smiled, "I agree and it is another reason I want you close to my son. De Brus is clever. If we had to fight him then it would be your archers who would achieve the victory."

The Prince and the Archer

I spied hope in his words, "So, I would not be needed for some time?"

"We get the trial over. Go home and enjoy your family. In the spring we shall muster an army and make Scotland secure. Then you can be my son's advisor."

"Yes, my lord."

"And the manor at Sadberge…"

I had not acknowledged the recent gift and I realised it was remiss of me, "Thank you for the gift, my lord."

He smiled. It was the smile of a wolf, "Warbow, the manor is to place you close to the border. Enjoy your time at home for I wish you to visit your new manor. De Brus has a manor not far away at Guisborough. Visit with him and let him know that King Edward has placed a guard dog close to him."

"Visit him?"

"If he knows that King Edward has sent his dog of war to his threshold then it may curb his ambitions. Besides, when we muster the army it will not be in the northwest but in the northeast. I am giving you a shorter journey from your new manor." He waved a hand, "You are dismissed. Enjoy London and the trial. Send in my guards."

I was dismissed and I left. "The king wishes you within."

"Thank you, Sir Gerald." They returned to their post inside the room.

While the door was open I heard him shout, "Someone fetch me Bishop Langton." The bishop was his treasurer. The poor man had just emerged shortly before I was admitted.

I headed back to the hall. It was late in the day and most of the petitioners had gone.

Harry was waiting at the door for me. I walked over to him, "I found an inn, Sir Gerald, *'The Peauterpotte'* in Cheapside."

"Does it suit?"

He grinned, "They serve rabbit as well as steak and oyster pie and the doxies still have all their teeth. It suits, Sir Gerald."

I nodded, glumly, he would have the best of it. "The trial is set for the twenty-fifth. You have until then to indulge your appetites."

He patted his purse, "And I have the means to enjoy myself. What else would I do with my coins? They are for me to enjoy."

I liked Harry. He knew that death could come at any moment for he was a warrior. With no family to worry about and a secure income from me, he could indulge himself in the pleasures of the flesh.

The king dined in the Great Hall but the ones who were seated close to him were his great lords: Aymer de Valence, the Earl of Pembroke,

The Prince and the Archer

Henry de Lacy, the Earl of Lincoln, Guy de Beauchamp, the Earl of Warwick and Robert de Clifford the Lord Warden of the Marches, as well as Bishop Langton, were all seated on either side of the king. They were, the bishop apart, all warriors and close to the king. None of them were courtiers. I sat at the lowly end of the table. Richard of Craven joined me. After the Bishop of Westminster had said Grace and the food was fetched, we spoke.

"Well, Richard, were you successful? Did you manage a confession which would save a trial?" I spoke quietly so that the lords close by would not overhear.

He shook his head as he took the grilled fish cooked in a lemon sauce from the platter before us. He spoke as quietly as I had, "He told me he had no sins to confess for he had not committed one since his last confession. He said that he has done no wrong and cannot understand why he is a prisoner."

I laughed, "I know that he does not believe that and so is guilty of the sin of mendacity. He fought against the king and should be punished."

"He has asked to speak to you."

"Me?"

"He respects you, Sir Gerald. He showed me the scarred hand that came from the combat. He regards it as a bond between you." I nodded. "I told the king of his decision and his request."

"And?"

He shrugged as he sucked the flesh from the bones of the succulent river fish. After he had washed the fish down with wine he wiped his mouth and said, "You know the king as well as I do but I think he will use you to get Wallace to confess."

"And that will never happen. Wallace is a warrior and a strong man. He could have stayed abroad and lived well but he chose to return to Scotland to fight the king. He will break but he will not bend."

It was the day before the trial when the pursuivant sought me out again. I was by the river watching the wherries as they sailed up and down to London Bridge. "Sir Gerald, the king would have you visit with William Wallace. He said you would know what was expected." King Edward had fixed Sir Richard and I with his eye at the meal. He knew that Richard would have told me all. Kings liked to play games.

I nodded knowing there was no way I could avoid this duty, "Lead on, pursuivant."

The cell was below the first floor and adjacent to the stores used for the storage of food. Two guards stood without. One said, "Your weapons, Sir Gerald."

The Prince and the Archer

I said, "Do you think he could take them from me?"

The man shook his head, "No, my lord, but it is the king's command." I sighed and took off the baldric and handed it to him. "When you are ready to leave just call and we will unlock the door." I nodded.

The pursuivant said, "I am waiting with a scribe for the confession." It was then that I noticed, in the corner, the tonsured man with ink-stained hands. I knew he would not be needed.

The door was unlocked and I could smell Wallace as I entered. He had not bathed since I had fought him and he stank. He was seated at a chair next to a table. A single tallow candle flickered giving off a smoky flame. It had burned halfway down and I guessed that the guards would ensure there was always one burning so that they could see him. There was a paillasse on the floor and next to the door was the piss pot. It stank of urine. I doubted that they would feed him enough to make much night soil. The door shut behind me and I heard the ominous turning of the key. I would be allowed out but I knew the effect of its turning would have on Wallace. When I had first come across him, all those years ago, he had been a bandit leader in the forests of Galloway. He liked the outdoors. This would not sit well with him.

He stood and I saw that his head almost touched the low roof. He held out his arm for me to clasp and I took it. His grip was still firm. I saw in the amber light of the candle that he was smiling. "I hoped you would come."

I nodded, "I am responsible for this incarceration and felt duty-bound."

"That is because you are a warrior." He held up the hand I had cut, "This is the clear evidence of that."

"It is healing?"

He gave a sardonic laugh, "It does not really matter, does it, Sir Gerald? We both know that I am doomed to die when this trial is over."

"Then why did you wish to talk to me?"

"Because, before I am sentenced, I would speak with another warrior. My life is like this candle and is reaching its end. The difference is that the candle can be replaced and I cannot. I will go to heaven for I have not sinned but I still wish my country to be free." I said nothing. "Would you fight for England if an oppressor tried to take it?"

"Of course."

"I suspect that you would have more success than I had."

"You did well enough. Stirling Bridge was a great victory."

The Prince and the Archer

"But that was Sir Andrew's victory and not mine. It was English arrows that did for me and you are the complete archer. Our men were brave enough. Our schiltrons kept your horses at bay but without armour, they could not hope to withstand your arrows. I knew we were doomed at Falkirk when your arrows harvested the brave men who fought for me and for Scotland."

I fixed his eye, "You tried to poison me."

He nodded, "And I regret that now. I wanted you dead but my men would not risk a combat. I confessed for that sin as soon as I could and I was glad that you survived." I accepted his words and nodded. "You will be at the trial, tomorrow?"

"The king demands my presence."

"Yet you would not choose to be there."

"No, I would not. You are doomed to die but just as I would not want a wounded hound to suffer so I wish that your end could be swift."

He hung his head, "That it will not be. I am like a pagan sacrifice and it must be a humiliating and painful public demonstration of the king's power." His eyes met mine, "I would like you to be there, at the end, Sir Gerald. Your presence will give me the strength that I need. You and I are similar in so many ways. I should like to look a warrior in the eye when my death is upon me and you are a warrior I respect. Will you do this for me?"

I nodded, "Aye, I will but know that I will not enjoy one moment of it."

We then spoke of our lives for he wished to talk. The candle burned down a little more and it measured the time we were there. The key turned and one of the guards entered, "I am sorry, Sir Gerald, but we need to replace the candle."

I nodded, "It is time I was going." I held out my arm and William Wallace clasped it and gripped it. "Farewell. You are going to a better place where you will be free of pain and this cage."

He nodded, "And you, I fear, are in for a harder time. Thank you for your company, Sir Gerald. You have eased my last hours."

Outside, when I had strapped on my sword, I said to the pursuivant, "Tell the king he would not confess." He nodded and left. I had not asked Wallace to confess for I knew that not only would it be pointless but it would also be dishonourable to do so.

The trial was a forgone conclusion. The king and his lords were dressed in their finery and seemed to mock the stinking rags that Wallace wore. They were the same clothes he had worn in the hut in Scotland when I had captured him. He argued eloquently for his life but I could see in his eyes that he knew it was a waste of time. It was a noble speech and should have earned him a pardon or a swift death at the very least. When the sentence was confirmed he looked, not at the king but at me and our eyes spoke. He nodded and I nodded back. I would be at the execution and I would not shirk from the promise I had made.

The king said, "Sir Gerald, you will lead the prisoner to his cell in the Tower of London."

I did not want to but my conversation with William Wallace made it easier. He would like my company. There were ten sergeants waiting outside for us. They were mailed and wore the king's livery. They held halberds in their hands. They parted to allow the shackled Wallace to stand between them. I pointedly stood next to him. It was not only his hands that were shackled but his feet as well and I said, "Lead on but go steadily. I am an old man and I would not trip and be mocked by these carrion crows."

"Yes, my lord."

Wallace murmured, "Thank you, Warbow." He knew that I had done it for him.

We marched towards the Ludgate. There were crowds gathering already. The sergeants held their halberds to keep them from us. It was a strange experience for they were not, as I had expected, shouting, but there was a buzz, a murmur of conversation as we passed. He was the monster who had destroyed an English army and evaded capture for so very long. I suspect I was almost of as much interest as the prisoner. They would be speaking of us, both notorious in our own ways. I saw Harry as we passed through Cheapside. I marked the inn as he waved. It was a relief to leave the city and enter the Tower. It was still white and rose like a huge monolith, a monument to the ambition of William the Conqueror. It would now be the last resting place of another William whose more understandable ambition had brought him to this.

The constable met us at the base of the Tower and said, "Thank you, Sir Gerald. William Wallace, come with me. There is a confessor waiting."

He nodded and smiled at me, "Thank you, Sir Gerald. I will try to bear all stoically tomorrow."

"May God be with you."

I turned and left. The crowds had largely dispersed but I was stared at. When I reached the tavern where I had seen Harry I said to the sergeants, "I will make my own way back."

"Are you sure, Sir Gerald?"

I laughed, "The day I am afraid of the men of London is the day I will become a priest."

They joined me in the laughter and I headed for the tavern's entrance. As I entered I was noticed and conversation ceased, briefly. Harry was at a table with a jug of ale. I wandered over and Harry shouted, "Another mug." I sat, aware that I was being studied as though I had two heads. "So, it is almost at an end, my lord."

"What is?"

"The hunt."

I nodded as the servant poured some ale into the mug, "Yet the effects will ripple on. We leave on the morrow, Harry, as soon as this is over. I would be rid of this stench that fills my nose."

"Stench, Sir Gerald?"

"Aye, the stench of baying hounds desperate to devour the still-living body of the hunt."

I spent the rest of the day with Harry and we spoke not of the trial or the impending spectacle but of Yarpole and what Harry would do. He waved a hand around the room, "Since I have been here, my lord, I have thought about my future. I have a mind, my lord, to build a tavern like this in Yarpole. With your permission, of course."

I waved an airy hand, "You have it but is there enough trade?"

"I care not if the only trade is myself and the men of your retinue. I am getting old. I have another year or so at most and then there will be someone more skilled or quicker and I will die. I have enjoyed my time here. I have spoken with Bald Peter, the owner, and he has told me all about the pitfalls. He was a warrior too and we have got on. He fought at Lewes, for de Montfort, of course, but that is in the past. He advised me to get a good alewife and that seems to me to be the hardest part. I have gold and I know the place I would choose to build it."

I finished my ale, "Then good luck to your enterprise. You have my blessing. I enjoy a good inn as much as the next man and I know that you will do as good a job as you did when you were a man at arms. I shall have to replace you first though."

"Of course, my lord."

Having spoken to Wallace it would be good to think of a warrior enjoying old age. Harry would not end up butchered on some battlefield but grow old and fat.

The feast in the Great Hall made me feel sick. It was not the food. It was the sound of men baying at the impending death of William Wallace. I saw men whom I knew had done nothing to apprehend him or fight for England, crowing as though they were the Achilles who had defeated him. I retired early.

I had a light breakfast. I needed something in my stomach, I heard gossip at the table about an argument between the king and his son.

The Prince and the Archer

Prince Edward, it seemed, wanted more money. King Edward had argued with his own father, King Henry, about the same thing. Hamo and I had never had a cross word about money. I decided it must be to do with royal blood. The breakfast finished, I followed King Edward and his retinue to the Tower. His sergeants kept the press of the crowds from us. The execution would not take place in the Tower but at Smithfield in the open place there. The king was doing as the Romans had done and giving the people a public spectacle. It was close to St Paul's and, perhaps, the proximity of the cathedral would afford Wallace an easier passage to heaven. I hoped so.

William Wallace was already waiting between the Tower and the Great Hall. He was no longer shackled but there were archers ready to pierce his limbs if he should try to flee. I saw a team of horses waiting nearby, held by a squire. The constable was next to Wallace and when King Edward arrived the constable nodded and said, "Strip him."

We all knew it was coming but it was shocking to me. William Wallace was stripped naked. He stood as proudly as a man whose manhood is bared can stand. I did as William Wallace had asked in his cell and looked him in the eye. He looked defiant. He gave the slightest of nods. The constable said, "Fasten the rope." I saw then that there was a rope attached to the horses and it was tied to his feet. When it was done the constable looked at the king who nodded. "Lead on!" The squire, now aided by two sergeants, led the horses towards St Thomas' gate and the city. It was impossible for William Wallace to keep his feet and he hit the cobbles. By the time we reached Smithfield his back would look as though he had been flogged. I hoped that a cobble might render him unconscious but it did not and I saw the whites of his eyes as he fought the pain.

We followed and entered the city. This time the crowds bayed, hooted, cheered, jeered and laughed. He could not hurt them and he was like a tethered bull baited by snapping hounds. It was as though this was a holiday. I saw the smoke rising above the cathedral as we neared Smithfield. The tar would be heated for the dipping of the skull. Soldiers were keeping back the crowd and a platform had been built. The hooded executioners waited there, the tools of their trade to hand. A worse job than theirs I could not imagine. They would be paid well.

When William Wallace was untied and stood I saw that his back and buttocks were bloody but he pulled himself erect as proudly as he could. He was led up to the platform and when he reached the top he shouted, "Scotland, I die for you." He was rewarded for his defiance with a blow to the head which almost felled him. He was quickly laid on the platform and then the grisly work went ahead. The executioners

The Prince and the Archer

would not risk another outburst. A garrotte was placed about his neck and the executioners pulled on it until Wallace almost expired. They knew their business and they released him before he died. I heard and saw him cough as he sucked in air. A man, especially a warrior, clings to life. The executioners worked quickly. He was first emasculated. The knife that was used had to be incredibly sharp for it was quickly done, and his parts were held up for all to see. Wallace uttered not a sound but the crowd cheered. The razor-sharp blade that tore open his chest might not have hurt but when he was eviscerated and his bowels burnt before him I wondered that he did not shout out. The chief executioner looked over to the king who nodded. I saw Wallace's head turn and knew that he sought me. As the executioner raised his axe our eyes met. The axe ended all of his pain. The head was picked up by the hair and held up for the baying crowd to scream and applaud. The grisly trophy was taken and dipped into tar. The executioner then chopped the body into four parts. The noise from the crowd almost hurt my ears. I could not wait to leave but I had to wait until the king left or risk his wrath.

When the king and his lords had gone, Harry, his bag over his back sidled up to me, "I thought I would be glad when he died but I felt sorry for him."

"As did I. Let us find our horses and leave." We returned to the palace and the stables. We saddled our animals in silence.

As we headed west Harry looked back to the walls of the city and asked, "What happens to his parts now, my lord?"

"His head will be placed on London Bridge and remain there until it is just a skull picked clean of flesh. His limbs will be displayed, separately, in Newcastle, Berwick, Stirling and Perth. They will be a reminder of the folly of opposing King Edward."

We rode in silence and did not speak until Oxford. Both of us had been affected by the execution and neither had enjoyed the spectacle. The ride would, hopefully, clear the stink from us. The horses had been rested and we pushed on.

Chapter 2

Yarpole 1305

I had intended to enjoy my lands but that was not going to be. King Edward's message had been clear. I was to go to my new manor in Sadberge sooner rather than later. We reached my home close to the Welsh border within two days. It was late afternoon as we headed along the road through the village to my hall. The crops were being harvested and with peace in England, Yarpole was a happy place. It was late afternoon as we entered the village with the sun dipping towards the Welsh hills.

Harry and I were greeted with smiles as we clattered through the village. Harry pointed to an empty plot of land. There had been a wooden house there when Mary and I had first arrived in Yarpole but it had become derelict and in the savage storm of 1300 it had finally been destroyed. "My lord, I have a mind to build an inn there." He hesitated, "With your permission, of course."

There was not enough land for it to be a working farm. I had thought to build something there for the empty plot looked unsightly but I could not devise a purpose. Harry provided the best solution. "I told you in London, you shall have it. I will have the documents written. Robert can do that." Robert was the French priest I had saved and who now acted as my doctor and clerk.

"Thank you, my lord."

We entered my walled hall and as I dismounted I asked, "Have you a name for it?"

He grinned, cheekily, "I thought the ***War Bow***, my lord."

I laughed, "Aye, that sounds about right. You have my permission. I see war in the future but not for a while. Make haste, Harry. Plans that are deferred often wither and die. Do not procrastinate lest time is stolen."

The groom came from the stable and took the horses. The door opened and Mary stood there. We were not a great lord and lady. She had been a slave and I had grown up in a tiny house in the Clywyd Valley. Our greeting was open and sincere. We hugged and kissed. Grabbing my arm she led me within, "I am glad that you are home. Come, I have some wine that is chilled and while food is prepared we can enjoy the arbour."

She squeezed my arm as we walked and led me through the house. Anna, a servant, followed us. Mary had been taken as a slave whilst still young but she had remembered the house in which she had grown up. It was much further south than ours and had olive and lemon trees. They would not grow here but, instead, she had planted some apple and cherry trees that were of the dwarf variety as well as a hedge of lavender, rosemary and thyme. The result was she had created at the rear of the house and facing west, somewhere shaded from the sun and yet with the most exquisite of aromas. The wooden bench was cushioned and we enjoyed fine sunsets, as it faced the setting sun.

Anna took my cloak and gauntlets, "I will bring some water, my lord."

Mary kissed my forehead, as I sat, "And I shall be the wine steward."

Left alone I enjoyed the sound of the birds and the view of the herb and vegetable garden. Bees and butterflies fussed around the flowers. It was the sound of peace. It was as far from the baying crowds at Smithfield as it was possible to get. I found myself smiling and that was rare. Anna arrived back first with a drying cloth and a bowl of water. I washed my hands and face and dried them. She left as my wife arrived with a tray. There was a jug of wine from my cellar, two goblets as well as bread, ham and cured meats.

"It will take an hour or so to cook your meal, my husband. I know how grumpy you are when you are hungry. This will stave off the pangs."

I smiled and shook my head, "Not so grumpy these days, my love." She handed me the glass and I drank the chilled white wine she liked so much. I preferred red but this was refreshing and I drank half of it in one gulp.

"And while you eat I will tell you all," She sipped her own wine and after placing the goblet on the table spoke, "Susanna and the baby, John, are thriving and Jack, thanks to Robert, is healing. I had a message, while you were away, that Hamo and Alice are both well as are their children. So, you can enjoy peace, here at Yarpole."

I put the goblet down on the table that lay close to the bench and took a hunk of bread and a piece of ham. I shook my head, "I fear that is not the case." As I ate I told her of the execution, although I omitted any details and made my story brief. I also told her of the king's demand for me to train his son and the need to ride north as soon as I was able. "They were not requests, they were orders. I am to try to teach the puppy tricks and also visit my new manor and let de Brus know that I have a home that is close to his."

"You can do it. You moulded his father."

"His father was different. Young Edward is…I do not like him. I do not think he will be a good king."

The Prince and the Archer

I chewed and swallowed and then finished the goblet. As she refilled it she said, "But he will be king and anything that you can do to change him can only aid the people of this land."

I nodded and took the goblet, "And that is why I will obey the order. Before that, I am commanded to visit Sadberge."

"And as that is in the north it will need to be sooner rather than later. You do not want to cross this land in winter."

I sighed, "The end of September is when I shall go. I will take some archers." I looked at my wife. We shared much and I trusted her judgement, "I need a steward."

"Harry?"

Shaking my head I told her of his plans. She laughed, "He will make a perfect innkeeper. Let me see." She sipped her wine and played with my fingers as she thought. "Then it must be Dick."

Dick was one of my best archers. He and Gwillim were my rocks. They led and trained my men. "I am not sure he would relish the role."

She sighed, "He married last year, remember? Betty is young but she has borne him one child and there is another on the way. He is getting old and perhaps it is time for him to enjoy his life."

I remembered that he had married but when we had been in Scotland he had not spoken of his wife. I realised that was my doing. I had never asked him. "Sadberge is a long way north of here."

"And the manor?"

"Small but it brings a good income. The problem is that it is close to Scotland."

"Ask him. If he says no then Gwillim is also getting older. He has no children but perhaps this opportunity might encourage him to take on a new responsibility and give him an occupation."

"You are the best of wives. I will speak to Dick."

Robert dined with us. We did not see ourselves as above those who lived in the house with us and we enjoyed his company. He was a witty man and clever, too. I told him of the execution and my visit north.

"I would come with you, my lord."

"Of course, I enjoy your company but why?"

"I have seen Scotland but not the land north of York. I would like to see the city of York. It is said to retain much of its Roman architecture. You will be passing through it?"

"Aye, for being September we can take the road through Craven. In winter it is impassable and now that Richard of Craven is the constable at Skipton we will have fine accommodation."

"And your new steward?"

"I have yet to choose him."

The Prince and the Archer

It was wonderful to sleep in my own bed and Mary and I snuggled and embraced before we slept. I would make the most of my time at home. After breakfast, the next day, I asked Edgar to arrange a session. There were matters of law to attend to and my absence had built up a backlog. As lord of the manor, I had to arbitrate over land issues as well as administer the law. That would be my task for the next day. That done I headed, with Robert, to Dick's home.

All of my archers and sergeants who were married each had a smallholding. There was a house, a hogbog and enough land to grow food. The unmarried ones lived in my warrior hall. Men like Dick and Michel had a home with enough land to raise crops or animals. Michel had a larger one than the rest. Dick was content with his for he had made many coins serving me and could augment what he grew with food purchased from others. Betty was just seventeen and Dick was more than twice her age but they got on well. As I neared the house I saw her at the door holding their daughter, Maud, as she watched him harvesting the beans. She had the clear bump of an expectant mother.

"A good crop, Dick."

"Aye, my lord, we came back from Scotland just in time. Any longer and Betty would have had to harvest them alone."

She smiled, "I could have managed. I was brought up to be strong. Would you come into our humble dwelling, my lord?"

"No thank you, Mistress Betty, I need to speak with your husband but I would not have him cease in his labours."

I began to help Dick to pick the beans and put them in the willow basket. Robert joined me.

"Dick, you know I have a new manor in Sadberge?"

"I do, my lord."

"How do you feel about being my steward there?"

He looked surprised and pleased but then a frown appeared as he looked at his young wife, "It is an honour, my lord, but Betty…"

His young wife laughed. Her laugh tinkled like a brook, "Do not worry about me, Dick of Yarpole. I, for one, would like to be the wife of a steward but it is your choice to make. You make the decision. I am your wife and I will follow you."

I smiled, "You chose a strong bride, Dick."

He nodded, "Many wondered at the disparity in our ages but she has an old head on her young body. She raised her three brothers when their mother died and held the family together after her father followed." He continued to pick and I did not disturb his thoughts. He was debating within. "We have no ties here. Her brothers serve you and I have no family."

The Prince and the Archer

Betty had three brothers. The eldest, Edward, her twin, was training to be a man at arms. Abel, just fifteen summers, was training to be a groom and the youngest, Joseph, worked in the warrior hall. When he was old enough he would train as a warrior. The three did not need their elder sister.

Betty said, "Maud needs food. I shall take her within. Let me know if you wish for some refreshment, my lord." She was allowing us to talk without her being close. Dick had a good wife.

When she had gone within Dick said, "Is it safe for her in Sadberge, my lord?"

"It is no less safe than here. True, you will have fewer men but Stockton has a fine castle and the Lord Warden of the Marches is a good warrior. Further north you might be in danger but I think that Sadberge could be made defensible."

"Yet you have not seen it, my lord." My Frenchman showed he had been listening.

"No, Robert, but I spoke, while in London, with Sir Richard of Craven who knew the manor and he said that there is a manor house with a ditch around it. The entrance is up a stair and the ladder can be withdrawn."

I saw Dick taking that in. "When would I need to leave?"

I paused in my harvesting, "Ah, there is the rub. You would need to be there well before All Saints Day. When is the baby due?"

"Christmas time."

I said no more. I would not persuade him. He would either accept or I would ask Gwillim.

"Can I ask Joseph to come with me? I will need men."

"Ask any that you wish."

"Archers too, my lord?"

"Archers too."

"Then I will accept." He held out his hand and I clasped it.

"You have not asked how you would be paid."

"You are a fair man, my lord."

"Then you may keep a tithe of the income. I do not know yet the value but I can ascertain that when I visit."

He looked at his fields. The beans were almost harvested and the cabbages and leeks could stay in the ground. "I will need to come with you, my lord."

I nodded, "Lady Mary will watch over Betty. We leave at the end of the week. I have manorial business to attend to first."

"Good, then I can finish the harvest and prepare Betty. There is much to be done."

The Prince and the Archer

As I walked back the two hundred or so paces to the lane, Robert observed, "You are a rare lord, Sir Gerald. You ask and do not command and you are a generous lord. A tithe is a fine income."

"That is because, Robert, I came from nothing. I began life as a man hunted for the murder of a bad lord and I determined that in the unlikely event of my elevation, I would be a better lord. Your words please me for they show that I am close to achieving that."

I ate a fine lunch and visited, first with Hamo and then with Jack. Neither was a hard ride and Robert came with me to attend to Jack. Hamo listened with interest to my tale. "Prince Edward is not his father. Still, with men like de Clifford and de Valence, he has good leaders. Tell me, Father, how will you ascertain the loyalty of de Brus?"

"He is a devious man and I do not trust him. I will see if he can trip himself with words."

"And Sadberge, is it in danger from de Brus?"

I smiled, "Ah, that is the one thing I am sure about. Guisborough is an English manor and has never been Scottish. De Brus may have ambitions in Scotland but he will not give up his richest manor. The Tees is safe from Scottish privations so long as de Brus has Guisborough."

Jack's arm was healing well and I knew that by the New Year, he would be ready to go to war.

Mary was happy to watch over Betty and all was resolved. I spent the next two days administering justice and arbitrating disputes. Despite the fact that I had been absent too long I had few cases. The majority of my tenants were either serving or former soldiers. They got on well and the cases were from those families who had lived in Yarpole when first we had come. There were fewer of them these days as they all knew me and the only cases were ones that needed the judgement of Solomon. I was pleased when they were over. I sat with Edgar to look at the manor's accounts and was satisfied that we were making a healthy profit.

"Pay the archers and sergeants, as well as yourself, an extra five shillings for their good work this past year and the servants can all have sixpence each. They should all be rewarded for their efforts."

"What if the king asks for a tax, my lord?"

I looked at the books, "We have more than enough in reserve." Edgar did not know about the chests I had stored in our bedchamber. I had accumulated gold and treasure whilst serving King Edward. Battlefields were a rich picking ground for a victor. I knew the value of armour and weapons. I had converted my booty into gold. The rings and jewels I had accumulated lay in the chest too. They were my reserve in case the king became greedy as King John had done and began taxing people hard. I could not see that with King Edward but his son…

I spoke with Gwillim. Now that Dick was leaving Gwillim would be my captain of archers and I paid him accordingly. "While we are away I want more archers. Find ten or so."

He nodded, "I will journey into the land of my birth. There are fewer Welshmen now who oppose us than there were and English lords pay more than Welsh ones."

"Harry is leaving me too although not soon. I will have him seek more sergeants."

"We have eight in training my lord, and they are better than those we do not know."

"Aye, you are right. Still, it will not hurt to ask."

Harry was more than willing to seek more men at arms. The extra pay my men had been given was a good enough inducement. Michel and his son were both good men not to mention Alice's brothers, James and John, and I only needed a dozen or so. By the time I was ready to leave, I felt I had done all that I could. I took Hob and Nob with me. They were good archers and close to each other. They were good scouts and reliable. Unlike Gwillim, they had their eyes on maids in the village and, like, Dick, would soon build their own nests. They would sire the archers who would serve Hamo and Jack.

The journey was two hundred miles and would take us five days. Chester now belonged to Prince Edward and that would be our stop for the second night. I knew he would not be there. He and his father were still wrangling about money. We had a sumpter and Robert led it. He had improved as a rider since our first meeting in France but he was not confident in the saddle. He looked like a badly tied piece of luggage. I hoped that leading a sumpter would stop him worrying about falling off.

It was September and the weather, especially in the northwest, could be variable. We had left Chester very early to take advantage of the daylight for the days were still longer than the nights. The rain swept in from the west. It was not particularly cold but it rained all day and I was glad that we all had oiled cloaks. Poor Robert only had a cowl on his cloak while the rest of us had beaver skin hats that kept our heads dry. Archers always kept bowstrings in their hats and chose head coverings that would keep them dry.

After crossing the Maersea at the bridge at Wallintun we stopped in the small manor of Newton to eat something in the shelter of a farmer's barn while we waited for the rain to stop. It did not and by the time we reached Westhalton, we were so weary that we could go no further. We stayed in the manor house. The lord of the manor was absent but his steward recognised my rank and accommodated us.

When we woke to clear skies I was happy and we pushed on to Skipton Castle.

The first thing that impressed me was the gatehouse. It was a castle in itself and its elevated position, not to mention its rocky base made it a very difficult castle to take. The Romille family had liked their comfort and the Great Hall reflected that taste. Sir Richard greeted us at the barbican. The sentries had spotted us from afar.

"Welcome, Sir Gerald, this is an unexpected but welcome pleasure."

"We are heading north to my new manor. Dick is to be my steward."

"My lord." Dick knew Sir Richard from our hunting of the bandit.

Sir Richard shouted, "Egbert, have our guests taken to their chambers."

The steward looked at the three archers somewhat disdainfully, "All of them, my lord?"

Sir Richard snapped, "If I have to constantly repeat my orders then, Egbert of Thorlby, you will have to find other employment."

"Yes, my lord, sorry, my lord. If you would follow me, gentlemen."

Robert said, "I will take your bag, Sir Gerald."

When we were alone Sir Richard said, "An inherited staff, I fear. They have been unsupervised for so long that they think it is their castle." He chuckled, "I will whip them into shape."

"And the garrison?"

"Ah, they are good soldiers all. Sir Robert de Clifford sent me good men and I have both a good squire, Roger, as well as Captain John, my Captain of Sergeants. What I lack is a large number of archers. Having seen yours in action I want to have parity of numbers."

We went into the hall and a servant appeared with refreshments.

"It is a good castle."

"It is and it guards this border. Sir Robert has Brougham and Carlisle to the north and the king's castle at Bowes is strong too."

We sat and I toasted Sir Richard, "Good health and death to the king's enemies."

"Aye, and speaking of enemies, I hear that Robert de Brus is plotting."

My curiosity was piqued, "Plotting?"

"We are at peace yet he is hiring men at arms and drawing lances to him like flies around a dunghill. Why?" He looked at me and the question hung in the air. He continued, "He is mustering them at

The Prince and the Archer

Guisborough rather than in Annandale. That sounds like plotting to me. If he gathered men in Annandale then Comyn would know. The two men do not like each other."

"And King Edward would not like that."

"No, indeed, he would not."

"You think he plans to take the Scottish crown?"

Sir Richard had been a pursuivant and was well versed in such matters. He nodded, "When the male heir of Duncan, Alexander, died there were no male heirs. That allowed King Edward to take control. John Comyn has the strongest claim as he is descended from Duncan's sister. He has another claim too, and that is shared by de Brus. Over a hundred years ago, Fergus of Galloway had two sons by different women, Uhtred and Gilbert. John Balliol and John Comyn are descended from Uhtred and de Brus is from the line of Gilbert. De Brus has a claim, albeit a distant one. Comyn is the one with the best claim."

I reflected on the recent alliance of de Brus and the English. It now made sense. "De Brus helped to eliminate one of the claimants, Balliol, and now he just has John Comyn left. He is a clever man."

"He is and he is not to be underestimated."

"Now I see that King Edward does not trust him either. The king will not be fooled by a fawning face."

"Just so."

"But his son…"

Richard of Craven was astute and he nodded, "Aye."

My men returned with an unhappy-looking Egbert the Steward. Richard dismissed him and the six of us enjoyed ale and wine before we ate. Richard of Craven understood the value of the men I had brought. Robert, of course, was a storyteller and an entertainer. It was he who held court and after one funny story I shook my head, "Robert, you were never meant to be a priest but a court jester would suit you well."

He laughed, "It is true, my lord I like to tell a story and to sing a ballad or a bawdy song but I have a mind which is easily bored. I enjoy being a healer too."

"I am not complaining, Robert, I have the best of it."

By the time we left, not long after dawn, I had a better idea of the land ahead of us. Richard had assured me that de Brus' presence guaranteed peace. Even if he made an attempt on the Scottish crown he would not risk losing his English manors. Dick and Betty would be safe.

Richard's grooms had fed the horses well and we rode a hard fifty miles to York. Though we stayed there but one night Robert got to see the Minster and the Roman walls. We could have saved a day by heading for the river directly from Skipton but I had to speak to the Sheriff of Yorkshire. It was courtesy and he needed to know that there was a new lord in his land. We then headed north, crossing the Tees at the old Roman Bridge of Piercebridge. I had my deeds with me but I hoped I would not need them. Richard of Craven had passed the manor and had described it well. It was a typical border dwelling, situated on the highest part of the huddle of houses that made up the village. I could see why the village had grown where it did. It had a fine view across the Tees Valley and yet was not hilly. The land was largely flat and had been cleared to create fertile fields. The manor house itself was built so that the entrance was up a ladder and the door was the height of a man from the ground. I had seen larger versions in Scotland. It afforded defence and meant the defenders would be safe from an assault. The house was small enough so that attackers would not waste their time on such a place. I saw that there were shutters to the right of the entrance and that suggested a large wind hole. There was a wall running around the outside and it surrounded the other buildings. There was a barn, a hogbog, as well as a cow byre, a stable, a bakehouse and a smaller dwelling. I also saw a pair of hives. That was good. Honey was like gold. I saw, as we passed through the village, no sign of another oven and I deduced that the manor's was used by the village. We were observed, surreptitiously, as we rode towards the open gate. That boded well for being open it showed that there was no danger. The sun was dipping in the west and we urged our horses towards the gates. They were open now but nighttime would surely see them closed and barred.

As we passed through them, a man and a woman, whom I took to be his wife, emerged from the building. He climbed down the ladder. A younger version of him came from the barn. We reined in and I dismounted. My clothes and horse, not to mention my sword marked me as a noble of some description and the man bowed, "Can I help you…my lord?" The younger man, a pitchfork in his hand came to stand close to the man I took to be the steward.

"I am Sir Gerald of Yarpole and King Edward has given me this manor." I did not mention that it was with the total support of the Bishop of Durham, Anthony Bek. This was the Palatinate and the manor was managed from Durham. The next moments would tell me much about the man.

He smiled and I was relieved, "Then I am happy, my lord. It has been some years since there was a lord here. Master Geoffrey died at Stirling Bridge and he had neither wife nor heirs."

"And your name?"

The Prince and the Archer

"I am Alfred and this is my son, David. My wife, Seara is yonder." He turned and waved at the woman who bowed. "My daughter Maryanne is in the kitchen preparing supper." He looked at us apologetically, "We did not know you were coming and…"

I nodded, "We will eat whatever you have. This is Dick and he will be the one who will manage the manor for me. He is one of my archers."

Alfred smiled, "I can see that and now that I think of it, are you not the knight called Warbow, Lord Edward's archer?"

"I am."

"Then we are blessed to have such a warrior as our lord."

Dick said, "For this night my lord, we shall sleep in the barn. It is too late to disturb these folk." Dick was being sensible. Seara and her husband would have only one man to accommodate.

"We can make room, my lord."

"No, Dick is right. Stable our horses and, Robert, bring my bags. Lead on Alfred." As we headed to the ladder I said, "Have you ever needed to pull up the ladder because of danger?"

"I have lived here since my son was born, sixteen years ago and there has been no danger in the valley."

I looked at the ladder. It was both an uncomfortable and undignified way to enter a home. I said, "Then tomorrow we build a stair. We can still make it hard for an enemy to attack but Dick's wife has two young children and I would not have her endure this."

He beamed, "My wife will be delighted with that, my lord. She does not like the climbing of the ladder."

He entered first. His wife must have tidied while we approached the ladder for it looked neat within. There was an open hatch which led down to the floor below. I knew that it would be partly below ground and, when the hall was built, would have been intended for the horses. There was one large room with a table. It looked large enough for ten people.

His wife bobbed, "If you will excuse me, my lord, I will help our daughter augment the meal. I fear there will be no meat for this is a Tuesday and we eat beans and vegetables."

"And that will do. Thank you Mistress Seara." She disappeared through the hatch and I deduced that there was another ladder there. The hall needed work. If the kitchen was without wind holes then it would be an unpleasant place to work. Added to that the ladder made it difficult to serve food. "Alfred, there is work to do here. We need a stair down to the kitchen. Are there wind holes?"

"Just two, my lord."

The Prince and the Archer

I nodded, "Where is the chamber I shall be using?"

He shuffled his feet, "We will need to vacate it first, my lord. My wife and I have used it since Stirling Bridge."

"And that is understandable. There are other rooms?"

"Yes my lord, follow me."

He led me to a large chamber with a comfortable-looking bed. There was a chest at its foot and a rail for clothes hung over a place which I assumed was above the kitchen fire for the wall looked warm. There was a large wind hole.

"This is the chamber of the lord of the manor. I will vacate it while we eat." He led me down a narrow corridor. There were two rooms on each side of it. I peered in and saw that two of them were occupied and each had a bed in while the other two had nothing but a paillasse. The empty rooms smelled musty.

"We need more beds."

He nodded his head apologetically, "We did not need them and…"

"And things change, Alfred." I sighed, "You will no longer be the steward but you and your family can work for Dick, if that is agreeable. You shall be paid and all will be written down so that there is no misunderstanding."

He smiled and looked relieved, "We have lived here so long that we are part of the village. I am no longer a young man and I would not wish to start again."

"Good. This night I would have your family dine with us. I am not staying long in the valley and both Dick and I need to get to know your family. There will be time to vacate your chamber after you have eaten."

"Yes, my lord."

My archers were resourceful men. They had stabled the horses and made their beds. Robert had brought my bag inside the hall and then Hob and Nob had brought the last of our ham to the kitchen to add to the bean and vegetable stew. Richard of Craven had given us skins of wine and ale. It would not be a feast but I guessed it would be better fare than Alfred and his family were used to on a Tuesday.

Robert still had the priory in his mind and he said Grace before we ate. It seemed to please Seara. The family might have been uncomfortable with the strangers around their table but for Robert. He had an easy way with him and his pleasant smile helped. By the time we had half finished our food, there were smiles all around the table. I learned that David was sixteen summers and Maryanne looked to be thirteen. She would be close enough in age to help Betty. She seemed a willing girl.

The Prince and the Archer

I was still a fast eater and, having devoured the food I picked at the last of my bread and sipped the wine, "There are changes, Dick and Alfred, that will need to be made." They both nodded. "Tomorrow I will help as will Robert but the day after I will ride to Guisborough." Alfred's face showed curiosity but he kept his questions to himself. "We will build two staircases, one down to the kitchen and one as a better, more functional entrance. I have not seen the kitchen but I am guessing, Mistress Seara, that it has not enough wind holes and the ones that are there are narrow."

"Yes, my lord and it is smoky. There is a chimney."

I nodded, "We will put two large wind holes in the walls, on opposing walls. They will allow the smoke to be dispersed and make it more pleasant to use."

Alfred said, "But, my lord, will that not make it more vulnerable to assault?"

"When the fields around here are ploughed do you find rocks?"

It was David who answered, "Yes, my lord, Baldor the smith makes many coins from repairing the damaged plough shares."

"Then we use those rocks and make the perimeter wall higher. We also put a ditch around the house. The days of raiding Vikings are long gone and we are far enough from the border so that we do not fear the Scots." I let them take it in and then said, "We are all agreed?"

Seara said, "It will suit, my lord, but why ask us for this is your manor. You command and we obey."

"That is not my way, Mistress Seara, and besides I will not be living here. Dick, or, should we call him, Master Richard, will command in my absence."

Hob grinned, "I like that! Master Richard!" He and Dick got on well.

Dick shook his head, "I am happy to be called Dick."

They all seemed pleased. I added, "And David, it is also my practice to have the young men trained to be warriors. It is late to make you an archer but Dick can train you as a man at arms if you will."

"Yes, my lord. I should like that. I can use a sling and I sometimes add to the pot that which I hunt but I know not the way of the sword."

"We can teach you."

The family left us and I was able to speak to my men, "You are happy, Dick?"

"It feels right, my lord, and I think that these are good people. I sensed no resentment."

"There is land for building too." We all looked at Robert. He was a constant source of surprises. "If you added a building close to the chimney then you would not need to make wind holes. You could have a door to the new building and put wind holes in that. I have not been down to the kitchen and storage area but in my experience, they are always damp places. Damp causes illness. The building would also be closer to the bread oven."

"Thank you, Robert. Your advice is always sage, especially for one so young."

"I told you, my lord, I have a mind that never ceases working. It can be a curse as well as a blessing."

I looked over to Dick, "There is a lot of work here."

"I know and as much as I wish to return to Betty and the bairn…"

I had already thought this through, "Then here is my suggestion. We will all stay for a week and work from sunrise to sunset. At the end of the week Hob, Nob and Robert shall return with me, to Yarpole. We will procure a wagon for your family and I will ask for volunteers to return here for a month and toil for you."

I saw the relief on his face, "That is most kind, my lord, but can you spare the men?"

"You forget, Dick, that this is my manor. I am being selfish allowing you to make it safe, secure and profitable." He nodded. "Robert, while the other three labour with me you shall go over the accounts. Looking at the squiggles makes me ill. You can tell me the state of the manor and use that agile mind to make suggestions."

"Of course, my lord."

"And now," I rose, "as I will be labouring with you tomorrow I shall retire. You have me for one day before I leave for Guisborough. Use that time well."

Chapter 3

It was a comfortable bed but it was not my bed and I rose early to make water. Alfred had placed a pot in the corner. I dressed and went into the room where we would eat. Seara and Maryanne had enjoyed less sleep than me for there was the smell of freshly baked bread as I entered the dining hall. It was not manchet but, as I had expected, raveled. I knew it would taste good. The butter, when I spread it, was delicious. The cow byre and the animals within were unexpected but bode well for the manor. With fresh milk, Dick could enjoy cheese, good butter and wholesome milk for his children. There was fried ham and eggs cooked in ham fat as well as porridge and I ate well. I was halfway through when my men joined me.

By way of explanation, Dick said, "We thought to explore the manor before we ate. We have found a stand of trees that can be copsed and Robert located some stones."

"You are the steward, Dick. Today I labour. How many cows are there?"

"Two. They have a sow and a boar as well. The sow is ready to drop her litter. They are not the largest of pigs but they look hardy. David told us that they have hard winters up here."

"There are no horses?"

"No. There are chickens and a small pond with ducks."

"It is not a fishpond?"

"I think not, my lord, but David pointed out a stream to the northeast that empties close to the bishop's first castle at Bishopton. Perhaps, in the fullness of time, we can build a fishpond. The remains of the bishop's, so David told us, is still there but he is not sure if it is stocked."

"It would not do to poach the bishop's fish. When I have the chance I will speak to Bishop Bek." Alfred came in. "I wish Robert to go over the accounts, Alfred. Be so good as to furnish them and while we labour he can give them his attention." I saw the look of horror on his face. I smiled, "The past is the past, Alfred. For me, the manor begins today and all that Robert will do is to see how to make it more profitable, in the future. I need to know how we can make the manor yield more crops and animals. I want Sadberge to grow. I will not be able to meet the villagers this visit but Dick will and he knows my mind well enough to let them know how my rule will change their lives. He has seen Yarpole and knows the acorn that it was. It will be the same here."

"Yes, my lord." The relief was palpable.

The Prince and the Archer

My three archers had finished and I rose, "To work. First, we hew the timber for the stairs. I am too old to clamber up a ladder. Robert, you have until noon on the accounts and then we use your mind to design the stairs."

The six of us headed down to the stand of trees. David had the tools. There were just two wood axes and so while my archers and I took it in turns to chop down the trees, the spare archer strung his bow and hunted the birds we disturbed. Between them, they brought down five pigeons. The stew would have a better taste that night. When the timber was hewn, we used the shaping axes and adzes to strip the bark and take the worst of the roughness away. Then we sawed. I saw that we needed more tools. I would have to speak to Baldor, the village smith. I had gold with me and that would need to be spent.

By noon and with so many of us working we had timber cut into varying lengths. In a perfect world, we would have allowed it to age. We needed it now and Dick and Alfred would have to live with the warping. We had more than enough timber. When we had copsed the stand of trees we had seen seedlings that would, in the fullness of time, yield trees. Dick could ensure that they were trained to be straight and avoid wastage.

Seara and Maryanne brought out more fresh bread, cheese made on the farm, the last of the wild strawberries, blackberries and the first of the autumn raspberries as well as honey cakes. We feasted like kings. Seara was an alewife and her brew was delicious. Although it was hard to get back to work, I for one was keen for a nap, we did so to make as much progress as we could. Robert came to join us and offered advice about the construction of the staircase.

It became clear, during the afternoon, that we did not have enough nails. When we stopped for an ale break I said, "Now is as good a time as any, Dick, to meet the blacksmith."

I sent Robert up the ladder to fetch my purse and we headed into the village towards the sound of hammering. The smell of charcoal was also a good indicator of the workshop. Baldor, like all smiths, wore a huge leather apron and like every smith I had ever met was huge. A youth worked the bellows as he hammered what was clearly a ploughshare. I guessed that the valley had been peaceful long enough for weapons to be of secondary importance.

He stopped work and laid down his hammer. He came from the furnace and wiped his hands and face on a cloth that was laid on the bench, "Keep the furnace hot."

"Yes, Father."

"How can I help you, my lord?"

The Prince and the Archer

"You know who I am?"

He smiled, "We knew you were a lord from your arrival but word has spread that we have a new lord of the manor, Sir Gerald of Yarpole, Warbow. We are honoured."

"I will not be living here but my steward will be, Dick." I waved a hand at my archer.

Dick nodded, "I look forward to working with you, Baldor."

The smith frowned, "And Alfred?"

"Alfred is not losing his job, Baldor. The only change will be that there will be someone who looks to the defence of this land and to the number of coins sent to the Bishop of Durham."

He looked relieved, "And how can I help you, my lord?"

"For today it will be nails that we need but, in the future, we will need axes, spearheads, arrowheads and swords."

"War is coming?"

I shrugged, "Who knows, but a lord who does not prepare for war will lose all that he has when it does come."

"Wise words." He turned, "Falco!"

A smaller version of the bellows boy came running from the house, "Yes Father?"

"Fetch Sir Gerald a bag of nails." He scurried off.

"How much?" I could see that he did not know what to say. Normally a smith would barter and negotiate a price but I was his lord and master. I said, "Know this, Master Smith, I value a good workman and I will pay what is fair. You need to make coins and I do not need to be robbed. How much?"

"Two shillings, my lord, for they are strong nails. If any break I will pay back a shilling."

"Good." I handed him the coins and Falco handed me the heavy bag of nails. "Farewell, Baldor. Your furnace is still hot."

"Aye, Galdr knows better than to let it cool."

While Dick distributed the nails I said to Alfred, "Baldor, it is an unusual name as are those of his sons."

"They are of Danish descent. There are three or four families who live in the manor of Viking or Danish descent. They tend to intermarry and the result is that they have strange names but they are all loyal Englishmen."

"I did not doubt it. And the wapentake?"

"We were a liberty of Northumberland until a hundred years ago, lord, and then we became a liberty of Durham. The men here are yours to command."

"That does not answer my question. The Sunday practice?"

He looked down and shuffled his feet. He could not meet my eye, "We have allowed it to lapse, my lord."

"I told you this morning, Alfred, that the past is the past and your life begins anew now. Where does the village go to church?"

"Redemarshal is the closest church, my lord."

"And I am guessing that they do not observe the practice either."

"No, my lord."

"I can do nothing about Redemarshal but rather than enjoying the inn there they can hasten back here and Dick will put them through their paces. I will need men to follow my banner when I come north."

He was a clever man, "You will come north for war, my lord?"

"Perhaps. I have done so many times and always have I been forced to leave my manor of Yarpole undefended. If the king commands me north then I shall have men with a shorter journey and more reason to fight for this border."

The sun was about to set when the stairs were finished and attached to the outside wall. Robert had designed a small drawbridge that could be pulled up and would act as a double door. It made the hall more secure. They needed to have oil rubbed into them but that was a job for a hot day with nothing else to do. As was my right, I was the first to ascend. The meal, that night, was enjoyable for we had a pigeon-enriched stew and we had not only worked hard but also achieved something. I had been there for one day and my mark was already on the land. I had the family dine with us.

"Tomorrow, I shall take Robert and ride to visit Guisborough. We may be back by dark but if we are not then fret not. Dick, you decide on the work for the next days."

"Aye, lord. Robert has given us plans for the kitchen extension. We can dig the foundations and plant the supporting timbers. That will be a day of work."

"Alfred, are there woods on the manor with deer?"

"Yes, my lord, to the north and the east there are three such woods. The woods belong to this manor. The land beyond them belongs, like this manor, to the Bishop of Durham."

"Dick, we can hunt some deer. The rutting season will be upon us soon. Now is the time to cull the older hinds."

"A good idea. Any wild pigs, Alfred?"

"They have been hunted out. The manor of Elton has some, I believe."

I shook my head, "That is for the future. Let us not upset the other lords until we know how the land lies."

The Prince and the Archer

When the family left us Dick expressed his concerns, "My lord, you ride abroad alone. It is dangerous for there are enemies in this land and de Brus might be one of them."

I smiled, "I have Robert." They all laughed for, while a clever man, he was no warrior and they knew that I was joking. "But I think I will be safe. De Brus might see me as a threat but I am close enough to King Edward that any harm that came to me would bring down retribution. The king has sent me north for a reason."

Robert listened beneath my words and he suddenly said, "You mean the king sends you as bait?"

"Not as such but a temptation? Yes. Anyway, I am resolved for, once tomorrow is out of the way, I can spend the rest of the week toiling and then return to Yarpole. I will have Christmas with my family."

It was just sixteen miles to Guisborough, although we had the river to cross. I counted on getting there and back in a day but I knew that de Brus might ask me to stay.

"How do I cross the river, Alfred?"

"There are fisherfolk and fowlers who live not far away at Preston. There are just four families but they have boats. I would not like to do it but those who cross the river allow their horses to swim."

I nodded, "It is a quick way to cross and stops us from having wet breeks."

We travelled light. Dick insisted that Robert wear a short sword. It looked incongruous on the Frenchman. The fishermen who lived by the river were more than happy to take the copper coins and row us across the narrow stretch of water. We carried the saddles in the boat and the horses happily swam behind their fowling boats. The short crossing would save us a couple of miles. While we saddled our mounts Robert looked back at the hamlet. "A strange existence lord, fishing the river, taking birds' eggs and hunting. It seems a little primitive to me."

As I tightened my girth I said, "There will be those who live this way in France too, Robert. A man does what he must to provide for his family. The coppers we gave them will be added to their treasure. I do not doubt they keep it beneath the floor of the house. When they need it they have money to spend on that which they cannot catch or grow."

Alfred only had a vague idea of where the manor of Guisborough and the priory were to be found but he had given me a landmark to head for. There was a peculiarly shaped hill called Othenesberg that lay beyond the manor. As soon as we passed the now deserted hamlet of Thornaby we saw the hill in the distance. It looked like a bird's beak. We found a road heading east and followed it. The road was not Roman but well-travelled. When we passed the first dwelling on the road I asked for directions to Guisborough. The farmer confirmed that we were, indeed, on the right road.

"Robert, I know that you can write but can you scribe maps?"

He ruminated for a moment and then said, "I have not done so but I cannot see the problem. Once you know where east, west, north and south lie then all that remains is to use symbols for the places." He looked at the side of the road and pointed, "It would be easier if this was a Roman Road for they have the distances marked."

"The distance can be estimated. When we return to Sadberge I would have you make me a map of this area. If we have to return it would be useful. My memory is not what it once was."

"Then I will make you one."

"One thing more, Robert, speak as little as you can at Guisborough but keep your eyes and ears open. If you have to play dumb then do so but learn as much as you can about the Lord of Annandale and his plans."

He smiled, "The jester will play the fool for you, my lord."

Guisborough was a busy place. The priory helped to make it so but, as we headed towards the substantial manor, I saw more soldiers than I had expected. Even the Mortimers had fewer soldiers at their castle than I saw in the village and, as we neared the hall, in the grounds. It was not an army but the forty or so warriors were more than enough to guard a hall. The garrison at Harlech had fewer men than we had seen.

There were sentries but, as I had fought many times in Scotland and had a distinctive shape for a horseman, I was recognised. "Is Lord de Brus at home?" I asked the question with a smile and as much innocence as I could manufacture.

"He is, my lord, but he and his familia are out hunting." He pointed to the hall, "David the Steward will accommodate you and your servant."

"Thank you."

As we led our horses towards the hall I thought that if de Brus was out with his closest knights then there were even more men here than I had expected. The steward came to the door but unlike the sentry did not recognise me, "I am Sir Gerald of Yarpole and I would like to speak to his lordship."

"He is hunting but pray come in for the sun is warm today." He turned and shouted, "Walter, take these horses to the stable." A man came from a chamber which lay close to the entrance. I guessed he was a porter of some kind. He hurried out and took our reins. "If you would follow me, my lord." He led us down a panelled corridor. It was a fine hall. We reached the Great Hall and Walter said to Robert. "Wait here." He then led me into the hall and to a chair before the chimney. It was a warm day but the fire was laid ready to be lit when the evening chill came. "I will fetch you refreshments, my lord. Your servant will be accommodated in the servants' quarters."

Left alone I studied the hall. The tapestries on the walls were not there merely as wall coverings to keep it warmer, they reflected de Brus' ambitions. They showed scenes of glory from Scotland's past and were well-made. The furniture was also beautifully crafted. They had adornments and finishes that mirrored the fine tapestries. De Brus was a rich man and he was a patriot. He might bend the knee to King Edward but, in his heart, he was a Scotsman. I could have left there and then and given a report to King Edward but I knew that I could discover more if I stayed. Walter brought in good French wine and the bread was manchet. The cured ham looked delicious and the platters were pewter and not wood. Robert de Brus liked luxury.

"I will leave a servant at the open door, my lord. If you require anything then summon him, his name is Absalom."

"Thank you, Walter."

Eating and drinking gave me the chance to think. The journey had been an easy one. If we had to return to Sadberge we could be there before dark. Bishop Bek and the king had to have colluded in the gift of the manor. There were manors closer to Guisborough but mine was just far enough away for some secrecy and, I hoped, safety. However, the plans Dick and I had made to add a higher wall and a ditch now seemed prudent.

I was not alone for long. The priory's bells told me when it was Nones and I heard the clattering of horses' hooves on the cobbles not long after. I did not stir but I heard, in the corridor outside a conversation. The door opened and Robert de Brus stood there in hunting garb. The blood spattered on his tunic told me of his success. I stood for he was higher in rank. He beamed, "Sir Gerald, this is a most unexpected pleasure. Did the king send you?" The question seemed innocent enough but I saw the look in his eye.

I shook my head, "No, my lord. The Bishop of Durham and the king have been so kind as to make me a gift of the nearby manor of Sadberge. I thought to come and speak to a neighbour. I hope you do not mind the uninvited visit."

"My dear man, I am delighted. The hunter who captured the traitor, Wallace, makes my humble efforts today at hunting, pale into insignificance. You will stay and dine with us. I will not take no for an answer." He did not know I had no intention of refusing. He turned, "Walter, have a room made up for Sir Gerald."

I played a part, "My lord, I am in my travelling clothes and…"

"Walter, find a tunic and breeches for his lordship."

"Yes, my lord."

"There. It is settled. And now I must change too." He strode towards me and clasped my arm, "I am delighted to welcome you to my humble home."

His grasp was firm.

"And I am honoured that you welcome me so."

He turned and left. The servant, Absalom, said, "If you would follow me, Sir Gerald." I followed him down a corridor to the bed chambers. I could hear others already in the rooms as we passed them. We stopped at the door of a small but well-apportioned room. There was a bed and on it lay a pair of breeches and a tunic. I smiled. Walter had done well to find one big enough for my chest. I wondered who they belonged to.

"There is water, soap, cloths and towels, my lord. Should I wait or can you find your own way back to the Great Hall?"

"Thank you, Absalom, I shall manage."

I had been asked before why I did not have a squire. The fact was that I didn't need one. I never regarded myself as a knight. I had been dubbed but in my heart, I was still an archer. Jack was a squire but not mine. It was a title. One day he would become a knight but I guessed that was far into the future. Like me, he had no need of a title. We had manors and we had land. What more did a man need?

I washed and shaved myself and then dressed. I lay on the bed which was comfortable. It was not, however, my bed. That lay in Yarpole and I yearned for it. I closed my eyes. I would not sleep but I was finding, increasingly, that lying down and closing my eyes in the afternoon made for a better night of sleep and kept me more alert while I ate. I would need all my wits when I dined with de Brus.

I must have dozed off for I was awoken by a knock on the door and Absalom's voice saying, "My lord?"

I rose and said, "I come." I had not been woken by the bells for Vespers and so I knew that I had not slept for long.

I followed the servant back to the hall and said, "Is my servant catered for?"

"He is, my lord."

There were ten or so warriors in the hall. None wore spurs but then we were indoors. I guessed from their apparel and the fine daggers on their baldrics that some were knights. Robert de Brus said, rather too

The Prince and the Archer

loudly for my liking, "And here is our guest of honour. The man who caged the beast that was Wallace." The knights all cheered. I was not fooled by the feigned friendship.

I understood why he wanted Wallace out of the way. It left him less opposition when he made his claim to the throne but I wondered if all those in the hall shared his views.

I was led to the table and saw that I was seated at his right hand. The Prior of Guisborough Priory was at his left. The others took their places as was determined by rank. I wondered if they would be introduced to me. I did not recognise any of them and that meant they had not served in King Edward's army. There were three men who seemed close to de Brus and I noted their names as they were introduced: Sir Richard Edgar, Roger de Kirkpatrick, and Sir Robert Fleming.

The prior said Grace and the food was fetched in. We would not be eating the day's hunt. That would be hung but we were served venison as well as fine fish. We were close enough to the coast for freshly caught fish from the sea. De Brus and his familia ate well. The wine continued to be plied but I controlled my intake. I was here for information and a dulled mind was the last thing that I needed. The conversation began about the hunt but de Brus quickly shifted it to English politics and the public row between the king and his son. I was able to adopt an innocent stance. I had not witnessed the row but I knew it was about money. From de Brus' questions, I gathered that he thought it might cause a problem for the king.

I kept my voice even as I spoke as though it was of no matter, "You have met the king, my lord. He is a strong-willed man. He knows how to control his son. Prince Edward needs to learn that being a prince does not bring riches without effort. The prince is young and he will learn."

"Yet the king is no longer a young man."

"Neither am I, my lord, but I hope that diminishes neither my mind nor my skill."

He laughed, "Aye, my archers, few in number though they are, speak of you with awe in their voices."

"It is many years since I had to draw a bow in anger, my lord. An archer needs to practise every day to maintain his skill."

"But you can still draw a bow."

"Draw? Yes but stand with my archers and send flight after flight over a great distance? I think not. I leave that to my son and my captains of archers."

"You do yourself a disservice and I hear that you are a good swordsman."

The Prince and the Archer

"I was never trained with a sword, my lord."

"Yet you defeated Wallace, who was younger, taller and had been trained as a knight. How was that?"

I shrugged, "Perhaps I have some natural talent or, more likely, a desire to stay alive. When I was younger I fought at Lewes and Evesham as well as in the Holy Land. There you either learned to use a sword or died."

The prior said, "I heard that you and two others travelled across a vast desert to meet with the King of the Mongols. That must have been quite an adventure."

I nodded, "It was and most perilous too. He was not a king then. His father still ruled England. They called the Mongol leaders khans and we were lucky to reach the court safely. It was a bold stroke from King Edward and was almost the undoing of the Turks."

Robert de Brus said, "Aye, we can learn much from King Edward."

Was there a hidden message beneath his words? They were certainly weighted words and I stored them.

I learned nothing more for they spoke of the hunt they would enjoy the next day. One of the king's huntsmen had found traces of a boar and they were going on a boar hunt.

"You must come with us, Sir Gerald. With an arm like yours, you could easily skewer a boar."

I shook my head, "And as much as I would enjoy the hunt I fear that I have much work at my new manor."

"Will you stay long?"

"Just long enough to make it secure and then in a few days I will go back to Yarpole."

He nodded, "Remember, you are always welcome here. The archer who helped King Edward keep his throne is a good friend of mine."

The next day, as we left, his words still echoed in my head and I did not believe one of them.

Chapter 4

As Robert and I headed back to the river I questioned him about the household. "They are all English, my lord, even the steward. The Scottish warriors we saw have been arriving since Wallace's capture. The earl, it seems, will head north to Scotland to spend Christmas in his lands there."

I said, "Does that not sound curious to you?"

"No, my lord, why should it?"

"His lands in Dumfries, Annandale and Galloway will be colder and wetter at Christmas than here close to the Tees in the east. He has a purpose in returning home and he has with him the makings of an army. It is not one to threaten the King of England but I think it would be bigger than any of his rivals for the crown."

"He would start a war?"

"That I do not know but I am suspicious of the man and this visit was worthwhile. The king may be getting older but his instincts are still as sharp as ever. He was wise to send me north."

Our early departure and the slightly more familiar road enabled us to reach Sadberge not long after sext. It was a hot day and the men were working on the foundations for the new kitchen. They stopped as we approached and Dick said, "We have prepared the opening for the stairs and we have the timber but we did not want to start them without Robert's wisdom and sage advice."

Robert dismounted and gave a half-bow, "You are too kind, Dick, for this is not something I have studied." He pointed to the manor house, "It will be the same as the one we built the other day. I have work to complete for Sir Gerald while it is fresh in my mind, but I can help start you off if you wish."

"The map can wait, Robert, until you have helped Dick. I will see to the horses."

I became an ostler and unsaddled the horses while Robert advised the men and they began to make the stairs. We could not eat until that work was finished. We had decided that we would make the extension first and then break through to the kitchen. I think Seara was quite excited at the prospect of having light in her kitchen. By the time the horses were unsaddled, fed and watered, the men were happily banging and hammering under Robert's supervision. With no prospect of food and no desire to endure the hammering, I shouted, over the din, "I will walk to the site of the fishpond. Call me when the hammering ceases and the food is ready."

The Prince and the Archer

I strode over the fields towards the stream. Its course was marked by both weeds and shrubs that grew alongside it. I must have walked two miles or more. I saw, in the distance, the mound that marked Bishop Odo's first home and the light reflected off the former fishpond. My men were right, it had fallen into disrepair. I saw that the stream had a natural curve where it passed through some low ground. It would be a perfect place to build a fishpond. I saw a lone elder tree and walked over to it. The branches whilst sturdy enough were easy to cut and, using my dagger, I hewed four of them and stripped the foliage from them. I walked to what I determined would be the four corners of the pond and planted my four markers there. I doubted that it would be started before I left but this way Dick would know where I intended it to be built. This was my manor and I knew what I wanted.

"Sir Gerald!"

Dick's voice carried over to me and, my stomach complaining about the lack of food, I headed back to the hall.

Seara and Maryanne had improvised a trestle table outdoors and it was shaded by the hall. Cold food was laid upon it but there was plenty and the ale would refresh the men. I pointed, before I sat, "I have marked the fishpond with four elder branches. The ground is low and if you build up the banks then the pond will naturally fill up. When are the heaviest rains, Alfred?"

He gave it some thought and said, "The end of September through to November, they are very heavy, my lord."

"Then next week you should begin the work."

Dick glanced over at me, "There will be just three of us, my lord."

"I will leave money for you. Hire men from the village. Once the crops are in then they will be happy to have an income."

Alfred said, "That is generous, my lord, but this is your manor and you could demand that they serve you."

"I want a decent job on the pond. It is better to pay them and know that they will work more cheerfully than being forced to labour and have a poor job. This evening, Alfred, I will go through the accounts with you to determine where the priorities of the manor lie."

Until I had been given Yarpole such matters were like Greek to me but now I understood them.

By the time Robert, Hob, Nob and I loaded our horses and left to return to Yarpole, the walls of the extension were up and the roof was in place. It still needed to be covered with a turf roof. Slate or pot were preferable but that would necessitate a visit to Segges Field or Stockton where they made tiles. Turf would suffice for a while. Alfred knew

The Prince and the Archer

what was intended and I think that all were happy with the new arrangements. We headed for Skipton.

I think Robert was loath to leave the manor for he had enjoyed the stretching of his mind and the physical labour. Certainly, he had been in good humour the whole time we laboured.

"My lord, it might be useful if I were to accompany Betty and the wagon when she comes north."

"We need you in Yarpole, Robert."

"She has a child and has another on the way. I think her needs outweigh any others."

"So now you tell me what to do on my own land?"

Robert was always confident, "No, my lord, but if I came back and spent, say, a month at Sadberge, I could be there when the baby was born and help Dick. You saw how much he relied on me and there is still much work to do."

He was right and I nodded, "But I want you back in Yarpole within days of the baby's birth."

"I shall be like Bellerophon and my steed Pegasus."

I snorted, "Just get back safely, eh?"

The horses had enjoyed many days of rest and we reached Skipton before dark. We went the direct route home. Before we ate, however, I asked Richard of Craven for the use of parchment and a quill for Robert. He procured them and the three of us retired to his solar. I dictated a letter to King Edward outlining my suspicions and fears. When I had finished, Robert said, "This is all conjecture, my lord. There is no tangible evidence of a plot."

"I know and the king could well ignore it."

Richard said, "He will not, Sir Gerald for he trusts you above all men."

I smiled as Robert sealed the letter and melted a blob of wax upon it, "I know." I pressed my seal into the wax and then blew on it. When I was satisfied that it was hardened, I said, "I know that you will have missives from the Lord Warden to send to the king. Include this with the others."

"I can send a rider with it."

"And that would draw attention to the letter. This way we hide the letter amongst others. Whatever is going to happen will not take place until Christmas. The letter will be delivered by then, will it not?"

"It will. We send a rider every two weeks. The king is keen to be kept informed about the border and the Lord Warden is a vigilant man."

We did not take the same route south as we had north. Hob and Nob knew the reason but, despite the fact that he had travelled with me in

France, Robert was still not used to my ways. He asked, "Why the change in route, my lord? I know why we did not return to York but why this way?"

I turned to Hob, "You could tell him could you not?"

"I could, my lord." He smiled at the Frenchman, "We rarely ride the same way twice. Sir Gerald likes to be unpredictable. We have enemies aplenty in this land. I was not at Guisborough but I will wager a bag of arrows that he has enemies there. If Sir Gerald is ambushed and killed then King Edward loses not only a good leader of men but also one who knows how to use archers."

"Surely you cannot think that de Brus would have us attacked, my lord?"

"I do but if not him then any one of a dozen Scotsmen. John Comyn was asked to hunt Wallace, nay, he was ordered to hunt Wallace, yet he did nothing. He supported Wallace. There will be many others who saw in Wallace, not a leader to rule them but a figurehead to inspire them. I was the one who caught him. Make no mistake, Robert, I am a marked man."

My words sobered them all. By association, they were targets too. I think they remembered the fanaticism of those who had defended Wallace at the end. They had thrown their lives away recklessly to save Scotland's last hope. There would be other fanatics too.

We were all reflective as we headed south towards Wallintun and the crossing of the river there. Robert was a deep man and his mind would wrestle with all that he had encountered since meeting me. Hob and Nob had a decision to make. Did they stay with me in Yarpole or volunteer to join their friend, Dick, in Sadberge? My thoughts were different. Despite what I had said in Skipton I did not fear Scottish vengeance. I had endured and survived the enmity of Simon de Montfort and he had been a far more dangerous enemy than these Scottish patriots. I would, however, be careful and view every stranger with suspicion. My thoughts were on my future. I did not want to be a mentor for Prince Edward. I was too old to take on such a duty and I did not like him. The problem I wrestled with was how to get out of the task appointed to me. I realised I had not sworn an oath. King Edward must be slipping for he would have known that an oath would bind me irrevocably to his son. If I could avoid him I might be able to avoid the onerous burden.

We were close to Newton, not far from Wallintun when Robert suddenly reined in. "A problem with your horse, Robert?" My two archers smiled. They had watched his awkward attempts at riding north and then south.

The Prince and the Archer

He shook his head, "My lord, is there any other way across the river?"

"You mean apart from Wallintun? No, why?"

"Since Skipton, I have ruminated on your words about our route. I do not doubt that you are right and your Scottish enemies wish you harm. We were not followed." He nodded at Nob and Hob, "Your archers ensured that."

My two men had trailed us when we had left both Sadberge and Skipton to ensure that no one was following us.

I sighed, "And they found no evidence of pursuit."

Robert shook his head, "And they did not need to follow us, my lord, for they could get ahead of us. You have varied the route we took but we crossed this way when we headed north. I remember staying in that village and crossing the bridge at Wallintun. If this is the only crossing then they know where we will be. They know not the time but they can wait." He paused and looked at our three faces. "I am not a warrior. Tell me that I am wrong and it will ease my troubled mind."

I looked at Hob and Nob. Their faces told me that Robert, the novice, the man of peace, had spotted what we had not. "No, you are right, Robert, and I have been a complacent and overconfident fool." I peered ahead; although I could not see Wallintun, I knew that it was but a few miles away. If it was just the two archers and me we could simply swim the river. We had done so before but such an act would be the death of Robert and I could not allow him to try the crossing of the bridge alone. He had been with me at Guisborough and would be recognised. "Robert is correct, they would not know when we will arrive and therefore they must wait."

Hob said, "And it will be north of the river for there are too many men at the river to risk attacking us there."

My archer, now prompted by Robert's observations, was a hunter and knew the best place to ambush. Nob nodded, "You are right. It will be close to the road and there will be woods."

Hob pointed, "The road from Wargrave is wooded all the way to Wallintun. There are, if memory serves, just two settlements and both are small: the chapelries of Wargrave and Burton Wood. The road to Winwick lies to the east and the road we take is a smaller one. That is where they will ambush. The road from Winwick joins the road from Wargrave and they will be south of that junction."

Hob had a good memory. He could not read words but he knew how to read the land. I looked at the sky and made a decision, "It is just a couple of hours until sunset. I had hoped to spend the night this side of

The Prince and the Archer

the river and cross in the early morning. That is not a choice we can now make. We must ambush the ambushers."

Hob and Nob nodded. Robert said, "But you do not know where they are."

I smiled, "We are less than five miles from Wallintun. We ride the short way to Wargrave and ask the people who live there if they have seen any strangers pass. We leave the horses there with you and then the three of us stalk the Scotsmen and," I paused, "make our journey safer."

There was a chapel and just three houses at Wargrave. They eked out a living in the forest making charcoal and foraging. I had copper and it loosened their tongues. They told us that two days earlier six men, they called them northerners, had passed through. They said that they had poor horses and that the horses looked lathered. That was enough for us. Northerners meant Scotsmen and lathered horses that they had ridden hard. If you had poor horses you husbanded their strength. We rode half a mile beyond the village and dismounted. While Hob and Nob strung their bows I tethered the horses.

"Robert, make yourself comfortable but I would not light a fire nor sleep. We will return when all is done."

He shook his head, "My lord, you are not a young man and there are six men. The odds are two to one."

"The darkness is our ally and besides Hob and Nob are master archers, even in the dark." I took off my cloak and unsheathed my sword. "We will return."

My archers were ready and they each had an arrow ready to nock. I just nodded and let them lead. When I had first been an archer I would have been the scout. My ears, nose and eyes would have detected an enemy quicker than any. Age had dulled those senses and my two archers would be the ones to find our foes. We did not take the road but passed through the woods to the west of it. The ambush would need to be at least a mile and a half from the crossing. There would be guards at the bridge and the sound of an altercation would be investigated. The enemy would be somewhere within a mile and a half of us, probably where the Winwick Road met the smaller one we were on.

I was getting old but even my old nose could smell the smoke from their fire as well as fresh horse dung. The men of Wargrave had said that no other horsemen had passed. The wind brought it to us and that meant it would keep our smell from them. We stopped and held a whispered conference.

"They are ahead but I would not murder innocent travellers."

The Prince and the Archer

Nob shook his head, "No innocents would camp this close to the crossing."

"Nevertheless I will give them the chance to identify themselves. You will know, from their response, what is needed. Obey me." I was King Edward's man and I had to obey the law, even if it put me in danger.

"Yes, my lord."

I nodded and they took off south. I headed to the road and counted to twenty. That would give them the opportunity to get into position. I walked south and the smell of woodsmoke and cooking food grew. I also heard the murmur of words and they were loud enough for me to detect Scottish accents and words. I heard the sound of horses and saw their shapes in the woods beyond the fire. They must have been sitting around the fire for when one stood I saw its flickering flames. I moved from the road and into the woods. I was able to count the shadows against the glow and when I counted six I knew that they had not set a sentry. It was now too late for the crossing. The bridge would be closed during the hours of darkness. The ambushers would be relaxed.

I stopped just twenty paces from them and sheltered behind the bole of a tree. I studied the faces I could see. I thought I recognised one as being a man I had seen with Jack Short but I could not be sure. I saw the crossbows stacked against a tree and that was enough for me to speak, whilst still hidden, "What are six Scotsmen doing with crossbows and swords camped close to the road?"

They jumped to their feet and grabbed their arms looking around wildly. The tree hid me but they knew the rough direction from which my voice came. The one I thought I had recognised shouted, triumphantly, "That is Warbow! I recognise his voice! Kill him!"

The first arrow that slammed into the back of the speaker penetrated through to his chest. A second man fell to another arrow and that made three of the others turn. The fourth had drawn his sword and raced to the place where he had heard the voice. I drew my dagger too and stepped out as another of the Scottish warriors fell, pierced by an arrow. The man must have had keen sight for he either saw my shadow or, perhaps, the blade of my dagger reflecting the fire's glow. He swung his sword at me and I blocked it with my dagger. His speed of attack had brought him close to me and I could not swing my sword. Instead, I punched the crosspiece of my weapon into his face and broke his nose. He reeled and I lunged with my sword. He was young and he was quick. His blade deflected my sword but I still scored a savage cut on his leg. This was no time for mercy and I slashed my dagger across his head. He jerked his head back but I still managed to slash his cheek. He

The Prince and the Archer

was a reckless fanatic. I had more skill but that did not stop him and he ran at me, his sword aimed at my middle. I simply blocked it with my sword and rammed my dagger under his chin and into his brain, "Go with God!"

As he fell I saw Hob and Nob examining the dead. It was over. I wiped my sword on the dead man's kyrtle, "I will wait here. Fetch Robert and the horses." I smiled, "Try not to terrify him." They hesitated. "They are all dead, are they not?"

Hob nodded, "Yes my lord."

"Then I shall put the crossbows on the fire and see if they have any food." I saw that one of the men had indeed been with Jack Short.

The crossbows burned well and I saw that they had a pot with a hunter's stew. They had poached animals from the land of the estate that had belonged to Robert de Ferrers, the Earl of Derby. His support for de Montfort had cost him his title and his land. If you are going to murder four men then poaching seems an inconsequential act. I gathered their weapons and purses. I had seen emptier ones. They had been paid well for their task. I would let my three men share the booty. They had done most of the work. While I waited for them I examined the animals. They were sumpters and poor ones at that. They had pressed them to reach here before us and it showed.

I heard the horses coming down the road. The men had chosen a good place to ambush. The camp was close enough to the road for them to hear the approach of their prey and yet they would be hidden from a casual glance. I saw Robert make the sign of the cross when he saw the bodies. Hob and Nob tied up our horses and then went to the stew. Robert knelt next to each body and murmured prayers. I had no sympathy for the dead men. They had gambled and lost.

The stew was tasty but Robert did not partake. I think that his stomach was turned at the sight of the dead men. When we had finished eating we poured water on the fire and slung the bodies on the backs of the sumpters. We headed down the road to Wallintun and reached it just as the first rays of dawn appeared in the east. The sentries were alerted by the sound of our horses approaching. They were not the same men we had met while travelling north but when I announced myself they recognised my name.

I pointed to the bodies draped over the horses, "We were ambushed by these six men. They are dead. We would leave them here for a priest to bury them." I handed over a handful of copper coins we had taken from the dead. "Here is the fee for the priest." My men laid the bodies next to the guard house.

The Prince and the Archer

"Thank you, my lord, we will see to it." The priest would only get half of the coins.

"Is the bridge open yet?"

"When the light from the sun illuminates the roof of the guard house it is open."

I saw that we didn't have long to wait so we tightened our girths and waited. When we were waved across I knew that the dangerous part of the journey was over. Soon I would be home.

Chapter 5

Yarpole 1306

Hob and Nob chose to leave Yarpole and go to Sadberge. Both were closer to Dick than Gwillim. The two maidens that they had been courting were happy to go north. Betty had been popular and whilst both Mags and Bella would both be missed by their families the chance of a large smallholding in the north held appeal. Both Edward, Betty's twin, and Joseph also chose to go north. Only Abel from Betty's family would remain at Yarpole. I think he enjoyed working with horses and, after talking to Hob, he realised that he would not have as much opportunity to do so at Sadberge. The six sumpters were fattened up and rested so that four of them could return north with the wagon I gave to them. It took three weeks to prepare them for the journey as two hurried weddings had to be arranged. There were tears, for Betty, as well as Mags and Bella were popular. Abel looked torn but he was almost a man and a man stuck by his decisions. Mary was a kind woman and Betty, as well as the other two new brides, were given all that they would need to begin a new life. They left us with the sun shining and hope for a brighter future.

I made the most of my time at home. Gwillim's foray into Wales had been rewarded by the addition of fifteen archers. All were young men who were lured by the attractive pay I offered, the warrior hall that would house them and, as Gwillim told me, the chance to work with the most famous archer in the land. With King Edward planning a campaign in the north, we had to find more young men who could be trained with swords and spears. Luckily there were those who had not been trained as archers and yet they wanted the pay that came with being a man at arms. Many lords used the profit from their manors for luxuries or silken robes. Mary and I were more practical and we both knew the value of men to defend our home. The Welsh were now at peace but we had suffered at their hands and we lived too close to the border for us to be complacent.

With Betty and the rest of the party gone, we prepared for Christmas. Robert went with them. He would be missed. Even though they had their own manors it was understood that Jack and Hamo would return to Yarpole for the feast. I had lost my daughters. That was understandable. They had good husbands who were not warriors. We might not even see them and while that was sad Mary and I would make up for it with our son, stepson, grandchildren and step-grandchildren. The hall would be noisy. It was a better noise than the clamour of battle.

The Prince and the Archer

I enjoyed walking my land and now that I was home I made the most of the peace. Michel and his son were now well settled. Jean Michel was courting Alice, the daughter of Walter the Archer. My wife had watched them grow closer and she approved. Walter had no sons and it meant that when Jean Michel and Alice married, as we all knew they would, he could farm the archer's lands with him. I spent hours talking to the archers who had served me when we were all young. They, like me, had given up the bow but they had not done as I had done and taken up the sword. For them, their warring days were over but that did not stop them from enjoying talking about it. I must have told the story of the capture of Wallace a dozen times and the ambush at Wallintun eight or more. I might have tired of the story but they did not.

I also spent time with Harry. He had begun to raise his tavern from the empty plot. While I had been away he and some other warriors had cleared the land of the ruin and dug the foundations. While I had been with Dick helping to build a kitchen, my men at Yarpole had hewn great oaks for the eight beams that would give strength to the tavern that would double as a house and now I was able to help them build the low walls at the base that would give it strength. Once the walls were mortared they would be filled with small rocks. There were always large numbers to be found after a ploughing. When the walls had set then we would be able to build the wattle and daub walls, while the men with the skills that were needed would build a roof. Harry was confident that he would be able to serve his first jug of ale by the New Year. He had even found an alewife. Elizabeth's husband, Alan, had been a man at arms. He had come back from the Scottish wars with a wound. We thought it had healed but it had not and he had died. She and Harry got on and Harry promised he would care for Alan's children but that was as far as their relationship went. Elizabeth would not lie with another man. Harry would continue to be a bachelor.

Christmas came and we celebrated. We had new children to welcome and those like Michel and his son were introduced to our customs. They were not theirs but they found them agreeable. The one thing Michel disliked about England was the lack of wine. I always bought a barrel at Christmas and so he and his son enjoyed the taste that reminded them of their homeland, albeit for a short time. As we toasted everyone I told Michel that I would arrange for my son-in-law, the merchant, to buy more wine. His face lit up like a bone fire. Hamo and his wife Alice gave us the good news that she was with child once more and that meant a new baby would be born in May. It was the most convivial and happiest of times. There were no frowns and, given the number of children who now raced around, few tears.

The Prince and the Archer

Everyone stayed for the feast of St Stephen, the day after Christmas. The French did not celebrate it in the same way we did and my two Frenchmen were a little bemused by it all. As I sat drinking with Michel while Jack and Hamo played with their children, I asked him if he was happy he had come to England with me.

"You wish to be rid of me?"

I then realised that I had still to learn how to phrase my questions. I shook my head, "Quite the contrary, I enjoy your company and you have proved more than useful. You add something to my retinue I had not had before. You and your son have roots here now but I still wonder if you yearned for your homeland."

"For my part, I am more than happy to live here and I am grateful that you gave me the chance of a new life. This is not the life I imagined. It is better. You saved my son and me from a life which was desperate and I know that had you not come upon us we would now both be dead." He held up the goblet of wine. "I miss this but that is all. We have begun a journey, here in England, I do not know where it will end but I do not care, for life is about the journey. We all know the end will be, hopefully, heaven."

I liked that philosophy. When Jack and Hamo had departed and Michel and his son returned to their smallholding, the house felt empty. With short days and the wintry winds from the west bringing sleet and snow, January was as dark as ever. I began to make arrows. I had learned to fletch whilst a young archer for I could not afford to buy them. I was no longer an archer but I liked the discipline and the arrows would be used by my son. It was how I passed my days. I knew that arrows would be needed. It was just the time that I did not know.

Robert returned at the end of January. He brought news of the birth of Betty's baby. I think that while he had enjoyed the visit he had not enjoyed the journey south. He was almost blue with the cold and it took many days for him to recover. I had tried to warn him of the difficulties he had heaped upon himself but the best way to discover such things was by experience. The next time he would heed my words. I was glad to have him back.

We had fallen out with the Mortimers long ago and I was treated like a leper. They lived close to me and yet we never spoke. When they or their messengers rode through my village their eyes were always ahead. I knew that messengers had come from London at the beginning of March to give the lords of the land news from the court but did not know why. It took a visit from Sir Richard of Craven for me to be enlightened. He had been summoned to London and was on his way back to Skipton when he called to visit.

The Prince and the Archer

His face told me that this was a serious matter. "Come inside, Richard, and tell me your news. I can see by your face that it is grave."

"It is." We went to my hall and while Mary organised food, drink and a bed, Robert and I sat with the former pursuivant to hear his tale. "It is almost old news now but that is because it relates to Scotland. On February the 10th John Comyn was in Greyfriars Church in Dumfries. The two most important leaders in Scotland were meeting, at de Brus' behest, to settle their mutual grievances. Promises had been given and safety was guaranteed. Dumfries is one of de Brus' castles. While Red Comyn was praying in the church de Brus walked up to him and stabbed him. Comyn's uncle, Sir Robert rushed to help him and he was stabbed by Robert de Brus' cousin, Seton. Robert de Brus left the church to tell his companions what he had done and one of his knights, Robert Fitzpatrick, returned to ensure that John 'Red' Comyn was dead. Finally, Sir Robert Fleming went into the church, decapitated Comyn and brought the head out of the church."

I shook my head, "Those three men you mention were all with de Brus when I saw him at Guisborough. Does the king know?"

"He received the news two weeks after the murder. As you can imagine he is angry beyond words. He has ordered Aymer de Valence to take action. The king is related to John Comyn and he has made the son a ward. He is to be raised now, in England, by Sir John Weston, the guardian of the royal children. If de Brus thinks he can end the lineage of Comyn he is wrong."

"This means war."

He nodded, "I was in Winchester on behalf of the Lord Warden. It was a lucky visit that meant I heard the news. The king asked me to tell you on my way home that King Edward will need his Warbow and his archers. He said to prepare for a war."

My mind was filled with all that I would need to do but I could not help but wonder that if the king had acted on my suspicions then Comyn might still be alive. When next I saw him I would have to ask him, privately of course, why he had ignored my warning.

"When I return to Skipton I will send a rider to Sadberge, Dick should know of the threat."

"Thank you, Sir Richard, I do not think that de Brus will cast his eye south of the border. He has his own internal enemies to eliminate first but I thank you for your consideration."

He stayed the night and the talk around the table was sombre. I had expected something but to murder a rival in church...It evoked a memory, "Before I left for the crusade and met you, my love, another man was murdered in a church. That was Henry Almain, the king's cousin. Then the king could not act on the atrocity until, well until we returned to England and he was king. That callous killing was cold by then. This one is hot. King Edward is a hard man and de Brus will be punished."

That depressed the mood even more until Richard smiled and said, "The king has been given some good news, my lord." I raised an eyebrow. "Queen Margaret is with child. The king shall be a father again."

That did make me smile and Mary too. Queen Eleanor had borne him many children and it seemed the king was not yet done.

Richard then gave us the gossip and the news that had nothing to do with de Brus. "The king has taken the lands of the Earl of Derby from him and given them to Edmund of Lancaster." Edmund was a member of the royal family and it strengthened the king's grip on the lands close to the Scottish border. That affected Wallintun and, to a degree, Richard of Craven. "The new Pope has issued a papal bull which removes from the king the need to fulfil the oath that was forced upon him by Parliament and Robert Winchelsea. With the money from the Scottish nobles who bought back their estates, the king is now financially secure once more."

"And that means he can pay an army. De Brus may have prodded the bull a little too early, eh, Richard?"

When Richard left us the next morning, I sent word to Hamo and Jack. As soon as they arrived we sat in my hall so that we could talk. "Your arm is fully healed, Jack?"

"It is, my lord, and thanks to Robert's skill feels stronger than before."

"Good, for war is coming. We have not yet been summoned but I know that we shall. You, Hamo, will be needed to lead the archers and I think that you, Jack, could lead my men at arms."

Hamo asked, "You will not be going to war?"

I laughed, "Of course I will. I am still the archer that King Edward has relied on for these many years. I may not still be able to draw a bow but I have a mind that is sharper than some who are younger. With you two leading our men I can put my mind to devising strategies to defeat our foes. I do not know who will command the army with Aymer de Valence but he used my mind the last time we went to war and will do so again. You need to have arrows made, horses schooled and weapons and mail prepared. When the command comes it will have to be obeyed swiftly. De Brus is at his weakest now. There are many men who supported Comyn and others who support King Edward. De Brus is a clever man and he will only get stronger."

The Prince and the Archer

I had my own preparations to make. I went to my weaponsmith. My mail hauberk needed attention and I had learned the advantages of a good helmet. I gave him instructions and I was happy that he would carry them out. I also commissioned a shaffron for Felix. He was a good warhorse and I wanted the two of us to be well protected in battle.

The letter which arrived in April was from the king himself and addressed directly to me. The pursuivant who brought it waited for a reply and so he stayed the night. While he refreshed himself after his long ride I read the letter with Mary. I was, it seemed, confirmed as an advisor to his son, the Prince of Wales. The king and Edward were reconciled, he had been given Gascony, and the king wanted me to be close to him in the coming campaign. The date for the muster was given as July at Carlisle Castle but Aymer de Valence, so the king's letter said, was already in the northeast gathering local forces. The part that surprised me was the invitation to attend a ceremony at Westminster Palace on the 22nd of May. I was to present myself along with Jack and Hamo. The Prince of Wales would be knighted and the king wanted as many squires as possible to be knighted at the same time.

I put the letter down and shook my head, "Jack may think he is not ready for spurs but the king does. He cannot refuse."

Mary frowned, "But it is an honour. Why the sour face, my husband?"

"Because of the commitment it implies. It ties my son and stepson not to the king but his son and that worries me."

"His son may change."

I did not believe that but I said nothing. I wrote my reply promising the king that the three of us would arrive by the 20th. The pursuivant, having delivered the letter was in a chatty mood. He boasted of the king's actions, "The traitor de Brus had himself crowned on the 25th of March. The king became very angry and said, *'Robert de Brus will pay a price for his traitorous act'.*"

I said nothing. The pursuivant had drunk too much and was speaking words that the king would not like. Robert de Brus was only a traitor if he rebelled in England. Like Wallace he only sought Scotland and that, as yet, was not part of England. Perhaps King Edward thought it was.

After he left, the next morning, I rode first to Hamo and then to Jack to tell them of our impending journey and honour. Neither was particularly enamoured at the thought. Like me, Jack and Hamo did not enjoy dressing up and suffering great ceremony. They both knew they would have to endure it. "We three will ride with just Robert and Jean Michel. The rest can be ready to march north. If we are to be there by

The Prince and the Archer

July then we cannot leave after Midsummer's Day. We will have to leave by the middle of the month. The men will have to ensure that their farming duties are complete."

Jean Michel was honoured to be at such a ceremony and we left on the 16th. It would take a good three days to make the journey. It was not only their wives who fussed over Hamo and Jack but my wife also. They had new clothes made for the ceremony. I had fine spurs made for them and I reluctantly endured the making of new clothes. It was a relief to be on the road and away from the chattering magpies who had made such a fuss before our departure.

My son and stepson were the lowliest of the esquires to be knighted. Piers Gaveston, Hugh le Despenser, John de Warenne, 7th Earl of Surrey, Roger Mortimer, 1st Earl of March and his uncle, Roger Mortimer of Chirk were amongst the squires to be knighted. I knew that the Mortimers would not be happy that they would be knighted along with my son and stepson. They thought that we were common and low-born, not deserving of the honour.

There were so many people at Westminster Palace that we all had to cram into one chamber. Robert procured paillasses for him and Jean Michel, and my sons and I slept in the one bed. While they took the opportunity to explore London I was sent for by the king and his son. The two men were alone in a small chamber. The prince, to me, seemed even more arrogant than when I had last seen him.

The king pointed to a chair and I sat. The act did not go down well with his son.

"Before we begin, Warbow, I want to thank you for your letter concerning de Brus. I should have heeded the message but I was," he briefly glanced at his son, "distracted, at the time. Now that matters have been settled I can address the issue. This time we shall scotch the snake before he can do more harm. I wish you to ride with my son when he leads his army north. Your sage advice will guide him and mould him into a great warrior."

Before I could answer the prince snorted, "I do not need old men around me, Father. Send him with de Lacy and the other old men, King Edward, but do not burden me with a common old archer. I want young knights and fine warriors around me when I face and defeat de Brus."

Many men might have reacted to the insults but I let it wash over me. I did not respect the young man so why should I worry about his insults? His father, however, did not like it and said so, "You will have to learn to take advice, my son, and there is none who gives better advice than Gerald Warbow."

The Prince and the Archer

"Then send him to Aymer de Valence, God knows he needs all the help he can be given."

I saw the king colour and I intervened, "King Edward, I know Aymer de Valence and I have fought alongside him. I would not burden your son with an old man if he does not wish it. I will happily take my men and join with Aymer de Valance, the Earl of Pembroke, in the east."

The king looked from me to his son. We both knew that even if he ordered his son to take me it would only cause problems and having given him a solution he eventually nodded, "Thank you, Warbow. The earl will be grateful for your advice." I nodded. "You may leave us now. I fear this means that you and your retinue will have to leave sooner than the rest. The earl is already mustering his army in the north."

"As soon as the ceremony is over, my lord, we shall leave."

The prince said, "But I would have your sons with my men! They are not old men."

It was my turn to smile, "And they are my sons. They will follow my banner, is that not right, King Edward?"

The king nodded, "Warbow is quite right. If you wished his sons then you should take the man who helped me to keep my throne." I saw irritation flick across the face of the prince. The king waved a hand, "You may leave us, Warbow."

It was a tiny victory but I had learned that any victory, however small, was worth celebrating.

Both Hamo and Jack endorsed my decision and were more than happy not to be serving with the prince. "It means, of course, that we shall have barely two nights at home. We will need to get to Berwick as soon as we can."

The Feast of the Swans was an elaborate event and more than just a dubbing of squires. The king first knighted his son who then knighted the other two hundred and fifty-six esquires. The ceremony being completed, we went to a feast and two swans were brought in. The king stood and stated, "I swear before God and the swans to avenge the murder of John III Comyn, Lord of Badenoch and the desecration of Greyfriars Church in Dumfries by the Earl of Carrick Robert Bruce and his accomplices. When that is done I promise to take the cross once more and to fight the infidels in the Holy Land."

That brought many shouts and promises from others who promised that they, too, would take the cross. I knew that the king would never go to the Holy Land again. He might intend to, for he was a man of his

The Prince and the Archer

word, but I knew that he was too old. Perhaps the offer was part of a deal he had brokered with Pope Clement for the papal bull.

Prince Edward then stood and vowed, "And I swear never to sleep two nights in the same place until the Scots are vanquished."

Robert and Jean Michel were acting as squires and Robert whispered to me, "I can see that the prince has read the Grail legends." I looked at him. He explained, "That is the oath that Sir Percival swore when he sought the cup of Christ. The prince sees himself as a hero, eh?"

The swearing of the oaths had an effect and many other newly knighted squires also swore oaths. Jack and Hamo were too wise for that. They did not need to put on a show to prove their courage. They had done that many times already. They did not promise to take the cross.

Chapter 6

Berwick on Tweed 1306

My early preparations were rewarded. The men were not discomfited by our early departure. Their fields were tended and arrangements were made for those not going to war to help them out. We had plenty of horses and instead of a wagon, we packed sumpters with our arrows. It would make for a faster journey. I had not summoned men from Baldon but I would take men from Sadberge and Coldingham which both lay in the northeast. The men I led from Yarpole, Lucton and Luston numbered fifty-three, fifty-five if you included Robert and Abel. We had three knights but none of us had a squire yet. Their sons were infants and there was no rush for we had Hamo's brothers-in-law, James and John, who would serve as men at arms but they could also take on the duties of squires. As well as Felix I would take my hackney, Arthur. I would keep Felix for the purpose for which he was bred, war. The many leagues to the muster would be ridden on a riding horse. I asked Harry if he wished to come. His hesitation told me that he did not. I understood. He had an inn to build and once he had decided to give up the sword then his heart would not be in it. The moment a man chose to give up the sword then he could never go back. He did not need the coins and he had proved his courage more than enough. I was happy that I was leaving a good warrior who could, in the unlikely event of trouble, defend my manor and organise the men we had left.

Each warrior took their own supplies. The warrant I had from the king's officials allowed me to make demands on the castles and villages through which we passed. Our supplies were to augment that which we requisitioned. The last thing the king needed was an army living off the land and taking from the people.

We did not leave at the crack of dawn. That was not fair to the ladies. We left from Yarpole and we looked glorious. We had three banners and with spurs on three of us were the noblest band of warriors to ever leave Yarpole. Mary held in her tears. She was used to this. Susanna and Alice were not and they wept. Alice was nursing her newborn, Robert. I was just pleased that Hamo had been there to see the baby born. His son had arrived the day we returned from the Feast of the Swans. The other bairns were not yet old enough to realise the importance of our departure and they were just mesmerised by the colours of the livery and the jangle of mail and weapons. Michel's wife Anna was there too. She would give birth while he was away but I knew

The Prince and the Archer

that Mary and the women of my manor would rally around her. We all rode. I had learned that speed was often crucial to victory and besides, as a young archer I had tramped behind sergeants and knights too often. I had resented it and I wanted my archers to feel equal. We headed north and west, first to Wallintun and thence to Skipton. Our first day would be an easy twenty-eight miles to Shrewsbury but the next day, to the bridge at Wallintun, would be a gruelling forty-seven-mile ride. We reached Skipton Castle in the early afternoon after a four-day ride. Sir Richard had not yet left. He would be joining the muster at Carlisle. He was, however, able to give us good intelligence about de Brus. My knights and Robert dined with him while James, John and Abel acted as our servants. I think they enjoyed the privilege of hearing for themselves what would soon be gossip to be spread around the campfires.

"He does not enjoy universal support, Sir Gerald. His familia and family are his greatest allies. There are many Scotsmen who liked Red Comyn and others who, while they did not like the man, were appalled at the manner of his death. De Brus is busy subjugating those he cannot suborn."

"And the Earl of Pembroke, what has he done about the rebels?"

"Henry Percy and the Lord Warden of the Marches have raised the northern host."

"Is Bishop Bek with them?"

"No, but his men are. The earl has in the region of three thousand men."

It was not enough. "And de Brus?"

"That is harder to estimate but between four and five thousand men are loyal to him."

"Then the sooner we join the northern barons the better."

We made Richmond Castle and stayed in that northern fortress. Being a royal castle most of the garrison had joined the muster. The relatively short journey from Richmond to Sadberge meant we reached it at the ninth hour of the day. Dick and my men had done well and with the extension finished the wall now looked formidable.

Dick nodded as I dismounted, "We heard about the muster, my lord. Do you wish us to join you?"

"My archers? Yes. The rest of you, no. Keep Betty's brothers here. I will take Abel as a groom."

Betty was reunited with her younger brother and I was touched by the affection they showed to one another.

My men made shelters and began to cook their own food. I went with Dick to inspect the progress he had made on the manor. The

The Prince and the Archer

kitchen was now a much better place to cook. It had light and it had air. Whilst the hall was not as secure as it had been, the raising of the wall and the addition of a fighting platform made the manor easier to defend.

"We have trained the villagers and they know that if there is danger then they are to come within the walls and defend it. They see the sense in that." He pointed to a new set of foundations. "This will be the warrior hall you wanted, my lord."

"Good. Where do the archers sleep at the moment?"

"The barn and the stable are both warm and secure my lord. They are happy and now that you are taking them to war we have the chance to erect the walls for their new home."

He led me across the fields, now filled with crops that were ready to be harvested: there were beans and oats and I saw that he had managed to sow wheat. When I asked him about it he shrugged, "I am no farmer, my lord but Alfred assured me that as they grow wheat not far from here we could try it. It cost just a sack of seeds. I thought that it was worth the investment."

"Good."

I saw that the fishpond had been finished but it was not yet full. "We will stock the pond when the autumn rains fill it. Robert advised me about the fitting of a sluice gate to control the flow of water and we finished it last month. I visited the manor of Bishopton and the steward there was happy to let us have some of their smaller fish and eggs. Alfred and I thought that they would have the best chance to grow. We will not be eating the fish for a year or so but when we do they will be a good size to eat."

As we walked back to the hall I reflected that I had appointed the right man. I found myself envying him. Yarpole was finished and I wanted to see the changes wrought here at Sadberge. That evening my son, stepson and Gwillim dined with the family. Gwillim was an old friend of Dick's and I saw, in his eyes, the envy. Dick was happy and had something Gwillim would never have; children of his own. His wife, Myfanwy had a son but Gwillim had never managed to sire a son. I knew he regretted that.

We left for Durham. I knew, from Richard of Craven, that relations between the bishop and the king were not as good as they had been. A dispute with a prior had escalated and it had taken the intervention of the Pope to save the bishop from arrest. The Pope had then made Bishop Bek the Patriarch of Jerusalem. As such he was the most powerful churchman in England and immune from further punishment from the king. All was now, it appeared, settled, but it explained why the Prince Bishop was not with the army. The bad feelings lingered. I

The Prince and the Archer

dined alone with Bishop Bek. We had fought alongside one another and I think that he trusted me. It would have been wrong to involve my son and stepson so we dined alone so that we could speak openly.

The bishop was unhappy that the king had not supported him against the prior, "Sir Gerald, you know the service I did the king. The least I could expect was his support."

I was never a diplomat but I knew it was incumbent upon me to pour oil on troubled waters if I could. "The king is getting old, Bishop Bek. His mind is as sharp as it ever was but Queen Margaret is not the influence that was Queen Eleanor. Had Good Queen Eleanor been alive then you would have had the support. We cannot have division with the threat that is de Brus."

He nodded and drank some more of the excellent wine that had been served, "De Brus is a very real threat, Sir Gerald. His lands straddle the border both here and in the west. He was constable of Carlisle Castle and he knows well the strengths and weakness of our defences."

"More, he fought alongside us and knows the strengths and weaknesses of our army."

He smiled, "And that is why I was pleased when I heard that you were coming north. Falkirk was as much your victory as anyone's."

I shrugged, "I just played my part, Bishop."

Our last stop before Berwick was Alnwick Castle and we enjoyed a good welcome and fine food. Like Richmond and Durham, the castle had been stripped of most of its defenders. If the Earl of Pembroke lost then we might lose the whole of the north for there would be few men left to defend it. Aymer de Valence had a great responsibility upon his shoulders.

Berwick was an armed camp. My band was a small one but we were recognised and cheered. Everyone knew the value of men led by King Edward's archer. In many ways, I was seen as an extension of the king. I let my men take my horse for I was waved over to join Aymer de Valance, Robert de Clifford and Henry Percy. They were conferring in the barbican of the fortress.

I was older than all of them and I had seen them progress from squires and lowly knights to captains in the army. I knew that they respected me and the Earl of Pembroke's words confirmed it. "Your banners were seen as you approached the crossing. We have waited here for you. Come to the Great Hall so that, now we are all gathered, we can plan our strategy."

The earl's bodyguards cleared a path as we made our way through the mailed men who milled in the outer bailey.

The Prince and the Archer

"Clear the hall and fetch refreshments. Then William, guard the doors so that we are not disturbed."

A grizzled warrior nodded and said, "Aye, my lord. Rafe, you heard his lordship."

I took off my cloak as the doors were closed. I knew I stank of horses but I would probably do so until this campaign was over. I sat and waited. Henry Percy unfolded a map. The wine and food were brought and, when we were alone the earl said, "We left the king some time ago. Were there any further instructions from the king?"

"Instructions, my lord?" I had received no instructions prior to my departure from Westminster.

Robert de Clifford said, "We were told to take no prisoners and use every means in our power to defeat this man. His exact words were, '*show no mercy and execute all who bear arms against us*'."

I shook my head and, after pouring myself some wine and sipping it, told them the tale of the Feast of the Swans and the ceremony of the spurs, "The king wished me as a mentor for the prince but the prince wanted only young knights with him. Prince Edward will lead the main army in July. We have until then to defeat de Brus."

The three men looked at each other. They probably shared my opinion of the prince but one day, unless he fell in battle, he would be king. Nothing was said directly but the earl's words confirmed his opinion, "Then let us try to defeat de Brus before the army reaches us." He turned to the Northumbrian, "Percy."

Henry Percy had the northern tones that had many similarities with that of the Scots but I knew that the men of Northumberland had been Scotland's enemies since time out of mind. While Robert de Clifford might know the western side of Scotland, the east was the land that Henry Percy knew. He spoke, "De Brus has gone to Perth. The king may have taken the Stone of Scone to Westminster but the Scots still see the place it was held as special. He is gathering men there in great numbers. The lowlands are not too enamoured of him but further north they are. He has four thousand men."

The Earl of Pembroke used the eating knife with which he had just sliced some ham to point at the map. "He may outnumber us but I intend to take the battle to him. The less time he has to rally support the better chance we have of quashing this uprising before it has begun. Wallace and Murray inspired the people and that led to the defeat at Stirling Bridge." He looked at me, "So, Sir Gerald, have you any observations?"

"How many archers do we have?"

The Prince and the Archer

The earl looked at Robert de Clifford who said, "I know not how many you brought but we have a hundred or so."

"They are not mounted?"

"No."

It was woefully inadequate. Falkirk had not been won by knights but by archers. "I would have my son, Sir Hamo, command the archers who fight on foot." I looked at their faces for any dissension and there was none. "I suggest that we use my mounted archers as scouts although it seems to me that the enemy will be easy enough to find."

"Good, then we leave on the morrow. We have a chamber for you here, Sir Gerald."

I shook my head, "My lord, I have a manor just north of here, at Coldingham. One of my archers, Mordaf, is the steward there. I will visit with him. He may have local men trained as archers and, in any case, he might have information that will help us. I will sleep amongst my men."

Percy shook his head, "You would shun a soft bed for one made of rocks?"

I smiled, "My lord, as much as I would enjoy a night in a soft bed for I am an old man whose bones ache no matter where I sleep, unless it be in my own bed, while we are on campaign I will endure the same conditions as my men. It is my way and I am too old to change now." I paused, "Do we know, my lord, why Comyn was murdered?"

"For the Scottish crown, of course. What we heard was that Comyn and de Brus came to an arrangement. If de Brus rose in revolt then Comyn would not oppose him and in return for this complicity would be rewarded by de Brus land. The king heard of this and was about to have de Brus arrested when he fled. As for the murder…when a man wants a crown then all else goes from his head. He was absolved of his crime by Bishop Wishart."

I had my answer and I headed to my camp, recognisable by my standard littering above those of my son and stepson. The king was slipping. He had been given two warnings about de Brus and he had acted too slowly. "Abel, saddle me a spare horse, not Felix. Robert, mount and accompany me, we have a visit to make." As they both hurried to obey me I said, "Hamo, you command the archers. There are a hundred but they are not mounted. Gwillim can command the mounted archers. They will be the scouts."

"Aye, my lord." My son would organise them and assess them. They would not be as good as my archers but there might be some who could be used in the same way as mine.

The Prince and the Archer

We headed north to the manor I had been given some years earlier. When we reached it I saw that, like Dick, Mordaf had made the best of the gift of a home that I had given to him. He and his men were in the yard winnowing. The air was filled with the dust from their labours and they had cloths about their mouths. When we clattered through their gate they stopped.

Mordaf had aged but not in a bad way. He looked contented, "Sir Gerald! I wondered if you be with the army. Betty! It is Sir Gerald."

It was clear that Betty had been baking for she came from the hall with her hands covered in flour. She beamed, "My lord! The house is a mess and…"

I dismounted and held up my hand, "I come for a brief conference. I will visit but only when the threat of de Brus is ended."

My words sobered them all. She nodded, "Then I will bring ale for you."

Robert had dismounted and Mordaf viewed him with a face that showed the questions he wished to ask. "This is Robert. He thought he would be a priest but took up instead with Warbow!"

Robert bowed and said, "It is good to meet you, Master Mordaf."

"A Frenchman! Well, I'll be…"

I laughed, "And I have two more Frenchmen who serve as sergeants, Mordaf. The world has changed whilst you have husbanded my manor in the north." I put my arm around his shoulder, "We go to Perth to find de Brus. Have you any men I can lead?" I added quickly, "Not you, old friend. I will not tear you from Betty's side."

He nodded at the men with him, "Donald, David and Robbie here are all good archers and trained by me." He added, "And loyal to both King Edward and to you, my lord."

"Good. Have they horses?"

"I can provide them."

I looked at the three men he had named, "Then fetch your bows and gardyvyans."

The three grinned and ran off leaving the other two men with Mordaf looking disappointed. Mordaf explained, "These would be spearmen but they are not yet ready to go to war, Sir Gerald."

I nodded and seeing their faces said, "When we return we shall bring war gear for you so that the next time I come north you can follow my banner." Their faces brightened. Betty came out and she was followed by a couple of small children. "Yours?"

"Aye, Sir Gerald, God has blessed us with a boy and a girl: Gerald and Mary." He looked worried, "I hope you do not mind the impertinence."

The Prince and the Archer

I laughed, "Why should I? I am honoured."

We drank in the shade of the hall and I told Mordaf of the recent events. He smiled, "So Dick is a steward too and he has married a Betty. It is a strange world, eh, my lord?"

"I have long ago given up trying to work out the way that Fate directs us. You found a bride here, Gwillim found one in Wales and mine came from the heart of the Mongol Empire, while Dick tripped over his at Yarpole."

The three archers returned and they were leading three horses.

"When this is all over Gwillim, Jack and Hamo will return with me to enjoy your hospitality."

Mordaf nodded. He had viewed Jack as a son, "And now I will have to address him as Sir John, eh, my lord?"

I shook my head, "Hamo and Jack are like me. The title means little. They are still Hamo and Jack. The men call them 'my lord' but I think that is pride from our men that the two have been elevated." I mounted, "Farewell. I am more than happy at your blessings, Mordaf."

As we rode back to Berwick, Robert said, "I have not known you for long, Sir Gerald, but I get the impression that you have never changed. Your men, even those who have not seen you for some time, seem to view you as a friend."

"And why should I change? I am the man I always was. Those who have their heads turned by titles and land are not to be trusted. I have been blessed with land and riches but I know that I have been lucky. Both land and riches can be taken away at the whim of a king but friends and brothers in arms? They are the rocks on which I can rely."

Food was being prepared as we rode into the camp. Gwillim, Jack and Hamo were keen to know how Mordaf fared. Hob and Nob took care of the three new archers and, all around my camp, there was harmony. When men began to sing songs I took it as a good sign. They were in good heart. The men of Sir Gerald Warbow were going to war again. So long as I led them then they would be confident in victory. It was a burden I had to carry but every one of my men was as precious to me as Hamo and Jack. It was that bond that brought success and the Prince of Wales would need to learn that lesson or he would be doomed to failure. His father had surrounded himself with wise and loyal warriors. The prince, it seemed to me, was merely looking at glitter and youth. I hoped he would change and I knew that his father had intended for my guiding hand to move him down the path to wisdom. That guiding hand would now be the recently knighted Sir Piers Gaveston.

Chapter 7

Methven June 1306

De Brus made his first mistake when he did not try to stop us from investing Perth. It had a castle as well as good walls and the Earl of Pembroke was too good a general to allow the enemy to use it. We now had a base. It took a couple of days for the new Scottish king to realise what we had done by which time we had the small deficiencies in the defences repaired and the walls manned. When de Brus woke up to the fact that the Earl of Pembroke had brought an army into his heartland he reacted quickly and brought his whole army to the gates of Perth. I made sure that my archers were prominently seen on the battlements. Their bows were not strung and the arrows were not nocked. It would be enough. His heralds sounded for a parley and the earl, along with Henry Percy, Robert de Clifford and myself spoke to him from the gatehouse.

"My Lord de Valence, I invite you to bring forth your army so that we may do battle here, before the gates of Perth."

When we had heard that the King of Scotland had come we had discussed our response to any demand that he would make. It would be prevarification. The earl shaded his hands against the sky and said, "It is late in the day, my lord. Let us say we shall array here on the morrow and do battle."

De Brus nodded, "Good. Shall we say the hour of terce?"

"The hour of terce it is."

As the army slipped away the earl said, "Can your archers follow without being seen?"

It was almost an insult but I knew that the Earl of Pembroke meant nothing by it. I nodded, "Of course, my lord."

"Then have some follow him and find out where he is camped."

I turned and headed for Gwillim, "Gwillim, choose two scouts to go with Mordaf's men and follow the Scots. We need to know where they intend to camp."

"Mordaf's men?"

"They are Scottish." If they were stopped their voices might confuse the enemy.

"Aah."

I left the details to Gwillim. The men would slip out of a sally port and walk rather than ride. As at least half of the Scottish army was on foot they would have no problem keeping up.

The Prince and the Archer

I joined the other leaders and our Scottish allies in the Great Hall. With the doors guarded, the earl began to outline his plan, "I have no intention of allowing Robert de Brus the opportunity to use his overwhelming numbers to defeat us. I intend to make an attack at dawn on his camp when Sir Gerald's men have discovered its position. We need his sentries eliminated. Another job for your archers, Sir Gerald."

It was not a pleasant task that we had been given. My men would have to sneak up and slit the throats of the sentries to allow our horsemen to charge into their camp.

"We can do so, my lord."

"Let your archers know that they will enjoy the rewards we accrue."

I nodded. That was only fair. The men they killed would not have the purses, weapons or armour that would come into the possession of our victorious knights and men at arms. The king had said no prisoners and that meant no ransom.

My men returned not long before the sunset. It was Hob who reported. The earl listened attentively to my archer. "The Scots have moved six miles away, my lord. They are in a wood on some high ground. Mordaf's man, Donald, spoke to some locals and discovered the river is called the Almond. The tiny village nearby is called Methven."

He beamed, "You have done well, archer." He placed a handful of coins on the table, "Take these for your pains and let the others know that there will be a greater reward when we have ended this Scottish threat."

"Thank you, my lord." Hob glanced at me and I nodded for him to leave.

Now that we knew where they were we could plan our attack. "We rouse the men before lauds and the archers can eliminate their sentries before prime. I shall have the horns sounded for the attack and we shall sweep into their camp while they are still asleep."

It was neither honourable nor chivalrous but we had our orders from the king. There was to be no mercy and the Scottish soldiers led by the murderer, Robert de Brus, would pay the price for defying King Edward.

I joined my men and held a council of war with my leaders. "Hamo, you will lead my archers to eliminate the sentries. The ones who came with Percy and de Clifford are of unknown quality. I doubt that they will have more than twenty or so sentries." Hamo nodded. "Jack, you and I will lead the sergeants. We will use spears rather than lances. When we have passed your archers, Hamo, then follow. The earl is confident that we can catch them unawares but de Brus is clever. He

The Prince and the Archer

may have been fooled by the earl's words but, equally, he may have plans of his own."

Hamo looked at Jack and then Gwillim. He cleared his throat and said, "Father, you do not need to lead us. Why risk a ride in the night and a fall from a horse?"

I could tell, from the looks they shared, that this was a conspiracy. Even Robert looked away. I stared at them one by one before I spoke, "The day that I do not lead my men into battle is the day that I hang up my sword. My king is older than I am and he has not given up on being a warrior and neither shall I. I will have no more talk like this. Do you understand?" My voice had an edge to it and they all nodded and murmured their agreement. "And as I have never fallen from a horse in my life then I think that such an event is unlikely now that I ride the finest horse that I have ever owned."

What I did do was ensure that I had a sleep after we had eaten. That was a sensible thing to do. I knew that once I was mounted and heading into the fray my body would respond to my commands but I was not a fool. I was old and needed more rest than when I was younger.

It was Robert who roused me. He had food and wine. "You have slept well, Sir Gerald. It is two hours to Lauds and the men will be roused soon." He smiled, "I thought you might need longer to rejoin the land of the living."

I snorted, "I did well enough before I took you into my service, Robert."

He was not put out by my chastening tone, "And now that I am here you shall do even better."

I made water and then ate and drank.

"As you are here you might as well help me into my mail."

"Of course."

I slipped on my gambeson, the padded undergarment that would absorb the blows from heavy weapons. Then I raised my arms and he slid the mail hauberk over my head and arms. I did not put my hands in the mittens. That would be done just before I rode into combat. He shook his head, "This weighs so much that I do not know how you can move in it."

"The weight is spread and besides I was an archer. My body can cope." I strapped on my sword belt and looped the end through it. I donned my arming cap and then Robert placed my mail coif over my head. "You can carry my helmet and shield. Come, let us see if Abel has saddled Felix yet."

By now the camp and the castle were roused. If de Brus had any spies then he would know what we were about. Felix was saddled and

The Prince and the Archer

Abel was fastening the shaffron on his head. The caparison with my coat of arms was on his back. It might deflect a glancing arrow but that was all.

Abel said, "I have given him a couple of apples, my lord. He likes the treat."

I nodded, "Just so long as he makes his dung now and not when we attack then I shall be happy."

Hamo and my archers appeared. They wore no mail and their bows were carried unstrung. They wore dark cloaks and each had a short sword and dagger. Hamo was not wearing his spurs but he had his sword. I nodded, "You know what you are about?"

"Aye, we do."

"Then go with God."

That was all that was needed and they slipped away. It would take a little over an hour for them to reach the woods.

Robert said, "Would you care to be shriven?"

I shook my head but, taking my sword from its scabbard, knelt and held the blade like a cross before me, "Almighty God I pray that you watch over my son and my men and, if it pleases you, to keep me from harm. Amen."

Robert shook his head.

I used Abel's arm to help me to my feet and sheathe my sword, "God knows my heart, Robert. I do not need long conversations with him. I leave that to priests with flapping lips."

I walked to the muster point and Abel led Felix. Robert still carried my helmet. Jack was there already and he wore his helmet. He also wore poleyns on his knees, cannons on his arms and schynbalds over his shins. I knew that Mary had paid for the armour. She had tried to have a set made for me but I would have none of it. I did not even bother with the metal sabatons which Jack wore but, like most of my men at arms wore my buskins. I was pleased that Jack was so well armoured. I wanted him to survive.

"Are we ready then?"

Jack beamed, "We are, my lord." I saw, behind him, that Michel and his son were attired much as I was but both wore a helmet.

"Robert, I shall not need my helmet." I took my shield from him, "Fetch me a spear."

Robert rolled his eyes but he and Jack, wisely, said nothing.

The earl and the other leaders rode to join us. I saw that there were Scottish nobles with us. I recognised Sir Philip Mowbray. He was an avowed enemy of de Brus.

The earl said, "Let us be about them, Sir Gerald. Your archers?"

The Prince and the Archer

"Are even now slitting throats, my lord."

The earl led as was his right. His household knights and the other leaders flanked him. We followed. I did not need to show my courage by being among the first to charge. We had left our foot soldiers in Perth. If we failed then we would still have a home. We rode through the dark. To an archer, the noise of metal and hooves seemed deafening. If my archers failed to eliminate the sentries then we would have a warm welcome for they could not fail to hear our approach. I saw the woods rising in the distance. Dawn was still almost an hour away and we would need to be in a long line before we attacked.

The horsemen before us stopped at the foot of the slope and as I nudged Felix through the gap, I saw Hamo speaking with the earl. It was at that moment that the sun began to flare in the east and, even as the earl ordered his horn to sound the charge, I heard shouts of alarm in the Scottish camp. Even though the sentries had been eliminated we had been heard.

We hurriedly formed a line and began to ride towards the Scottish camp. It was all coming to life. I found myself in the second rank but close to the earl. Jack was on my right and Michel and his son to my left. James and John were just behind me. As we rode towards the camp I heard the sound of Scottish horns. Horsemen were coming to meet us. I wondered if de Brus had been up early and this was just bad luck. Such things happened.

I couched my spear and followed the earl. I recognised Robert de Brus leading his household knights. I even recognised the livery of Sir Christopher Seton. In any battle, you look for your own enemy. Mine was the Scottish standard bearer. He would be a good knight. When we clashed de Brus had the advantage that he was charging downhill. He was a skilled knight and in that first encounter, he unhorsed the Earl of Pembroke.

Sir Philip roared a challenge at the newly crowned Scottish king and rode at him. I concentrated on aiming my spear at the standard bearer. If the flag fell then they might lose heart. He was the nearest man to me and so I rode directly at him. He saw me coming and lowered the standard to use it as a lance. My right arm was still a powerful weapon and I had a good eye. I rammed the spear at him a heartbeat before he tried to strike at me. My spear struck his right shoulder and must have penetrated to his skin for he lowered the standard even more and when the end touched the ground, it was torn from his grip. I punched at him with my shield as we passed and he fell to the ground. I reined in and shouted, "Do you yield or shall I end your life?"

The Prince and the Archer

He was lying on his back and he said, for he had no choice, "I yield to you, Sir Gerald."

As I turned I saw that Robert de Brus had been unhorsed by Sir Philip Mowbray but before the Scottish warrior could claim the victory, Sir Christopher Seton rode at Sir Philip and de Brus, with all the luck of a cat, caught the reins of the standard bearer's mount, mounted and galloped off. He would live to fight another day.

The earl had remounted and he shouted, "After them! Let none escape!"

The flight of their king ensured that the whole army tried to follow him. The problem was that Robert de Brus was mounted and his men were not.

"Warbow! Stay with me!" We had not taken our banners and I used my war cry to ensure that my men stayed with me. We fought better when together. The earl's men and those led by Henry Percy and de Clifford were all good men but they were not our brothers in arms. As we cleared those who had tried to prevent us from pursuing de Brus, Jack and Michel closed up with me. I had better vision than they did for I had no helmet to restrict what I saw. I veered to the left as I shouted, "To the horses." I knew that men would try to get to the horses. We would be able to hurt them more if we took their horses and slew the men who were trying to mount them. A man cannot hold a weapon and mount a horse. A Scot rose up ten feet before me. He must have been lying in wait and in a flash of sunlight from the rising sun I saw his axe swing towards me. I hurled my spear and both my arm and eye were good. The man was naked from the waist up and my spear struck him squarely in the chest. He had not had time to dress. He was a big man and tough too for he did not drop the axe immediately, but as the spearhead found something vital the axe slid from his lifeless hands and he fell to the ground.

Drawing my sword I prepared to lean from the saddle as I saw another warrior scurrying for the tethered horses. In the last moment before he died, he half turned and saw death swinging his sword. I hacked across his spine and he fell. There was a mass of men close to the horses. Some, foolishly, tried to saddle them. The wiser ones just slashed at the tethers to ride bareback. One or two managed to escape but we slaughtered the rest. I knew that some of the younger ones would baulk at the butchery and I shouted, "King Edward said, no mercy and no prisoners! Remember Stirling Bridge!" They were all too young to have fought in that disaster but they remembered the stories and it must have hardened their hearts for they hacked, stabbed and slashed with renewed vigour.

The Prince and the Archer

The wall of enemy dead slowed us up. I heard the horns of the earl and the other two commanders as they raced north and east pursuing de Brus and the ones who had managed to flee. Hamo and my archers had now joined those of us who were clearing the Scottish camp of the odd survivor. There were prisoners for many of the nobles who were unhorsed shouted that they had surrendered and we held back from killing them. It went against the grain to kill an unarmed man. I knew that if the earl wished it then they would be executed. There would be no trial.

I shouted, "Gather the prisoners. Jack, Hamo, have men search the camp."

I looked around and saw that there were none left to oppose us. Our men were already stripping the dead of their mail and their weapons. The dead horses would be butchered for food. I dismounted and tied Felix to a spear I rammed into the ground. "Those apples worked, Felix. You fought well today."

I slipped my coif from my head and removed the arming cap. The air felt cool as it flowed over my thinning hair.

Michel came over to me. He had blood spattered on his surcoat but he had no wounds that I could see, "An impressive victory, Sir Gerald. It was a good plan."

"Aye, Michel but had we not executed it well then it would all have been in vain." Jack and Jean Michel, along with four other sergeants pushed the prisoners towards us. One was the standard bearer. All looked dejected. "Your names?"

"Alexander Fraser."

"David de Inchmartin."

"Hugh de Haye."

"John Somerville."

The standard bearer proffered his sword, "I am Alexander Scrymgeour, the royal standard-bearer. Will you demand ransom?"

I shrugged, "King Edward demands your death but who knows? The Earl of Pembroke commands this army and your lives are in his hands. For my part, I would ransom you."

I looked at the two who had not spoken. "Thomas de Randolph. King Robert is my uncle."

"And I am Hugh, the king's chaplain."

I thought that he alone might be spared. I felt sorry for the others. I was still haunted by the thought of Wallace's death. Some of these might be lucky and just be beheaded. Others would be hanged, drawn and quartered. I doubted that they would bear it as stoically as William Wallace had done.

The Prince and the Archer

When the earl and the hunters returned they were all in an exuberant mood. The mood soured a little when the earl saw the prisoners. "Sir Gerald, the king ordered us to be merciless."

I shrugged, "Then, my lord, have them executed but I am a warrior and not a butcher. Perhaps the king wishes to pass judgment on them."

The earl did not want to execute them either and he saw, in my words, a way out. "A good idea. Sir Henry, have some of your men escort them back to Berwick."

He looked at me, "And you, Sir Gerald, are needed to find de Brus. He has headed north and has a start. You found Wallace. I would have you find his successor. Bring him and his family back to us."

I shook my head, "I can follow and I can hunt but I cannot promise anything, my lord. To the north of here is a wild country and he has supporters."

"Just do your best and remember that the prince is closing from the west. I will send a messenger to tell him of our success. If you can then hold him and send for us. I will send for ships. If he heads for the islands we can search for him."

"Very well, my lord. We will take fifteen of the horses we captured. We will need the remounts." I did not ask nor did I ask permission to keep the treasure we took. He nodded. I turned to Hamo and Jack, "Break camp. Send Hob and the men from Coldingham to find the trail of our enemies. If they have women with them then they cannot move as fast as de Brus might hope." They both nodded and left me with Abel and Robert. I smiled, "Well Abel, I can promise you that you will learn more about horses here than you would at Yarpole."

He was an eager young man and his grin was infectious, "I have already learned much, my lord, and this is like a dream."

"Then see to Felix."

He left us and Robert looked north and west where the highland peaks rose like dragon's teeth, "This will not be easy, will it, Sir Gerald?"

"No. We have more than fifty men but the advantage will always lie with our prey. They know where they are headed and we do not. Enough of them survived to ambush us and that is why I have Hob leading our men. He has a nose for ambush. Do you regret following my banner?"

He laughed, "Regret? Not for an instant. I am in a world where despite my lack of martial prowess I am accepted by warriors. More than that, they call me a brother. I feel privileged to be one of them. Like Abel, I am learning. In my case, it is how to be a doctor. No, my lord, you saved my life and gave me a life."

The Prince and the Archer

I was weary already when Donald rode in. We were on a flatter piece of ground. A cottage stood close by and there was water. We had stopped to water our horses. "We have picked up their trail, my lord. They made good time and they are twenty miles ahead of us. Hob and the others are close by them."

I looked up at the sky. It was getting late.

Donald said, "They have taken the pass to the Spittal of Glenshee through the mountains. It is not a place where we can get close to them and they have one hundred and ten men with them."

Hamo said, "Defeated men, Father."

I shook my head, "They are men protecting their women and in a land that they know and we do not. We will camp here and make an early start. Donald, take a remount and go back to Hob. Tell him that we will follow. He is to keep hidden."

"Yes, my lord."

When Donald came back I gestured for him to approach, "Where does the road finish?"

"It drops to the Dee Valley and the castle at Braemar."

"Can that castle be defended?"

"I am sorry, my lord, but I have never been there. I know where it is only because we were told."

I nodded and patted the rump of his horse. "We camp here. Robert, you might terrify the farmer less than we do, ask him if he has food we can buy. Discover if he is a threat."

"Aye, my lord."

We had no tents with us but there was an animal byre and, most importantly, grazing for our horses and water. We would make hovels. The sky looked clear. It might be chilly, later on, but we had blankets.

Robert came back with a sad look on his face, "The man is fearful for his life. The ones who passed north, de Brus and the others, told them that the men who were pursuing ate babies and raped the women. I think I persuaded him otherwise." He held up a round of cheese, "His wife offered us this. I paid for it."

"Good. Then we can expect little help and more importantly, dangerous opposition as we ride north. De Brus' lies will make a wall of silence for us and we will be forced to rely on our scouts."

It was a frugal meal. Our foresight in bringing our own supplies was justified but we would have to forage soon and that meant taking from the locals. If the farm where we rested for the night was an example then pickings would be slim.

"What if de Brus holes up in Braemar Castle?"

The Prince and the Archer

"Then we have him. If this is the Dee Valley then our men can simply block it off and we send to the earl for men to take the castle. No, I do not think that he will make a stand there. He will push on. We may have to fight but I do not intend to stay long."

"You seem to know what he will do."

"I followed Wallace, remember. De Brus will be heading to the islands that surround the Scottish coast. Wallace did and escaped by taking refuge with the Vikings. De Brus is no less resourceful. We have to catch him before he can take a ship."

We passed the Spittal the next day and dropped down to Braemar Castle. As soon as I saw it I knew he would not be there. It was too small. They would have enjoyed a night with a good roof and beds for the women but that was all. Whoever the lord was in the castle, he was an enemy of England for he had the walls manned. It was easy enough to avoid the poor bows and ancient crossbows his men had and we followed the clearly marked trail. It was easy for us to see as Hob had left us signs. Nob knew them and he pointed to the trail. "Hob has left us marks, my lord."

As we crossed the river and headed along its northern bank Hamo said. "As I recall, Father, Aberdeen lies fifty miles to the east of us. Do you think he might be making for there?"

"If he does then he has lost for the earl will have ships by now and they can cover the distances far more quickly than we can. We will see."

When the marks left by Hob turned north we knew that de Brus was not going to Aberdeen and, a few miles later, when Hob himself emerged from the trees we realised that something was amiss.

"They are waiting for you, my lord. The road forks just a mile away and they have secreted men in the woods."

"They saw you?"

He shook his head, "You know me better than that, my lord. A rider came over the tops of the hills from the south-west and we watched him. He joined them and pointed in this direction. We were hidden and he could not see us."

Hamo nodded, "The castellan at Braemar saw us and sent a rider."

"Aye. The others are watching the ambushers?"

"They are."

"De Brus is clever. This buys him time. If the road forks then even if we dispose of his men we have to discover his true trail." I said, "Gwillim, take the archers and go with Hob. Ambush them. We will follow and fall into the trap. Hamo and Jack, ride with me."

"Yes, my lord."

The Prince and the Archer

"The rest of you, arm for war. Abel and Robert stay with the remounts at the back of the line."

I donned my arming cap and coif. I let my shield hang from its guige strap but I did not take a spear. When all was ready I had Jean Michel unfurl my banner, "Let us tell de Brus who it is that follows him." We rode up the road four abreast.

The ambushers were too eager. They heard us coming and neared the edge of the wood. Light, coming from the west, reflected and glinted from their weapons. Even without Hob's warning we would have known they were waiting. The road divided before the wood. One arm of the road went north and west, the other north and east. The ground was naturally flat and so I raised my sword to wave us into a line. I wanted the ambushers' attention on us.

"At the walk, forward."

We began to move towards the waiting men. We were still a hundred and fifty paces from them when our archers began to slay them. We heard the cries as they died. By the time we reached the eaves of the wood, the fighting was over and the dying had begun. We saw the survivors fleeing from the woods towards the road that led to the northeast. We knew the direction that de Brus had taken.

I cupped my hands and shouted, "Gwillim, clear the woods and follow us."

I spurred Felix.

Jack was next to me and he said, "Is this wise, Sir Gerald? There are too few of us to face de Brus."

"We do not face de Brus. We chase his ambushers. Do not fear, Jack, I have no intention of trying to take on de Brus with a handful of sergeants. We keep our sword in his back and hope he makes a mistake."

Gwillim and my archers had done well and we found a warrior just a mile from the woods. He was lying on the ground, his foot still in the stirrup of his horse. The arrow that had hit him in the back had made him bleed from within.

"Michel, take his weapons and his horse."

He dismounted and said, "My lord, he has mail beneath his surcoat."

"Then take it and follow us."

We hurried on but as the sun dropped dramatically behind the hills to the west I knew that we could not risk a longer pursuit. We stopped at a narrow river that went from west to east. The ground was open and would give us grazing. I set sentries and had fires lit. It would be a hunters' stew made from foraged greens, beans and some ham. It would be the warmth of cooked food that would nourish us. Gwillim and the archers rejoined us as the stew began to bubble. Some of my archers had discovered food with the ambushers and that was added to the pot.

"There were just twenty men, my lord, that were slain."

"Then that is twenty less to defend de Brus. The question is which direction have they taken? They could go east, west or north from here."

Hamo pointed, "They went north, Father. I saw the heavily muddied ground. It led north."

"Good for that tells me that we are closing in."

Robert asked, "How so, my lord?"

"The course he is taking is now clear. Where the road allows, he is heading north. If memory serves me there is a castle twenty miles from where we camp, Kildrummy."

"How do you know, Sir Gerald?"

"When we hunted Wallace, it was one of the places we thought he would use. He did not but I stored its name. Braemar was new to me but not Kildrummy. Gilbert de Moravia is a supporter of de Brus and although I have never been there I have heard that it is a formidable fortress. It is no Braemar."

Chapter 8

I was proved right when we neared the impressive castle the next day. The royal standard flew and the walls were manned. De Brus, his family and his loyal knights, it seemed, had run enough. "What do we do now, Father? There are too few of us to besiege it."

I turned, "Robbie, take a remount and ride back to Perth. Tell the earl what we have found."

"Aye, my lord."

"Donald, take the road to the southwest and find Prince Edward. Let him know that we have de Brus in a castle."

"Yes, my lord."

"Gwillim, have the archers surround the castle. If they sortie then we will stop their flight."

"Yes, my lord."

Robert shook his head, "That is it? We use fifty men to surround a castle that may house four times that number?"

"I do not think it does, Robert, but for once we have the advantage. De Brus does not know how many men are following us."

"There are none!"

I smiled, "But he does not know that. He may think we are the advanced guard. My men have often performed that duty for the king."

I placed my men at arms before the main gate but the sally ports and the walls were watched by my archers. Their horses were close by. I split the tiny force we had so that we were in threes. One watched while the other two rested. Working this way was the most efficient way. After a day of watching no one had attempted to leave and they had not tried to dislodge us.

I sat and ate with Robert and Hamo. Jack was on watch for it was his turn to be the Captain of the Watch. "They must have planned this before they fled Perth."

"How do you know, Sir Gerald?"

"They have women with them, de Brus' family. They had to have laid supplies into this castle to keep them fed. What is de Brus up to?"

"Surely he has lost, Sir Gerald."

"The man wants the crown and he will not give up so quickly. No, he is planning something. It could be that he wished to lure us here, far from our base where our supplies are threatened so that he can bring another army to defeat us." I shrugged, "If that is the case then we shall have to be prepared to run."

The Prince and the Archer

It was the next day that Donald returned. He galloped in, "My lord, it is the Prince of Wales and the main army, they are just a few miles down the road."

I wondered if I had misjudged the prince. He had not tarried in Carlisle but hearing the news of Methven must have pushed on north and east. We would soon reduce the castle.

The prince and his companion, Sir Piers Gaveston, were splendidly dressed in the finest armour on the two most expensive warhorses I had ever seen. The young knights who followed were the ones dubbed at the Feast of the Swans and their glistening mail put that of Hamo and Jack to shame.

The prince reined in but did not dismount, "You have done well, Warbow, to have stopped the flight of the traitor. Have you spoken to him?"

"Not yet, Prince Edward, I thought to make him think I was the advance guard. I have but fifty men or so here. I sent to the earl to tell him of the position."

He then completely ignored me and turned to Sir Piers, "You and I will take our heralds and demand the surrender of this castle and all within. With the army we lead they cannot hope to thwart us for long."

I ventured, "My lord, have you brought equipment for escalade?" He looked at me as though I was speaking a foreign language. "Ladders, shovels to dig trenches and mines, timber for rams and the like."

Sir Piers gave me a patronising sneer, "We can fashion ladders and our men are resolute." It was Sir Piers who spoke. Their tone and haughty looks told me that my words were dismissed.

The prince confirmed it when he said, "You have done all that we required. Take your men and repair to the north side of the castle. Prevent their escape. I will send a message to the earl to tell him he is no longer needed here." He smirked at me, "Watch how young men reduce a castle." They both laughed.

"Yes, my lord. Hamo, Jack, break camp." As we mounted and headed north I said, "Gwillim, this will not be quick. Send our best hunters into the forests to the north. Seek signs of enemies and hunt for game. We will eat as well as we may while we watch these two popinjays blunt their swords on the walls of this castle."

It took all day for the prince and his advisor to surround the castle and erect their tents. My men had made do with hovels. My men smiled at their efforts. Prince Edward and Sir Piers clearly thought that they did not need to consult the men at arms they had brought with them. They organised their tents and lit their fires. As we ate the food hunted by

The Prince and the Archer

Gwillim's men, we heard the singing of ballads coming from the royal camp. The two leaders obviously had an idealised vision of war and his young knights were behaving as though on some extravagant hunt. We continued our three-man watch system but, during the day, we had men hunting and watching the woods and forests to the north. I thought it increasingly unlikely but there was a chance that the castle would be a lure to hold our attention while another army fell upon us. When it had just been my men then it had been a possibility but any Scot watching the castle would have seen that the prince's army was huge.

Two days after he had arrived the prince was ready to begin his assault. His men advanced behind shields and carrying ladders. I had seen the fires burning in the castle and knew what it meant. They were heating something. It would probably be sand rather than oil or water. The latter would be too precious to waste. The crossbows and bows from the walls had little effect, for the advancing men held their shields before them but once they began the escalade, then men began to be hurt. The ditch meant that they either needed longer ladders or the angle at which they would be placed was not the right one. A man can hold a shield and he can climb but he cannot hold a weapon as well. The men in the castle also had long forked poles and two ladders were pushed away before the men were halfway up. The other six had more success but that ended once they neared the top. Arrows and bolts sent from the side cut down the ones close to the top and then when the heated sand was poured over the top of the battlements it not only burned flesh as it insinuated itself beneath the mail, it also set fire to the wood. The escalade was a total failure. I had no idea how many men had been lost; it was probably a small number, but it was the fact that they had not succeeded that would be the most damaging. None of the defenders had been hurt and they had cheered and jeered as the attackers had withdrawn.

It was late in the day when Robbie returned. The earl had been ready to march north when the prince's messenger had arrived. The earl would stay in Perth and the castle would either fall or not to the prince.

The next attempt was one with crudely built rams. As we watched, even Robert recognised that they would fail. The tops of the rams were made of wood and brush. Hot sand would easily ignite it. It took three days to build the four rams and the prince's men pushed them towards the walls. It was as they neared the walls and ditch that they realised their mistake. They had to stop. They had not taken into account the ditch and they were jeered once more as they made their ignominious retreat. It was at this point that I rode over to the camp to offer my advice.

The Prince and the Archer

"Prince Edward, you need to use faggots to make a bridge and the rams must be covered with something like hides or even just wet blankets. If not then they will burn."

Sir Piers snorted, "If we need advice from you, Warbow, we will ask for it."

"My friends call me Warbow, Sir Piers. You are not a friend and I would appreciate my title, Sir Gerald." I said the words mildly but I saw some of the younger knights smile at his discomfort.

The prince said, petulantly, "Leave us… Sir Gerald."

I did but I would offer no more suggestions. I was angry that my men and I were wasting our time. We could be at home in Yarpole where we would be more productively employed. De Brus' attempt to wrest the crown had failed. Prince Edward's father would have ended the siege already.

When the rams crossed the improvised bridge I knew that they had heeded some of my words, but that they had not made the rams and the men within safe from fire, demonstrated the words that they had chosen to ignore. The defenders sent fiery arrows and soon the rams became three infernos. I do not think many men died but the failure would further demoralise the army. We noticed, as men returned that there were no longer any songs coming from the camp. They had ceased to sing. The mood in the main camp was in direct contrast to ours. My hunters had found deer and we were eating well. We had grazing for our horses and water for them too. The only thing we lacked was ale.

It was three days later when a messenger invited me, Hamo and Jack to a council of war at the camp. As we rode towards the camp Hamo said, "Will you help him?"

"I may not like either man but I was charged by the king with defeating de Brus and helping his son. I have to aid him."

Sir Piers was not present. I think it was so that he would not have to hear my suggestions. When they failed he could blame me. The prince asked bluntly, "Sir Gerald, will you help us to reduce this castle?"

I nodded, "Of course, my prince."

"Then how do we do this?"

I had already studied the castle and knew how to take it. "Have your men make two large bridges to cross the ditch."

He pointed to the blackened skeletons of the rams, "We tried that before and it failed."

I sighed and held my tongue. The answer I wished to give would merely end the meeting and I wanted it over and to go home with de Brus in chains.

The Prince and the Archer

"This time, my lord, my archers will clear the barbican. If your men advance behind shields they can weaken the gate and then use the enemy's weapon against them, we set fire to kindling and burn the gates."

He frowned as though he was trying to see the weakness. When he could not he said, "When can we assault?"

"As soon as you have made the bridges, Prince Edward." I shaded my arm against the sun, "You have the afternoon and many men. What say we attack at dawn?" All the other attacks had almost been heralded and taken place close to noon. A dawn attack would come as a shock.

He nodded, "Very well." He turned to a sergeant at arms, "Edmund, have bridges made."

"Yes, my lord." The sergeant looked gratefully at me. He knew that we now had a chance when before they had none.

When we returned to our camp Hamo and his archers set about making pavise. I knew my men had a greater range than the defenders thanks to both their bows and their skill but I did not want to lose a single archer.

Before dawn, we moved around the walls to the front gate. I left my men at arms to guard the road north and we joined the sergeants and their bridges. The prince and Sir Piers were noticeable by their absence. Perhaps it was too early for them.

"Captain Edmund, do you know what to do?"

"Aye, Sir Gerald. We advance behind shields and wait for you to clear the walls. When you give the signal we will cross our bridges and hack at the door. When they are weakened we soak them in oil, add kindling, and light the fires."

"Then you withdraw behind my archers." He nodded. "Good. Hamo."

Hamo set his pavise up and each archer stood behind the huge shield. It was still dark. The defenders must have been aware of movement and noise but they would not know what was heading their way. We were all ready when the first rays from the east struck the wall.

Hamo said, "Archers of Yarpole, choose your own target." With Hamo there were thirty-six of them which is not a large number but these were the best archers in the land. They all knew their own limitations and every archer chose his best arrow, nocked it and then aimed. The first eight defenders who died knew nothing as the fletched angels of death plucked them from their walls. The horn that sounded the alarm would avail them little. The men who raced to get to the walls had ladders and stairs to ascend.

The Prince and the Archer

"Now, Captain Edmund."

He and his men raced forward with shields held before them. The barbican had been cleared. More men would already be ascending the ladders but by the time they reached the walls then Captain Edmund and his men would be at the gate. The defenders reached the walls and looked over, their crossbows and bows ready to strike but my archers had their bows prepared and the archers and crossbowmen fell. When the defenders sent arrows blindly over the walls my men laughed. They saw them as they descended and the odd one that came close to an archer was easily avoided. Captain Edmund had lost men in the failed attacks and he was in no mood to be thwarted a third time. He took an axe and joined his men as they hacked and chopped at the gates.

Captain Edmund shouted, "Faggots and fire!" The men with the bundles of wooden faggots raced over the bridges to the gates which were scored and hacked by axes. The holes and splits they had caused would accelerate the fire as they would draw air to fan the flames. It was Captain Edmund who used the burning brand to light the wood and he waited until it was blazing before he joined his men to run for the safety of the pavise. A spearman rose to send a spear at his unprotected back. Three arrows threw him from the walls.

"Well done, Captain Edmund." He joined Hamo and me to see the results of their efforts.

"Now we shall see the mettle of the men within."

It was now a waiting game. As I had thought, they had little enough water to spare to douse the flames and having used their sand had nothing left to stop the inferno from destroying their gates. By now the two leaders of our army had dressed for war and stood with their knights.

The end when it came was an anti-climax. The royal standard was lowered and the garrison surrendered. There would be no slaughter and we had lost not a man in this last attack.

The prince and Sir Piers were the ones who rode into the castle as though it was their efforts that had brought us victory. Their knights cheered as they paraded inside the walls that had been won by sergeants and archers. The victory was a hollow one. We discovered that de Brus had not entered the castle at all, the standard had been a bluff. He had fled north with Sir James Douglas and Gilbert Hay, Brus' brothers Thomas, Alexander, and Edward, as well as Sir Neil Campbell and the Earl of Lennox. Apart from the women, the only men of note left in the castle were de Brus' brother, Neil and the Earl of Atholl. I was, of course, blamed.

The Prince and the Archer

The prince was incandescent with rage, "This is your disgrace, Warbow. You should have ensured that de Brus was within the castle. Take these prisoners to my father and explain your failure."

I bowed, "Of course, Prince Edward." My mild answer seemed to make him even angrier. He did, however, order a rider to head south and herald the news that he had taken the castle. He would take the credit for the victory. We left the next morning and the prince took charge of the castle.

"Where is the king, my lord?" It was Jack who asked the question. I knew he wished to return to his family. A ride to London was just too much to bear. It would be a long and slow journey as most of the prisoners were the women, de Brus' family.

When Robbie returned it was with the news that the king was headed for Northumberland. "We will go to the Tyne."

"But this unfair, Sir Gerald. You did nothing wrong."

"Robert, you will learn that princes and kings like to blame their failure on someone else. So long as this does not cost me my head I will accept it." I smiled, "With luck, we will be sent home in disgrace to Yarpole. I think we could all bear that, could we not?"

In the event, we discovered that the king was in Hexham Abbey. He was unwell and the monks there were tending to him. I left Mordaf's archers at Coldingham and went south, back to England, escorting the prisoners. We had gained horses, some weapons and whilst the purses we had taken were not heavy the men had all profited from the foray into Scotland. Despite my words to Robert, I was a little fearful of the meeting with the king. He could be unpredictable in his temper tantrums and if he was unwell then who knew how he would react to the news that de Brus had escaped.

We left de Brus' brother and the Earl of Atholl at Berwick. The Earl of Pembroke had ordered their incarceration. Their fate lay with the king. I learned, when we finally reached the king, that they would be hanged drawn and quartered. I had no desire to see that again. I wished to deliver my female prisoners as soon as possible and we hurried south. It was a cold journey because the women we had with us chose not to return our pleasant manner. We did not see them as the family of an enemy but women like Mary, Susanna and Alice. They refused to speak to us. By the time we passed Bamburgh, we had given up. They thought of us as gaolers and gaolers we would be.

When we reached Hexham we discovered that the king had moved to nearby Newbrough.

I was admitted to the chamber. He looked ill and was confined to a bed. He still had the same bodyguards I had seen in London and they

The Prince and the Archer

nodded gravely at me. They would have seen the deterioration at close hand. His eyes sparkled as he asked, "You have de Brus?"

As ever the king came bluntly to the point and I was as blunt and honest in my answer, "No, King Edward. He evaded us and is fled, I believe, to the islands."

His eyes dulled with disappointment. He nodded and said, "Sit and tell me all. Leave nothing out so that I may judge the blame."

I knew to be honest and I told it as it had happened.

He nodded and lay back on his bed with his eyes closed. Eventually, he said, "I thought to end it. When the messenger brought the news that my son had taken Kildrummy Castle my heart soared for I thought he had changed. I can see now that he had not." I had told him of the two failed attacks and his eyes had rolled when I did so.

"In his defence, my lord, he managed to scour the southwest of Scotland of de Brus' allies."

"With the army at his disposal that was not a surprise." He sat up and shouted, "Clerk!" A priest with ink-stained fingers hurried in. "Fetch your tablet. I have orders for you." He disappeared, "You can deliver these parchments for me and then you may return to Yarpole. There is little point in having my hunting dog waiting around when the prey has fled beyond our reach."

I was so pleased with the outcome that I ignored the insult.

The priest returned with the tablet and stylus.

"First, to the constable of Berwick. The brother of de Brus is to be hanged drawn and quartered. The Earl of Atholl is to be transported to London where he will be hanged drawn and quartered." He gave a grim smile, "That will anger many for the Earl of Atholl has the blood of King John in his veins. I send a message that no one is safe from my retribution." He seemed perversely pleased that he would be antagonising people. "Next, to the Earl of Pembroke, all those who participated in the murder of John Comyn are to be executed. Those who aided de Brus' escape are also to be killed unless they surrender. Finally, de Brus' sister, Mary, is to be held in a cage outside Roxburgh Castle so that the whole world may mock her. The woman who dared to crown him, Isabella MacDuff, Countess of Buchan, will be taken and held in a cage at Berwick Castle."

The priest said, "My lord!" He could not hide the shock in his voice.

"Priest, just write my words. I do not need your judgement. I was betrayed and all will pay a price. Now write out the parchments and bring them back for me to sign and seal." He scurried out. He turned his baleful eye to me, "Before you leave I want you to fulfil my commands;

go to Roxborough and then Berwick. The rest can be taken and held at Newcastle."

"And de Brus?"

"My son and the Earl of Pembroke can deal with him. He will have to return and when he does there will be a suitable punishment for him."

"And you, King Edward?"

"I will return to London and the queen. I still have a kingdom to rule."

I had known the man a long time and while I could never call him a friend I still viewed him as England's best king. He was certainly a better monarch than his father and grandfather. I spoke to him as a brother in arms, "King Edward, you are no longer a young man. Take this illness as a warning."

His face flared briefly with anger and then he smiled, "Warbow, you are an impertinent fellow, but you mean well. The illness is nothing. I paid a pound to have it healed and when I have my strength I will be the same warrior I have always been. Now go."

I left and sent for my son and stepson, "We are to deliver two of the prisoners to Roxborough and Berwick. Our work will then be done."

They were both pleased. We left as soon as the parchments were delivered. It would not be our task to imprison them: the two constables would have that duty. I thought that it was a mistake. The people of Scotland might endure their leaders being executed but to humiliate their women was something else. I wondered if the king, in the throes of this illness, had miscalculated.

Chapter 9

Yarpole January 1307
We reached home, happy to be alive and to be back in the bosoms of our families. Michel and his son still sounded French but they were, like Robert, now Englishmen and they were embracing the customs of our land. It meant that when we returned and he found he had a son the boy was christened, in our church, not with a French name like his father and stepbrother but an English one, Edward. My wife turned the christening into an opportunity for a celebration. The harvest, despite the absence of so many men, had been a rich one, and we had a surplus. In anticipation of the bone fire, we slaughtered an old cow which no longer gave milk. When the meat was stripped from the carcass the bones were boiled to enrich soups while the beast was brined for two days to tenderise it. Cooked for a whole day and a night, when the bairn was christened and the men of my manor crammed into the large barn, we dined on meat that needed no knife to cut it and even the old toothless men were able to enjoy the feast. With puddings made from our own flour, apples and autumn fruits it was as English a celebration as possible. Harry and his alewife had brewed ale. His inn was almost finished and Mary had bought some firkins of ale from him. This party would ensure that when his tavern opened he would have a regular supply of customers for the ale was good and all men were enjoying the brew. When English songs were sung, to allow the food to digest, I smiled as I saw my three Frenchmen trying to learn them.

I sat with Jack and Hamo. My wife sat with their wives. As one song, slightly bawdier than the rest finished and everyone laughed, Hamo said, "We would have a perfect world if there was no de Brus, Father."

I shook my head, "If there was no Robert de Brus then there would be a brother or another Scottish lord who would rise to resist the will of King Edward. There might be a lord in England who sought power too. The world is not like our world. There are many greedy and avaricious men."

"That is a depressing thought, Father."

I nodded, "It is, Jack, but King Edward needs to use border castles to keep the Scots away from England. Do you know why we have involved ourselves so much in Scottish affairs?" They both shook their heads. They had grown up with Scottish conflict as part of their lives. "It was partly to keep England safe from Scottish raids but had not King Alexander died, some say murdered, then it would not have left

The Prince and the Archer

Scotland without a king. The storm that took Margaret of Norway plunged Scotland into chaos. The king should have let that land tear itself apart. It is clear now that would have happened. He could then have taken the land when the dogs of war had finished tearing the carcass to pieces."

"But Scotland wants England."

"No, Hamo. Historically the Scottish kings wanted Northumberland, Cumberland and Westmoreland which they saw as theirs by right. They call the firstborn the Prince of Cumberland although none has lived there or been crowned as Prince in my lifetime."

I saw them both take that in. The village musicians were now playing jigs and some of the younger ones were dancing on the open ground before the barn. There was no rain and mead and ale fuelled the desire to frolic. There would be the starts of liaisons and they might lead to marriage. Those children would become the warriors: archers and sergeants who would defend Yarpole and, ultimately, England. I reflected on the change in my life from the young archer who had slain a lord and become an outlaw to a mighty lord who advised the king.

Hamo noticed my silence, "Does something ail you, Father?"

I smiled, "No, my son. I am at peace but I am looking across the years at my journey." I spread my arm, "When I was Jean Michel's age I could not have even dreamed about having this manor let alone the five others that have made me, us, rich."

"You sound like you think that your life is over."

I snorted, "Just because I cannot send an arrow as far as I used to does not mean I am ready to sit and play nine men's morris." I shook my head, "I do not feel old but the king looks and sounds old to me. My fear is his son." I held up my mug for it to be refilled with ale and when it was I said, "I am getting too maudlin. His son managed to clear Galloway of rebels. Perhaps I am too pessimistic. His father made mistakes when he was young yet he managed to change."

"He needs a wife."

"That he does, Hamo, for England needs an heir." Queen Margaret had borne the king three children, Thomas of Brotherton, Edmund of Woodstock and Eleanor but they were all under the age of seven. If something happened to King Edward and then his son, England would be plunged into anarchy. As far as I knew, no plans had been made to arrange a marriage and the Prince of Wales had shown no desire to be wed. Those thoughts filled my head as I retired to bed. They gave me a troubled sleep.

The Prince and the Archer

As winter approached we all prepared, as we normally did, for Christmas. It was not just a time for feasts but for the preparation of the ground, of the repairing of buildings for winter, especially in the west could be harsh. We often had deep snow and storms that could damage weak homes. For the women of the manor, it meant preserving as much food as we could. It would not be just for us but for the older ones in the village. There were few of them for most lived with their extended families, but there were a small number of couples who had no family. They would be cared for by the rest of the manor. Our larders were filled with pickled, brined and dried food. Weaker animals were culled and their flesh was saved. Skins and hides would be used and their bones, the ones that were unusable, would be burned, with the leaves, at the bone fire to make fertiliser for the land.

I set Robert the task of finishing off the maps he had begun many months ago. He had kept records when we had travelled in Scotland. It was not the copying of manuscripts he had been trained to do but it seemed to give him pleasure. They would not be for me. I had maps in my head but Hamo and Jack, when they led the men to war for the new king whenever he was crowned, could use them.

I thought about visiting my daughters and grandchildren but the rigours of the last campaigns meant that I did not relish the journey. We would see them when they visited at Christmas. Mary had written to them inviting them to stay with us. She had written the letter herself and I had smiled as she did so. The tone was of a lord demanding feudal duty from tenants. Of course, she couched it in sweeter words but the message was clear. They would come and they would celebrate as a family.

We had news, in late November of another row that had erupted between father and son, king and prince. Prince Edward, it seemed, had tired of hunting de Brus and the rebels. He had allowed many knights to attend a tourney and leave the campaign. They had all been punished by the king and Prince Edward and his now constant companion Sir Piers Gaveston, were not happy. I learned this from Sir Richard of Craven who had been sent by Robert de Clifford to report to the king on the progress of the campaign. The Earl of Pembroke, Henry Percy and the Lord Warden of the Northern Marches had not been able to cease in their endeavours. It did not take much to imagine their anger at the prince's behaviour. He was playing at war and the prince had clearly not changed. He had been lucky in Galloway, that was all.

When we were alone Sir Richard said, hesitantly, "It is rumoured, Sir Gerald, that the prince and Sir Piers share a bed."

"Many men do so on the campaign."

The Prince and the Archer

"No, my lord. I have it from Lord Clifford that they coupled like husband and wife."

That shocked me. It was not unknown but one would have thought the prince would be discreet. "Does the king know?"

"He suspects but I think there are more problems in his world than that one. De Brus is in Ireland and he rallies support. The caging of the women has angered the people and men now flock to his banner. His brothers, Thomas and Alexander, are both raising armies. I have been ordered to bring my men from Skipton to aid the Lord of the Northern Marches and Henry Percy. I do not mind for I have felt a fraud hiding behind Skipton's walls, but it shows how serious things are."

He left us the next day and my thoughts were dark ones. Was King Edward cursed? Three sons had died before Prince Edward had been named as Prince of Wales. Would Edward of Caernarfon be another King John, another John Lackland? I had heard the tales, from older warriors, of the chaos of his rule. His son Henry had been a child king and the land had been riven with dissent. Prince Edward seemed to me to be another that could cause the land to be riven.

Christmas drove those thoughts if not from my mind but to a recess at the back of it. I was surrounded by grandchildren and the ones who did not normally see me appeared to be delighted to be in my presence. I knew that my daughters were proud of me and would have regaled them with my tales. The exotic manner in which I had met their mother was now so embellished that when I heard it I found it hard to separate fact from fiction. I know that Mary was the same but we allowed the fantasy for it brought us closer to the grandchildren we saw so infrequently.

It was January when the messenger came from King Edward. It was a bleakly cold day. There was no snow but the ground was frozen hard and the messenger's breath hung before him. We brought him into the hall for to stand outside was cruel as well as making the house even colder.

"Sir Gerald, the king craves your attendance at the Parliament to be held in Carlisle." My heart sank even further. If it was cold in Yarpole then what would it be like in Carlisle?

"When is the Parliament to be held?"

The colour was beginning to come into the face of the messenger and he gave a wry smile, "If you leave quickly, my lord, then you should have an easier journey." He wanted me immediately.

My wife said, "Will you stay the night?"

"No, my lady, for I have to visit with Baron Mortimer."

"Then the least I can do is to give you ale heated with a poker and sweetened with honey." She hurried off and I saw the gratitude on the messenger's face.

"Why Carlisle?"

"The army, my lord, is mustered there."

I knew that he also needed my men but I was loath to make them endure the journey I would have to make. As the messenger gratefully supped the heated, honeyed ale and ate the sweet bun she had brought I worked out who I would take. Michel had his wife and new child. Harry was too busy with his tavern. That left Jean Michel. He would act as a bodyguard and squire. I would also take Robert. He had a quick mind and sharp ears. I would need both. Abel could come as a servant and groom.

When the messenger had gone I sent for Jean Michel, Abel and Robert. "Pack for winter. We leave for Carlisle on the morrow. Abel, we need four good hackneys and three sumpters. We have seven such animals?"

"Yes, my lord. All have their winter coats."

"Good. Jean Michel, ride to Lucton and Luston. Tell my son and stepson I need to speak to them."

The three obeyed and I was left with Mary. I told her all. "A Parliament?" I nodded. "The king does not always send for you when there is a Parliament."

"He sends for me when there is no one left and he needs me." I hesitated. "We managed to have many months away from the battlefield but I fear that this will mean the men have to go to war sooner rather than later."

"You have always been his rock. I will pack warm clothes. This is not the time of year for such a journey."

"I know." As she went to pack for me I planned my route. As much as I might like to go via Skipton it would add to the journey and besides Richard would be at Carlisle. I would stay with Thomas of Lancaster, the king's nephew, at his castle of Lancaster. I had known his father better than the son but I hoped I would be held in a high enough regard for a warm welcome.

My sons arrived within the hour and I outlined what I had been told and what I anticipated. "I expect that you will be joining me at some point. This time do not bring all the men. Leave Michel here, along with Harry to watch my lands and as you will be coming, Hamo, then Gwillim can attend to his own family." I knew that I was making demands on my son but that was part of our responsibility. We were the lords of the manors and had a duty to our people.

The Prince and the Archer

Hamo nodded, "Gwillim deserves the time at home. Jack and I are young. When Scotland is secure then we can live without fear of war."

I had doubts in my mind but I kept them there.

We left with brooding and blackened skies. We had barely reached Shrewsbury when the snow came. The last two miles to the castle were so hard that I feared for poor Abel who had never endured such a journey. The constable found rooms for us. We were lucky and there were few visitors. Jean Michel served me at the constable's table while Abel and Robert enjoyed the servant's hall.

The constable and I spoke of the border. I noticed that the threat from Scotland did not seem to bother him. He was just grateful that the Welsh were, at the moment, quiet. When Llewellyn the Last died and then the rulers of Gwynned died without issue, Wales had, effectively, become part of England. He hinted at some problems from Powys but he was unclear about the veracity of the rumours. It seemed remote and he was not as interested as he should have been. I think he saw it as the problem of the Mortimer family. There were always rumours. Prince Edward was now their ruler, the Prince of Wales, but with Gascony and Aquitaine providing income he did not need to exert any authority in Wales. I realised that when we had sought de Brus, mine had been the only warriors, Prince Edward's new knights excluded, not from the north. When I sent for Hamo and Jack I would ask for a token only.

The snowstorm lasted all night but the skies had cleared by the morning. The first ten miles were hard as we were travelling through virgin snow but by the time we were just twenty miles from Chester, the roads became passable. The prince, of course, was not in the castle and we had a fine welcome.

I had rarely visited Lancaster but I knew that it was a strong fortress. I had known Edmund Crouchback, the father of the present earl, Thomas. We had been at the Crusades together. I had heard that Edmund of Lancaster did not like Prince Edward and that became abundantly clear as he spoke when we dined. He poured his vitriol like wine. I was seen as being trusted because of my association with his father and the king. More than that I was known to be discreet. I think that part of the resentment was that the prince had been chosen to lead the army. Thomas of Lancaster felt that it was his right. I kept my counsel for I thought that they were both too young and lacked experience. He had fought at Falkirk but he had not issued orders. Prince Edward had demonstrated his lack of skill at the abortive siege and since then he had done little. However, I just smiled and agreed with the earl.

The Prince and the Archer

"I will ride with you and your men when you head to Carlisle. If other lords are arriving early for this Parliament then I will be there too."

I smiled but inwardly I groaned. I enjoyed the company of my three companions and the thought of riding with a member of the royal family did not fill me with joy. We would all have to watch our words.

The earl travelled with bodyguards and servants. He came from a rich family and his men were both well-armed and armoured. We passed through the land like a huge, metalled snake and as colourful and vibrant. When we passed along the pass close by Shap, however, I felt dwarfed by the hills and mountains that rose beside us. The ones in Wales had been higher but the fact that the road passed through them here made them seem even more intimidating. It was like a frontier.

Carlisle is a mighty fortress but even that huge edifice could not accommodate all those who needed beds. Abel and Robert had to find a bed of straw in the stables while poor Jean Michel had to join the other squires, camped in the inner bailey. I was happy that I was able to share a room with Sir Richard of Craven. A familiar face was always welcome. The treasurer, Walter Langton, was present and he and the king were busy in a meeting with Prince Edward when we arrived. Thomas of Lancaster was a man who cared about his appearance and before he presented himself he found a chamber in which to wash and to change from his travelling clothes. I was too old for such nonsense. If I stank then so be it.

Sir Piers Gaveston had ideas far above his station. As a favourite of the next king, he attracted those who sought to benefit from his proximity to power. It was as though he was holding court and not King Edward. I saw that Aymer de Valence, Henry Percy, Robert de Clifford and the Earl of Warwick were stood to one side and I headed, along with Richard of Craven, for them. A servant handed me a goblet of ale. I saw that these leaders of the land seemed isolated. Piers Gaveston was holding court.

The Earl of Pembroke nodded, "Good to see you again, Sir Gerald. You were unlucky to have lost de Brus. He is cunning." He shook his head, "To use your womenfolk as a way of escaping...does the man have no honour?"

Robert de Clifford shook his head, "I would have thought, my lord, that anyone who murders a man in a church would not worry about using his family to deceive his pursuers."

Just then there was a loud burst of laughter from Gaveston's court. Our conversation stopped and we all looked over. Thomas of Lancaster had just arrived and Sir Piers was mocking him. That explained the

The Prince and the Archer

laughter from the sycophants. Sir Pier's voice rose above the laughter, "If it is not Thomas the Fiddler. The Scots will be quaking in their boots now, eh?" His words were directed at Thomas but they were addressed to his fawning court.

"Sir Piers, I am an earl of the realm and I demand that you treat me with respect."

He laughed, "As I shall soon be the Count of Ponthieu, that is a moot point." He waved a mocking hand, "Go and fiddle elsewhere, little man!"

Aymer shook his head, "I have never met a more arrogant man nor one who has less right to be so, than him. You know that he took thirty knights away from the hunt for de Brus to a tournament? The king ordered them all punished until Queen Margaret intervened."

The Earl of Lancaster joined us and I saw from his reddened face how upset he was. I waved over a servant and gestured for him to give the earl some wine, "Have some wine to cool your blood, my lord. It does not do to allow such men to upset you. He can never be Count of Ponthieu for that is the king's title to give and he does not like Gaveston."

Robert de Clifford lowered his voice, "But his son does. In fact, some say that there is love there."

This was dangerous gossip and I wished to be elsewhere but I knew that if I left the others might take the wrong meaning from it. I resolved to keep silent and drink sparingly.

We spoke of safer things. The Earl of Pembroke told us that he had heard that de Brus had left Ireland and was in the Isles. There he would be able to gather support. It was what Wallace had done when he tried to enlist the aid of the Vikings who lived there.

"And I hear that his brothers are gathering clans further north."

The Earl of Warwick smiled, "Then more fool them, Sir Robert, for no one can campaign in this weather and all it does is to gather men who are cold and hungry. Any leader worth his salt knows that you campaign in the summer with long days, full fields and roads that are passable."

They asked me about the various campaigns I had been on. I had the most experience and I did not mind recounting our successes for I had been lucky and had endured few failures. It was as I was talking that I noticed that the ones who were gathered around Sir Piers were the young knights I had seen at the Feast of Swans and then at Kildrummy. They were hoping to pick up his crumbs.

Suddenly we heard a scream that was almost feral. It came from the chamber occupied by the king and his son and silenced everyone in the hall, including Gaveston. We all turned for the sound had come from the door guarded by two sentries in royal livery. The door was flung open and Prince Edward emerged, clutching his head. We saw just his hand but we heard the king's voice as he screamed, "Now you want to give lands away, you who never gained any? As the Lord lives, were it not for the fear of breaking up the kingdom, you should never enjoy your inheritance!" I saw, in King Edward's hand, a hank of Prince Edward's hair. The door closed and, before another word could be spoken, the prince had fled. Piers Gaveston followed him leaving the sycophantic knights lost without their leader.

We looked at each other in silence for a moment as a buzz of conversation grew in the hall. It was Aymer de Valence who broke the silence, "And de Brus would, if he heard of it, relish this dispute for a king and his son divided is not a good thing for his country."

The door to the chamber opened again and Walter Langton emerged. He came over, "Sir Gerald, the king would speak to you but, I pray you, give him a moment to compose himself. He is angry and as he is not as well as he might be that cannot be a good thing."

The Earl of Lancaster asked, "My lord, what caused the outburst?"

The treasurer and cleric looked around us and seeing that we were close to the king, lowered his voice and said, "Prince Edward asked that the County of Ponthieu be given to his, in his words, dearest friend, Sir Piers Gaveston." He shook his head, "The king has heard rumours and…I have said enough."

He left us and I downed my wine and headed for the door. I was expected and the door was opened by one of the sentries. The king had his head in his hands and I saw, on the floor, the hair torn from Prince Edward's head.

He looked up and said in a small voice, "Sit, Warbow." I sat and said nothing. "God has punished me. He took my brightest and best sons from me and left me with…I know not what he is." He drank some of his wine and looked me in the eye, "It is unfair. You, a common archer, are granted a son who is full of nobility and you even have a stepson who is applauded by all and what do I have?" He shook his head, "How did you do it?"

"Lady Mary and I did not treat him any different from any of the other children in the manor. When he was in the wrong he was punished. When he earned it he was praised. He worked."

"And Prince Edward did not. I was fighting for a country." I said nothing. I knew he could have raised the prince better. It had only been when Queen Eleanor died that Prince Edward changed. This was not the time for such honesty. He nodded as though he had made a decision,

The Prince and the Archer

"This... man," he could not bear to speak Gaveston's name, "is to be banished from the kingdom. I will take him away from my son. I want you to escort him to Dover. I will provide the men but it is you that I charge with overseeing that he reaches Dover."

"My lord..."

"You do not need to stay with the man, Warbow, God knows he makes my flesh creep. Just deliver him to the constable at Dover Castle and then you may return to Yarpole." I nodded. He added, almost as an afterthought, "I want your archers here by May."

I would be in the saddle for almost three weeks.

He saw my face, "There will be a reward. You shall become a hereditary baron, Hamo will inherit the title."

For once I saw the man behind the mask of king. King Edward thought that he was doing something for me. There was almost kindness in his eyes and I was taken aback. The title meant nothing and I suspected that it would mean little to Hamo, but it would make him safer from any mischief caused by the Mortimers. There were many barons but the hereditary title had been introduced by King Edward to reward those barons who were loyal to him.

"I am touched and honoured, King Edward."

He smiled, "I am getting old, Warbow. I know that my time on this earth is drawing to a close and soon I shall be with Queen Eleanor. She came to me in a dream at Christmas and told me that I had not done enough for you. As always she was right. Even in death, she is right. The escorting of Gaveston is incidental. Know that you would have had the reward come what may, but if you escort him then I know he will arrive in Dover and be kept away from my son."

"Then I shall do so."

"Richard of Craven and the knights of de Clifford will be the escort. There are ten of them and they should be enough. Bishop Langton will issue the warrants that you need and tonight, at the feast, I will announce your new title."

I left the room and re-entered the hall. The earls all hurried to my side, "Well?" Thomas of Lancaster was the most interested.

"Sir Piers is to be banished from this land and sent back to France, from whence he came. I am to take him to Dover." We saw Walter Langton appear and after nodding to us he entered the chamber. I was going to mention to Richard that he was my escort but thought better of it. King Edward would tell him.

Robert de Clifford shook his head, "And as much as I wish to see the back of him, I do not envy you your journey. To be in the company

The Prince and the Archer

of that creature for any time, let alone in the depths of winter, would be a torture beyond words. I do not envy you, Sir Gerald."

Just then one of the sentries came over and said, "Sir Richard, the king craves a word."

"Me?" he sounded surprised.

"Yes, my lord."

Robert de Clifford looked at me, "Well, Warbow?"

I smiled, "The king knows his business, my lord, and I know better than to gossip."

The Lord of the Northern Marches nodded.

Richard was in but moments and when he returned he said, to Robert de Clifford, "My lord, I am to choose ten knights to escort Sir Gerald and his charge to Dover."

"Then do so."

When he left us the talk turned from Gaveston to the prince.

"Perhaps without the influence of that Frenchman, all may be well. The prince is young and is not yet formed." Aymer de Valence was, in many ways, a kind man and thought the best of everyone.

Thomas of Lancaster was of a different opinion, "The prince is tainted, my lord, for good or ill we are stuck with him."

Guy de Beauchamp was a more practical man, "Then we will have to use Parliament to constrain him. We are all gathered here for just such a parliament and the barons, if we work together, can curb his excesses."

The Earl of Lincoln was unsure, "That reeks of de Montfort and his tactics. I do not want to go down the road of a civil war."

There was silence until I said, "My lords, Prince Edward is not his father. I think that there are wise heads that can hold this kingdom together. When Henry, King Edward's father was a minor then the queen and the senior marshals kept the land and the crown safe. We must support Queen Margaret and keep a firm front."

Their eyes were all upon me. They were born nobles and I had been lucky enough to be awarded my titles. I knew that, in their hearts, they believed that they had the right to rule. Did they see me as an upstart? De Clifford said, "You may be right, Warbow. Alone out of this august body, you know the people and their hearts better than we. What will the people do when Prince Edward rules this land?"

I sighed, "My lords, while the ordinary folk are loyal it is to England. When we had the civil war they suffered. They were not executed and they were not butchered on the field of Evesham but they went hungry. Their lands were burnt and their children died. They need

The Prince and the Archer

a land that is free from strife where there is peace and the chance to be prosperous. It is we who can provide that."

The servants came to clear the hall so that we could eat. I went to my chamber and Richard spoke to me about our task, "I know this is an honour but it is one that I wish I had not been given."

"Why?"

"I do not trust Gaveston. If he escapes and flees then the king will punish us."

I laughed, "Piers Gaveston will not escape, that I can assure you. The king has made me his gaoler and I will ensure that he does not flee. Your presence is the show of force for the ones who might seek to free him. Prince Edward will not be happy about this nor will the young knights they have gathered around them. We endure the Parliament and then leave as soon as we can after we have reached a decision."

Richard seemed to have almost forgotten the Parliament. "What decision?"

"The king will want a commitment from his barons and earls, that they will prosecute this war until de Brus is defeated."

I was seated at one end of the high table. Richard was next to me. Jean Michel's eyes were wide as he served at the table. To him, this was a high honour. He was rubbing shoulders with the squires who would, one day, inherit grand titles. Prince Edward was between his father and Bishop Langton. He still looked petulantly angry.

King Edward did not look well. The upset caused by the row could not have helped and when he spoke it was but briefly. "You may have heard that I have banished Sir Piers Gaveston from England. He will be taken to Dover by Baron Warbow." At my title, all the other leaders at our table turned to look at me. "The title is a hereditary one and a reward for a lifetime of service." He glanced at his son, "Would that others would emulate him. Tomorrow we hold the Parliament. I pray that this night you all search your consciences so that you make the right decision."

He sat and there was a buzz of conversation. Sir Richard said, "Well done, my lord. It is good for Hamo and the rest of your family."

"Do not forget, Richard, that with the title comes responsibility. I know that better than any."

Chapter 10

The king had his way. The Baron's Parliament agreed to prosecute the war against the de Brus family. Had he left it like that then I believe events might have turned out differently. However, the king was angry. I think it was the fight with his son which caused it, but he took his anger out on the leaders, the earls who had failed. Before the barons, the king castigated the leaders who been unable to bring Robert de Brus to battle. He mentioned both his son and Aymer de Valence in his harsh words. As if that was not enough he then included Robert de Clifford and Henry Percy. I saw the men recoil as though they had been physically struck. It made them angry and angry men do not make wise decisions. The result of the king's anger would manifest itself later.

I had other matters to contend with and I went with Sir Richard to the chamber occupied by Sir Piers Gaveston where he was guarded by the king's men.

I entered and he snapped as I did so, "I did not give you permission to enter."

"And I need no permission, Sir Piers, for I am now your gaolor. I am here to tell you that Sir Richard and I have been charged with escorting you to Dover Castle where you will await passage for a ship to France."

He laughed. His squire, standing in the corner, smirked. "You think that the two of you can make me do anything? Prince Edward will change his father's mind. Now get out."

I went close to the pompous and arrogant Frenchman, "Sir Piers, I know that you have a low opinion of me. I care not. It is true I had a rude and rough upbringing but know this: my king has charged me with the taking of a man he deems to be a threat to England, to Dover Castle. I will do so. Now how you are taken is your choice."

His eyes narrowed, "My choice?"

I turned to Sir Richard who had brought, on my orders, a Bible, "Sir Richard." He placed the Bible before the Frenchman. "Now the easy way is that you will swear on this Bible that you will not attempt to escape and you will obey my every command."

"Or?"

"Or I shall take your sword and have you bound to your horse and led by one of my men."

He paled, "You would not dare."

I laughed, "You are speaking now to a man who was commanded by King Edward to ride across a desert and bring forth a Mongol horde.

The Prince and the Archer

I am one of the men who faced Simon de Montfort and his killers on the battlefield at Evesham. Do you think I am afraid of a pathetic lump of dog turd like you?" I raised my voice and slammed my hand on the table, "Now swear or I will bind you here and now!"

I am not sure if it was my crude language, my voice or the slapped table but he stood and placed his hand on the Bible. "I swear, by Almighty God that I will not try to escape."

"And?"

"And I will obey all that Sir Gerald demands of me."

"Good."

"I also swear that one day I will have my vengeance on you, Sir Gerald and you will die at my hand."

Sir Richard started forward saying, "How dare you."

I held up my hand and smiled, "Pick up the Bible, Sir Richard. Let him make such an oath." I leaned forward to put my face close to his. He reeked of perfume, "You have made an oath and I hope that you try to fulfil it. Many men have sought to kill me. The latest one was William Wallace and we know how that ended. Know this, Sir Piers Gaveston, that if you come for me it will cost you your life." I held his gaze and then said, "Now pack. We leave in the hour."

As we left Sir Richard said, "You should tell the king. Gaveston will embroil the prince in this."

"The king has much on his mind. I will deal with this. He will do nothing until he has left England. Once he has done so then I will watch for the killers that he will send."

He stopped and stared at me, the Bible still in his hand, "You know that and it does not frighten you?"

I sighed, "Richard, I will be in Yarpole. There I am surrounded by men I trust. If any killers come for me then I will know and they will die." I smiled, "I am a good friend but a wicked enemy."

We headed east along the road that was to the south of the wall built by the Romans a thousand years earlier. It was bitterly cold but Sir Piers, his squire and the four servants he brought were all well wrapped in furs. They were a parting gift from the Prince of Wales. It was the king's roar of disapproval that made the parting briefer than either man had intended. I decided on the formation. Four knights preceded us and four followed. Abel and Jean Michel along with Sir Piers' servants rode behind those four and then two men formed the rearguard. I allowed Sir Piers' squire, Louis, to ride next to him. Robert, Sir Richard and I rode directly behind Sir Piers. I knew that it annoyed him. If he wished to speak to me he had to turn his head. He did not like it and he brooded all the way to Hexham where we would stay in the abbey.

He sought another way to get back at me. When we ate he tried to ingratiate himself with Robert whilst insulting me at the same time. It annoyed Sir Richard more than me for I knew what the prince's friend was doing.

"I cannot understand what an intelligent and witty Frenchman is doing in the service of such a brute as Warbow."

"Baron Warbow." I corrected him. He ignored the correction.

Robert just smiled. "My lord, Sir Gerald has shown me that he is the most chivalrous of knights and a true gentleman. I am honoured to serve him."

"Serve me and I will pay you twice what he does."

Robert nodded, "Very kind, my lord, but as Sir Gerald pays me nothing then it would avail me nought. Double nothing is still nothing."

"I will pay you gold!"

"When I thought I would be a priest I took a vow of poverty. I need no gold. I am fed, clothed and housed and I am welcomed in a house of strangers. Why change that to serve a man who has been banished? I like England and I have no desire to return to France."

Sir Piers did not take the rebuff well and spent the rest of the journey south trying to cause a split between myself and my two Frenchmen. I knew their loyalty. Sir Piers had nothing to offer them as an inducement. The weather remained clear but that just meant we were riding with chilly air that seemed to insinuate itself between our layers of clothes.

It was five miles south of York that Abel nudged his horse next to mine, "My lord, we are being followed."

"You are sure?"

"I thought we were when we passed Easingwold but now I am sure. When we left York I listened for horses and I kept a sharp eye out. There are riders and they are trying to stay out of sight." I looked ahead and saw, a mile or so up the road, a stand of trees that flanked the cobbles. I called out, "Sir Richard, I will stop in the woods to make water. You and the others carry on. I will catch up."

"Are you sure, Sir Gerald? A few moments will not hurt us."

"No, we need to keep a steady pace. I will keep Jean Michel with me."

When we reached the woods Jean Michel and I peeled off. I knew, from Abel's words, that our followers were too far behind to have seen what we did.

As we waited Jean Michel said, "What if this is just a party of merchants, my lord?"

The Prince and the Archer

"Then we emerge from the woods and tell them that I went to make water."

"But you do not think it is merchants."

"No, Jean Michel. At this time of year, merchants sit in their homes with blazing fires working out how to make even more coins next year. Men who ride in late February do so because they must. Neither of us would be here without the express command of the king. Do not draw your sword but have it ready."

I heard the clattering of horses and the jingle of mail before I saw the men who followed us. I watched the six men pass us, taking in that they had spurs and helmets hanging from their cantles. I recognised at least three of them as being knights who were given their spurs at the Feast of the Swans. They were supporters of Sir Piers Gaveston. I nodded and Jean Michel and I left the shelter of the trees. We were not mailed and there was no jingling. When we reached the road the hooves of our horses clattered on the stones and the two men at the rear turned.

I smiled, "My lords, you should not tarry so far behind us. If you wish our company then join us. I would prefer to have the friends of Sir Piers Gaveston with us rather than risking a blade in the back." Their hands went to their swords. I smiled, "My lords, we are on the king's business. Would you threaten us?"

One of them, Sir William de Frey, said, "We serve Prince Edward and he has charged us with guarding his friend, Sir Piers."

"Then you can ride back to the prince and tell him that my charge will be safe and will reach Dover unharmed for I have given my word to the king that it will be so and Sir Gerald Warbow is never foresworn." Their swords were replaced but they showed no signs of moving. "Let me add that if you continue to follow us then I will order my escort to take you as prisoners. I hope your families can afford the ransoms that we will demand."

"You would not dare!"

"It is you who is daring, Sir William, for every moment you delay me angers me and if I draw my sword it will not be for a ransom I do not need, neither your armour nor horse but your head and that I could take as easily as I might pluck an apple from a tree." My voice became harsher, "Now I have wasted enough time. Do you contest the road or will you turn and rejoin your prince, who is, no doubt, waiting for you to return with Sir Piers in York?"

I had hit the mark. The prince was also following. Their faces showed it and they jerked their reins around. As they began to turn their horses Sir William said, "When Prince Edward is king then all debts shall be paid."

The Prince and the Archer

"Then I hope that you are the popinjay who tries to claim it."

They turned and clattered up the road. I waited a suitable time and then spurred my horse as Jean Michel and I rejoined the others. All were curious. I said, loudly enough for Sir Piers to hear, "It seems, Sir Robert, that Prince Edward feared that Sir Piers might come to harm and sent six little chicks to guard him. I have sent them hence, assuring them that the appointed task would be carried out."

Our progress was not as quick as I would have wished. It was not due to any treachery or lack of obedience to instruction from Sir Piers but, quite simply, down to the weather. It seemed he wished to get to Dover as quickly as possible. Dover Castle was a royal palace and Henry II had made it a luxurious one. It was as good a place as any to be housed and be rid of the annoying gaoler.

Whenever we stopped I had two of Sir Richard's knights guard the door to the bed chamber of our charge. He had given his word but the six knights who had followed us had been a warning. They had not sworn an oath and if Sir Piers was freed through the efforts of others then he might argue that he had not broken his oath. Sir Richard, his squire along with Robert and Jean Michel would sit and talk with me after we had dined. Abel took his task as groom very seriously and he lavished as much care on the animals as he could.

"Has the prince given up, Sir Gerald?" Jean Michel was genuinely curious.

I shook my head, "I doubt it. He seems inordinately close to this Frenchman. He is treading on perilously thin ice for the king has a short temper. I would not put it past him to disinherit Prince Edward and make Thomas of Brotherton his heir. It would solve a problem."

Robert said, "I have been listening to Sir Piers and his squire. They seem to have forgotten that I am French. Sir Piers knew that the prince was following. Indeed, he has cooperated only because he expected some succour before we reached Dover."

I nodded for I had been wondering why Gaveston was so, apparently, compliant. "London." I said it out loud but the word was for me.

"What?" Richard was used to the world of politics but not necessarily to the politics of the people.

"De Montfort used the men of London when he made his play for the throne at Lewes. They are less loyal than those in the rest of the country and Prince Edward might seek to use them to his advantage. We have to pass through London and cross London Bridge. I will be happier when we are on the road to Dover and south of the river."

The Prince and the Archer

We rode through the gates of London and headed for the Tower. We were aided by the weather. It was pouring with rain. It was an icy rain with sleet and a biting wind from the east. Those who were outside were cowled and hurrying to get out of the rain as soon as they could. We reached the gatehouse and I presented my warrant.

The captain of the guard frowned, "My lord, Prince Edward is here already. He arrived by boat yesterday. He did not mention your arrival."

I shook my head, "It does not matter as we will be staying but one night. Is the constable in residence?"

"No, my lord. It is his deputy, Sir John de Villiers. He is entertaining Prince Edward in the new hall." He pointed to the new building that lay close to the river and the gate there. The original chambers had been in the White Tower but, subsequently, a Great Hall had been built close to the new St Thomas' Gate. That was where the prince and the deputy constable would be. The rooms there were much larger with better heating and better apportioned. I knew that the hall was magnificently furnished and more pleasant accommodation than the more austere and ancient Tower.

I waved my arm and led us into the grounds of the fortress.

"We will head for the White Tower."

The others said nothing but I saw an angry look flit across the face of Sir Piers Gaveston. He had heard the words of the captain and one thing you could not call him was a fool. When we reached the Tower I led our men inside leaving Abel and the servants to see to the horses. There were two sergeants in the guard room and they leapt to their feet as we entered. I was recognised. I had often visited the king there and my livery was well known.

I had no idea if they could read but I flourished the royal warrant with the king's seal, "We need chambers for the night."

They had been eating and one swallowed and said, "The deputy constable is in the Great Hall. The rooms there are better for such noble guests." He had recognised the friend of the prince.

"There are rooms here, are there not?" They both nodded. "There is a kitchen and food is being prepared."

"Yes, my lord, but food for the garrison and not great lords."

I smiled, "We are all warriors here and food that is good enough for warriors who guard the king's home in London will be good enough for us. Sir Richard, follow this man and find our rooms. I will wait here with Robert. I am sure that we will soon have visitors."

I sat and nodded to Robert, "Fill my coistrel with whatever they were drinking."

The Prince and the Archer

The ale was good. It did not take long for the door to the Tower to be thrown open and Prince Edward and the deputy constable stood there. I smiled.

"Sir Gerald, we have bed chambers for you and the other guests in the Great Hall. They would be more comfortable than the rooms here."

"We do not wish to bother you, Sir John. This will suffice and is, in any case, more secure."

Prince Edward coloured, "I am the Prince of Wales and I demand that you release Sir Piers to my charge while in the fortress."

I held up the warrant, "Do you see your name on this warrant, Prince Edward?" He glowered at me. Defeated. "If your father wished you to have contact with Sir Piers then he would have told me and given me written authority. As you can see it does not."

"Then I demand to see him, now!"

I sighed, "We have had a long and tiring journey, Prince Edward. You may see him… tomorrow before we leave. However, the meeting will be in the Inner Bailey when we mount our horses. There will be no contact between my charge and any other than his guards. Is that clear?"

He was defeated and he knew it. His eyes narrowed, "You are adding more grievances to my already long list, Baron Warbow, and when I am king…"

"And we all pray that the king will live as long a time as possible, eh, Prince Edward?"

"When I am king then you will regret these insults that you heap upon me." He turned and stormed towards the door. Of course, his dramatic exit was somewhat spoiled when the door, swollen no doubt by the rain, did not open immediately.

When he had gone, I said, "Sir John, I would have you command your men here, in the Tower to obey my every order." I tapped the warrant, "They come from the king."

"Of course, Sir Gerald, but…" he gestured towards the door.

"Ah, you mean Prince Edward? When pups bark it is to be expected. When they grow into hounds they learn to manage their noise. The prince is young."

Food was fetched and we ate in the guard room. As I had expected it was simple fare. It was a meal of beans and rabbit fortified with cider. I enjoyed it but I could see that Sir Piers thought that it was beneath him to eat such common food. He retired early and I went around the guards, "I want the doors barred and none, even the deputy constable, will be allowed in without my permission. Is that clear?"

Sir John had done as I asked and they all nodded, "Yes, Sir Gerald."

The Prince and the Archer

"It is one night and we shall be gone. You will all dine well on this story of the spat between the prince and the archer will you not?"

My words brought a smile and they nodded, "Yes, Sir Gerald."

Knowing that we would be well guarded I slept well. We rose early and when we emerged Prince Edward was there waiting for us. He had his knights holding the reins of four horses. Three were warhorses and the fourth was a hackney. His face lit up when he saw Sir Piers.

Sir Piers said, "My Prince, you cannot know the indignities I have suffered at the hands of this brute."

The prince frowned and jabbed a manicured finger at me, "More grievances, Sir Gerald. All will be paid."

That I had not done anything wrong was, apparently, immaterial.

He smiled at his friend, "I have gifts for you. There are fine horses and in the bags, there are good clothes. I would not have you live like a pauper. He took a purse from his belt and approached Sir Piers, "And here is gold to make life easier for you in this most hateful of incarnations."

I held up my hand, "No closer. Robert."

Robert dismounted and bowed before the prince. Robert held out his hand. Had I used a knight it might have caused a problem but Robert was a Frenchman, a clerk, and seemed harmless. He took the purse and presented it to Sir Piers.

"And now, we must ride." I smiled at the prince, "We will be staying this night at Rochester if you wish to follow but the same strictures will apply." I gave him no chance to reply but spurred my horse. Sir Piers had no time to mount one of the better horses he had just been given and his servants and squire scurried to bring them with us. I saw Sir Richard's knights laughing. Sir Piers was not a popular man.

I slowed when we neared the bridge and that was deliberate. The skull of the Earl of Atholl was still on a spike. I said to Sir Richard as we slowly passed, "Such is the fate of all traitors, eh, Sir Richard?" The words were intended for Piers Gaveston.

The prince knew that if he followed he would have to endure the embarrassment of not being close to Sir Piers and he did not follow. Sir Piers rode, pointedly, one of the gift horses as we rode the last miles to Dover. This was the end of my journey and I was glad to be rid of the man. He hated me and I disliked him. I gave the letter Bishop Langton had penned for the king. The castellan read it and nodded. It was unambiguous. Piers Gaveston would be closely guarded and when the ships sailed to France again he would be put aboard.

The Prince and the Archer

Sir Richard and I left the next morning. Before we did Sir Piers came to the outer bailey as we mounted our horses and pointed a bejewelled finger at me, "The next time we meet, Sir Gerald, you will die."

I had endured enough insults and I drew my sword, "I have done as my king asked and delivered you to Dover. You think of yourself as a good tournament knight and I am an old man. Draw your sword and let us settle it now. God will decide who is in the right. What say you?"

He was afraid. He took a step back, closer to the constable for protection. One of Sir Richard's men laughed.

I sheathed my sword, "As I thought, you are a reptile with no backbone. If we meet again, Sir Piers, and you draw a weapon, then it will be you who shall die, that I swear."

As we headed back to Rochester Robert asked, "Would you have fought him?"

"Of course, I do not make idle threats."

"And the outcome?"

Sir Richard answered for me, "Sir Piers would be a dead man and King Edward a happy monarch."

We left Rochester and headed for Wallingford. London had no appeal for me and the Wallingford Road would save us a day.

Sir Richard and his knights stayed with me for one night in Yarpole before heading back to the north. The campaign would begin again. As he left I said, "Tell the Earl of Pembroke that my men and I will join him…soon."

Chapter 11

Yarpole March 1307

I had much to tell my family and no desire to race back to the north. The muster was not due until July and that meant we would leave at the end of May. I wanted, no, I needed, some time at my manor.

Like me, Mary was not bothered by my new title. She had lived at the court of the Mongol Khan and was not impressed by titles. We both liked to judge people by their actions. The noblest person we had ever known was Queen Eleanor but that had nothing to do with her title, she was just a noble person who shone from within. My daughter-in-law, in contrast, was very impressed. She would have a title as would their children. She was, in many ways, an innocent soul.

I was able to work with my men at arms while Hamo stretched the skills of my archers. James and John, Alice's younger brothers, had developed into good warriors and would make excellent sergeants. Harry had been able to give them time, while he been building his tavern, to teach them all that he had learned over a lifetime. They had yet to finish growing so there was no need for a mail hauberk but we had leather jacks, studded with metal, made for them and I had the smith make them both a coif. We had captured enough swords over the years to furnish them both with a well-made sword. It was my livery that they wore and the shields they used had my sign upon them both. Abel had learned much in his time with my horse master and he schooled the two horses that Hamo bought for them. They were not coursers but they were good hackneys and Abel ensured that they were not frightened by the din of war. The helmets I had made for them were determined by my preferences. I did not like masks. I had always believed that they caused more problems than they solved. An open-face helmet, with a nasal, seemed to me to be a good solution. The two accepted my gifts. If they wished for a helmet with a face mask then they could either have them made or take them on the battlefield. As it was unlikely that they would be fighting knights it would have to be the former.

Harry's tavern was ready by the last week in March. He had worked hard and he asked me to be there for the opening. I was more than happy to oblige. My archers and men at arms all attended. I think that Mary would have made more of it but I knew Harry. My man at arms wanted it to be simple. It was a party atmosphere.

Robert was with me at the opening and he was bemused, "My lord, why should men pay Harry and his alewife money for beer when it is provided in the warrior hall? It does not make sense to me."

"True, the younger warriors have ale and mead supplied by me but what of the men with families?"

"Their wives make ale. I have heard it is good ale."

"It is. This tavern will be a place where older warriors can go and talk to their fellows. They will not have to moderate their words for fear of offending the womenfolk and they can unburden themselves. They can talk of their crops and their children."

"Will you visit the inn, my lord?"

I shook my head, "No, but I wish I could. The presence of his lordship would inhibit what they said."

"You mean that they could speak about you? Perhaps be disparaging?"

I nodded, "And I do not mind that. I am far from perfect. I am a bad-tempered old man and if they did not find fault with me then I should be surprised. If I had been a young archer then I would have relished just such a tavern. I am happy that Harry has built it and I hope he grows rich from the earnings. I doubt that he will but just so long as he can stand behind the bar and talk to the men alongside whom he fought he will be a contented man. He will not go to war again."

War would be the topic of conversation soon. One unexpected result of the building of the tavern was that travellers using the road to Chester and Gloucester began to call in not only to water their horses but take refreshments themselves. Harry's alewife made good ale and it was not expensive. The water trough in the village had always attracted visitors but the inn made them tarry and talk for longer. Within a fortnight of its opening, there was trade at noon. A fortnight after that Harry and his alewife began to sell food for the travellers. At first, it was just the soup that would be made on a Monday and topped up with water and more greens each day until it was finished on Friday. Then Harry employed Gwillim's sister-in-law, Meg, to bake bread. The word soon spread and more visitors used not only the village but also the tavern.

One such party had left the tavern in early May and Harry came to my hall. I was practising with James and John, Alice's brothers. Harry had, until the opening of **Warbow Tavern**, been able to train them. His increasing trade meant that the role fell to me. I enjoyed the exercise for while they were young, fit and quick while I was older and slower, I also had the cunning of age and I was learning to use that cunning to defeat those who should have easily beaten me.

"My lord, may I interrupt?"

The Prince and the Archer

I wiped my brow, "Aye, Harry, for these two are becoming more skilled each day. Any excuse to stop is welcome." I turned to them, "Continue sparring and remember to move your feet. A warrior who stands in the same place for too long may well be defeated."

"Yes, my lord." Unlike Prince Edward, the two heeded my advice.

He pointed down the road where I saw merchants leading their animals south, probably to Gloucester. It was safer to travel on the eastern side of the border than the Welsh one. "Those merchants enjoyed my ale and they had loose tongues. There is some good news, it seems. In February Thomas and Alexander de Brus were captured in Galloway. They were executed in March."

"Good for that is three of the brood accounted for."

"There is also some bad news, my lord. The Earl of Pembroke was defeated by Robert de Brus at Loch Trool in Galloway. The losses were not great but his lordship had to quit and yield the field."

The words hit me like a blow, "That is truly bad news. Since Stirling Bridge, the Scots have not enjoyed a victory. This will put heart into them. Did the merchants know how he lost?"

Harry gave a derisive shake of the head, "Merchants know nothing about war, my lord. They just said he left the field."

"The earl is a good commander but..."

James was the more curious of Alice's brothers and the one who was a little deeper. They stopped their sparring and he said, "Sir Gerald what does the *but* portend?"

I sighed. I had much to impart to the young warriors and not all skills were to do with weapons. I would have to teach them about their leaders too. "King Edward berated the earl and the other leaders in public for their lack of success in apprehending de Brus. Perhaps the earl was less patient than he needed to be and tried to force a victory."

"Less patient, my lord?"

"Yes, James, sometimes you can win a battle by not attacking. You can allow the enemy to make a mistake. A good leader watches his foes. King Edward has forgotten his mistake. It cost us dear."

"What mistake was that, my lord?"

"The Battle of Lewes, John. We had the enemy defeated. De Montfort was about to retreat when the king, he was Lord Edward then, saw the men of London retreating. He chased after them. Caution would have been better. De Montfort rallied and King Henry was captured. That was the only battle I saw him lose but it cost him his freedom and gave de Montfort England, albeit for a brief time." I tossed a couple of copper coins to Harry, "Thank you for the news, Harry."

The Prince and the Archer

He shook his head, "I do not need your coins, my lord, I am still your man."

I smiled, "And when I come to your tavern you do not allow me to buy my beer so let me buy information. Give it to your alewife if you wish."

The news made our preparations even more necessary. We were due in Scotland in July but all it would take would be another defeat and the king might send for me and my men early. Warbow had never been defeated. He might wish to use me as a talisman. Following our return, we had worked hard to train new archers and men at arms. Archers could not be hurried. We had to wait until their bodies had grown and developed before we could take them to war. Our success lay in the ability to send many showers of arrows to exactly the same place. Gwillim had already found trained archers in Wales and now it was the time for our homegrown variety to show that they were ready. I visited Hamo and Jack and told them both not only about the setback but also about the idea I had been growing.

"We will emulate the lords and hold a tourney. We will hold it on May Day in Yarpole."

"Tourney? You mean lists and the mêlée, Sir Gerald?" Jack had witnessed such things already.

"No, for we do not fight on horseback, my sergeants are not knights. We hold a competition to see who can send arrows the furthest and with the most accuracy. I will have prizes made. We will have knockout bouts with men using spear and shield, sword and shield, to determine the best men at arms."

Hamo saw what I intended immediately, "And this will show who is ready for war."

"Aye, those who are not can either be left here or taken with us as horse holders or arrow fetchers. I now believe that this border is safe but Scotland...that is another matter."

My weaponsmith was a skilled man. Bernard came from the land to the southeast of Yarpole closer to Wolverhampton and had been trained well. The land that had been Mercia once bred good weaponsmiths. He had come to my village with a wife and two boys, dragging a cart behind him on which was his anvil and tools. That had been fifteen years ago. He had fallen out with the lord of the manor at Codsall and was trying to find a new master. We offered him a place and I never regretted taking him. His sons had followed the father into the trade and their smithy now drew trade even from the land of the Mortimers for they all had skill. One of his sons, Leofric, had impressive skills in working with gold and silver. After I had spoken with Hamo and Jack I

The Prince and the Archer

visited them and took the sack of broken silver and gold I had accumulated over the years. Some of it I had kept since my time on the Crusade. Often, after a battle, a warrior discovered gold and silver that had been hacked into pieces during the combat by weapons. I had done so all my life. It was too valuable to leave on the field and so I had gathered it. It was now a sack weighing three pounds.

I walked into the smith and laid it on the bench, "Bernard, I would like your son, Leofric, to make me prizes for my May Day tourney."

The young smith took the bag and emptied the contents onto the bench. His eyes widened, "A rich prize, my lord."

"Prizes. I would have you make six but I want two of them, the one for the best archer and the one for the best man at arms, to be made of gold. You can take your fee from the purse. I want none back."

The three of them began to divide the ore into piles. To my eye, it was just gold and silver. Some of the silver was Viking hack silver, that was one variation I knew but the rest…They seemed to see differences that I did not.

Leofwine, Bernard's younger son suddenly held up something I had not seen, "A small ruby, my lord and there are tiny emeralds in here too. Do you wish them back?"

I shook my head, "No, incorporate them into your designs." I smiled, "I am an old warrior and I leave the designs to you."

Leofric rubbed his chin. "I thought we could make chains and medallions. The jewels would go into the two best pieces, the ones made of gold. I have a fancy to fashion a dragon. The jewel would be the eye and make it come alive. Your men at arms and archers do not wear rings and they could hang the medallions in their homes when they were not wearing them. I think that their families would like that. When their men were at war the hanging medallions would be a physical reminder of their prowess."

"Good, I like that idea. They will be ready for May Day?"

"They will, my lord."

We had always celebrated May Day. By that day the planting and the ploughing were done and it was the middle of the birthing season for both animals and my people. It was a time when couples married. All that I was doing was appending a tourney to the celebrations. Mary and the women of the manor would provide the feast and Harry and his alewife would provide the ale. I secured enough barrels with silver coins.

We had a village green and a large area of pasture. It was where my men practised on Sunday mornings and the marks were always in place. I decided to use that and I had my workers construct a stand where the women and non-participants could view, from safety, the combats and the archery. I had two large chairs made for Mary and for me. It was not that I wanted to stand out but this was a special occasion and my people would want to see us.

Jack and Hamo brought their families the night before, the last day in April. We had food laid in great store. I used my gold and silver, not to make my hall impress people, but to give all my people, family and tenants, better lives. The children were growing and the table was filled. As usual at such gatherings, there were squabbles and tears as well as laughter. Mary was the matriarch and it was not Sir Gerald, grandfather, who settled the table but my wife. There was a buzz of excitement around the table. The prospect of war and the defeat at Loch Trool were pushed to the backs of our minds for we would enjoy the spectacle of warriors showing their skills to their families. They all knew that their husbands, brothers, fathers and sons had such skills but they never saw them use them. The Welsh raid and the attack on Luston that had cost the lives of Edward of Ware and many others was a distant memory.

"Sir Gerald, who will judge the archery?"

I smiled, "Jack, no one needs to judge that. Whoever hits the mark with the most arrows wins."

"Then the man at arms competition? Surely that will need a judge."

"Yes, Jack and more than one. I thought to use Harry, yourself and me." He looked disappointed and I knew why. He had wanted to participate, "You are a lord now, Jack. You have your spurs. You cannot take part for it would be unfair."

He nodded, "I can see that. The day I ceased to be Jack of Malton and became Sir John of Lucton changed me, eh, Sir Gerald?"

"Aye, you may be the same man inside your skin but to the world, you have become something different. When we go to war the men at arms you lead just have to worry about staying alive. For you, there is always the threat of capture and ransom."

He was silent for the rest of the meal. I could tell he had not thought of that. Men would try to take him alive for profit.

I was dreading a wet or cloudy day but that May Day the sun shone from the first. The men trooped in from Luston and Lucton. As some arrived as the sun was just peering over the eastern horizon they must have left their homes well before dawn. It told me how much they valued the day. The marriages took place first, in my village church. The wedding feast, laid on by my wife, would be shared by all. That was the first meal of the day. I smiled as I noticed the archers and men at arms eating sparingly. The second feast, the one in the late afternoon

The Prince and the Archer

and early evening would see them indulge themselves. The participants were saving themselves for the combat.

There was singing and celebrations before the tourney and the women, in particular, looked happy. My wife squeezed my hand and said, "And our marriage is but a distant memory. I wish that we had employed someone to paint it then we would remember it."

I laughed, "And as we had little then that would have been a waste of silver."

She nodded and tapped her head, "I can see it here but I am not sure that you do."

"Ah, and there you are wrong. You wore white and were barefoot. On your head, you had a garland of English flowers and you smelled of Rosemary and Thyme."

She squeezed my hand harder and kissed me on the cheek, "You do remember!"

"Of course. You were the first and only woman I loved. Did you think I was a butterfly visiting every flower in the garden?"

"No, but you are so practical a man that I did not think you had remembered. I am pleased that you have done so."

Gwillim came over to us, "My lord, the sun is getting higher in the sky and the men are becoming impatient."

"Of course," I stood and clapped my hands, "To all the brides and grooms, congratulations. To the archers and men at arms, good luck, and may your skill shine through. It is time for the tourney. We start with the archery. Captain Gwillim."

My captain of archers roared, "Archers choose your five best arrows and come to the mark."

Their bows were in their cases and the archers all marched to the line that had been marked with white stones at the edge of the pasture. Gwillim and I had decided, after consulting with Hamo, that there would be two prizes. One for the best young archer and the best prize, the golden medallion with the dragon and the red eye, would go to the best archer.

"Young archers take your position."

The young archers had yet to go to war. Gwillim, Hamo and I would use this test to decide who would come to war and who needed more time to become stronger. Gwillim organised them into fives, there were fifteen of them. He had a rough idea of their skill and so the first five were the ones he deemed not yet ready. They loosed at the furthest target they could. Four of them proved Gwillim right, they were not ready but John of Luston hit a good mark. Gwillim praised him as he passed.

The Prince and the Archer

The next five hit the same mark as John of Luston. Those six could come to war. The last five were the ones we saw as the best of the young ones. Four of them exceeded the distance of the ones before them. The fifth was short. He would not be coming. The one who impressed everyone was Rhys, son of Owain of Pwellhi. Owain had been recruited by Gwillim and had brought his sixteen-year-old son Rhys. He hit a mark that was further than the rest.

Gwillim roared, "The winner is Rhys ap Owain." Gwillim was pleased that a fellow Welshman had won and his father looked so proud I thought he would burst.

He came over and I handed the silver medallion with the green emerald as the eye of the dragon to my wife. She hung it around his neck and I said, "You have done well, Rhys ap Owain. Are you ready for war?"

He beamed, "Aye, my lord."

The next archers were the serious ones and there were twenty-five of them. I had no idea who would win for they were all skilled. Twenty were eliminated quickly for five hit the furthest mark, the one that was so far away that the wind could easily affect an archer's aim. Owain, Hob, Nob, Iago of Ruthin and Peter Yew Bow had all hit the last mark squarely.

Gwillim came over to Hamo and me, "How do we decide, my lord? Do we put a longer mark?"

I shook my head, "No, the wind is too precocious, let us go for accuracy." I spied a pile of turnips. "Take a turnip and mark upon it, with charcoal, two eyes. Place it on the mark."

Hamo saw what I intended and said, "You had better use five, for fairness. I will do that."

While the two of them marked the targets I went to the five. "You have all shown that you have great skill. The golden medallion will go to the one who is the most accurate. You will each have a turnip," I smiled, "there will be two eyes on each one. You hit the turnip. In the case of a tie then the one who hits the target between the eyes will win. Are you happy with that?"

They all grinned and nodded. These were the best of archers and supremely confident.

I made my way back to the stand and I saw money being exchanged. The priest and Mary might disapprove but I knew that there would be gambling on the outcome.

I was more than intrigued. I expected David the Welshman and Garth of Cheshire to do well. They were potential vintenars. They both hit their target but David's was a glancing blow and Garth's stuck in the

The Prince and the Archer

side. Both were disappointed. Having seen his son win Owain of Pwellhi was confident. Perhaps he was overconfident. His arrow hit the turnip and knocked it from the mark but it did not penetrate the flesh. In war, the target would be dead but here it counted for nothing. That left a Welshman, Iago and one of Hamo's men, Peter Yew Bow. When Iago's arrow hit the turnip square in the middle there was a huge cheer and I saw money changing hands.

Hamo said, "An impressive hit."

Peter Yew Bow congratulated the Welshman. He had his name because Peter's father was a bowyer and had taught his son his skill. The bow Peter had was a handspan longer than most for he he had made it himself. As he chose his arrow I noticed that he must be a fletcher for he painstakingly fletched them with chevrons of red. It was the sign of a master archer who wanted to see the effect of his own missiles. There was a hush as he nocked his arrow. The creak from the bow as he drew back the string sounded like a crack of thunder in the silence. The sound of the release of the arrow came a heartbeat later and we all watched its flight, made easier by the red and white fletch. It struck the turnip and knocked it from its stand. The mark hid it and Gwilliam ran to pick it up. He held it up for us all to see. The arrow was between the two black charcoal marks. He was the master archer.

I let Hamo make this presentation for he was Hamo's man. As he hung it from his neck he said, "This is a prize from my father, Sir Gerald Warbow. My prize is that you are now my vintenar."

Peter beamed, "Thank you, my lord, I shall not let you down." The prize from my son meant that he would be paid more and be Hamo's deputy. He would prize the medallion but the rank would mean more.

I nodded to Jack who stood and shouted, "Men at arms, it is time for your competitions. There will be prizes for spear, sword and axe. The best two in each category will fight a round robin to determine who wins the golden medallion."

The weapons were all from my armoury and were all blunt. They could still hurt and limbs might be broken. That was where Harry and Jack would come in. They would stop any combat that looked as though it might result in an injury. In tournaments, knights were often killed. That was normally the result of arrogance and a misguided belief that honour was all.

When the combats began I saw my wife and the other gentler ladies, cover their ears. The sound was worse than Bernard and his sons working in their smithy. The axe competition was the briefest. Such weapons were hard to use and relied, often, on brute strength. Walter won and John, Alice's brother came second. We would award the prizes at the end. The spear category took the longest. There was a great deal of strategy involved. Michel won that category and his son, Jean Michel came second. I was most interested in the sword. When I had killed the knight and become an outlaw, I had used a sword. I was an archer but I had a natural skill. It became clear that the best two were James, Alice's brother, and Edmund Blacksword, named for his blade which had been tempered with charcoal. Edmund won.

The round robin was the final contest and would determine the golden dragon's home. The men chose their own weapons. Walter naturally chose the axe and it was a mistake. He was eliminated first. The rest chose spears or swords and it took longer to whittle them down. In the end, it came down to James and Edmund Blacksword. James fought a good fight but Edmund had quicker feet and faster hands, so he won. Jack and I presented the four medallions. There was no ill feeling and, as we headed for the feast I saw those who had fought each other discussing the combats.

Hamo and Jack flanked me. Hamo put an arm around my shoulder, "This must become an annual event Father." He waved his hand around the men who were making their way to the laden trestle tables, "if we went to war this day then no one could stop us."

Jack nodded, "Aye, Hamo, they are all brothers in arms and we have seen skills that will win the day for us when we fight the Scots."

I said nothing. I was happy with the outcome but I knew that, even with their skills, we might not win a war. It was not my men who would lose such battles but the men alongside whom we fought.

The day ended with singing and dancing. A Maypole had been erected and the maidens danced around it. For my three Frenchmen, this was all new. Robert was particularly interested, "This feels pagan, my lord, but your priest does not seem to disapprove."

"I see no blasphemy in this, Robert, do you?"

"No, my lord, but I can see nothing of the scriptures either."

I waved a hand around, "God made all of this in six days. We are privileged to enjoy it. All that we do is celebrate his work. If that is not in the scriptures then it should be."

He drank some wine and then nodded, "Perhaps you are right. The priory kept us from such observations. I am glad I went out into the wide world to see what is out there. There is danger but there is also beauty. Until today I never thought that sending an arrow at a turnip could be beautiful but, in a way it was. Tell me, Sir Gerald, you were an archer. How do they do it?"

I corrected him, "I am an archer but one who cannot send an arrow as far these days. To answer you it is practice. These men will send fifty

The Prince and the Archer

arrows a day every day and more than a hundred on Sunday. They will work their bodies hard and make them obey their will. Have you ever tried to pull a war bow?"

"No, my lord."

I saw that there was a bow that had yet to be unstrung lying on the ground. That alone told me it had been left there by one of the young archers eliminated in the first round. I picked it up, "This one is the easiest to pull. Just pull it back."

All my men, even the young ones had made it look easy. He took it confidently and held the bow the way my archers had. He was observant and he used, as my archers had, two fingers to draw back the bowstring. I saw his eyes widen as he strained to pull it even halfway back. He shook his head, "Impossible!"

"And yet you have just seen my archers do this with ease. It is practice." I watched his clever eyes take that in.

As lord and lady, we had to be present until the last guest had left. I had been ready for bed well before we finally headed to our bed chamber.

Mary squeezed my arm, "You are the best of husbands and the best of lords. You did not hear the compliments but I did. The people see you as their rock."

I smiled, "Then I am happy."

"But they do not want you to go to war. The women, especially Alice and Susanna, think that you have done enough. They think that others can shoulder the burden now."

I sat on the bed to pull off my buskins, "If today showed me anything, my love, it is that I am still needed. My men have skills, that is clear, but if they are badly led then they can still die and die badly."

"There are Hamo and Jack to lead them."

"And both are good in their own spheres but I am the one who can command archers and men at arms. Do not worry, my love, when Hamo is ready, then he will lead the men and Jack will offer him able assistance but that day has not yet come. When the time comes to leave I will lead my men to Carlisle and the muster."

The Prince and the Archer

Chapter 12

Lanercost Priory June 1307

By the time we headed up to Carlisle, we heard of another two disasters. The first was at Loudon Hill in Ayrshire where three thousand men led by Aymer de Valance had been defeated by six hundred Scotsmen. The first repulse at Loch Trool had been nothing for there had been few losses but Loudon Hill sent shockwaves through the country. De Brus had a further victory, albeit a minor one, also in Ayrshire.

The mood amongst my men was sombre. The joy of our departure was now sullied by the dire news. I knew that it would mean that the king would choose to lead us and he was not only getting old, he was unwell. He had been ill since Hexham. I feared that another campaign would be too much for him. Where was Prince Edward? He should be the one to be the figurehead and not his father. There were men who could command the army but we needed a member of the royal family to inspire the soldiers. Prince Edward had spurned his opportunity to change.

The king was not at Carlisle with the army when we reached the castle. He was at Lanercost Priory not far from the city. The muster had barely begun and there were less than a thousand men present but such was the mood of anxiety and despair that as soon as I arrived I was summoned to a council of war, not at the castle but at Lanercost Priory. There were the familiar faces I had served with before at the meeting which was held in the king's bedchamber: Henry de Lacy, Earl of Lincoln; Guy de Beauchamp, Earl of Warwick, Aymer de Valence, and Robert de Clifford, 1st Baron de Clifford. I barely took in their acknowledgements for King Edward was clearly ill. He was lying on a daybed with a blanket around his lower parts.

I could not restrain myself, "King Edward, what ails you? You should not be preparing for war but you need doctors."

He smiled, "I have more doctors than enough and I pay them well, Warbow, what my army needs now is King Edward and his archer." He waved an angry arm around, as though he was swatting flies, "These incompetents have all but handed Scotland to Robert de Brus on a platter. You and I will need to defeat him."

The Earl of Pembroke said, "My lord, that is unfair and we have yet to have all the muster. The army is but half-formed."

The king's eyes narrowed, "Tell me, my Lord Pembroke, how many men faced your three thousand at Loudon Hill?"

The Prince and the Archer

The earl could not meet the king's gaze and his eyes dropped. He mumbled, "Six hundred."

"Then if you are to lead the army then we shall need every man who can bear arms to join us and even then I am doubtful of the outcome. I will lead and Warbow shall be my guide. The rest of you can watch and learn."

The Earl of Warwick said, "Where is your son, my lord? He has many young knights in his retinue. With his help…"

The king roared, although it took too much out of him, "My son is lost! He is in the south-east of this land pining for his friend. It is his father and his archer who must pull this iron from the fire. I want the army ready to move within days. We will cross the river at Burgh by Sands and bring the arrogant Scotsman, who has bested my generals, to battle. Warbow I want your son to command the archers. As at Falkirk, their fletched missiles will sweep the enemy from the field. When they are weakened we shall see if my lords have the same steel as the yeomen of England and can charge home and give us the victory." He was putting every ounce of strength he had left into his words.

I felt sorry for the others but my intervention would have done little for them. They had lost and were now being punished. I had not suffered a failure, nor had the king. Lewes was a long time ago and we had both learned from that setback.

"Now leave me with Warbow. Prepare the men to march and have a litter made for me. I would ride to war but this damned dysentery means I must be carried like an invalid until we reach the army."

We were left alone and he said, "Pour us some wine, Warbow." I poured two goblets and handed him one. "Sit, looking up at you makes my neck hurt." I sat on the chair that faced his daybed. He drank some wine and then looked across at me. "We almost had Scotland. But for the distraction of my son and the poisonous snake that was Piers Gaveston, it would be ours and England would not have endured the humiliating defeat of Loudon Hill. Can none of my leaders do as I do and simply defeat these wild men from the north?" He sipped some more wine, "You could lead my army, I know, but because you are low-born men like the earls of Pembroke, Lincoln and Warwick will not countenance it. They respect you as a leader and value your advice, but as for taking orders from you…" He finished the wine, "Now let us get down to the planning. It is a simple one. You and your archers will find the Scots for me. When you have done so then I lure them into an attack using the Earl of Pembroke as bait and your archers will slaughter them." He smiled, "De Brus will think that he has the measure of the

The Prince and the Archer

Earl of Pembroke and your archers will be as a shower of icy water on his plans."

I could not help but laugh, "If battles always turned out the way that they were planned the world would be a different place."

"I know that I am being simplistic, Warbow. That is the basic plan. We have to find the right place to defeat him. He has shown that he is cunning. We need to find somewhere that looks innocent but where we have the advantage. When we cross the river that is your task. Ride ahead with some of your men and find the right place where we can bring the Scots to battle and defeat them."

I nodded, "Yes, King Edward."

"You will obey my orders, no matter what these others say." It was a command.

I smiled, "As I have always done, yes, King Edward."

Silence fell. I had my orders and he nodded his satisfaction. We knew each other well and King Edward never wasted words when he spoke to me.

"Is Mary pleased with your new title?"

"You know Mary, my lord, she is unbothered by such things."

He smiled. Perhaps the wine had eased his pain or the memory of the four of us in the Holy Land when we were young and the world had been a different place. "Queen Eleanor thought the world of her. She could not believe that someone held as a slave could forget that horror and live a normal life."

"Mary is strong, my lord, and I know that I was lucky that I was sent to do your bidding when I was sent to the court of the Mongol Khan."

"And of the three of you, you have proved to be the most resilient. I was lucky that you came to me all those years ago."

There was a knock at the door.

The king tried to bellow but it came out as a croak, "What is it?" It took a great deal of effort and he lay back in a stupor.

I shouted, "Come!" and a pair of the king's doctors came in.

"Sir Gerald, it is time for the king's medication."

"Then come and do it." I shook my head in irritation, "We need to make him well, for England's sake. You will have to endure his sharp tongue!"

"Yes, my lord."

"King Edward, I will speak with my archers but I shall return when all is done."

The Prince and the Archer

"The Scots support de Brus. Make them feel my wrath, Warbow. Any who support us will be rewarded but any who oppose us must be crushed. Do you understand?"

"Yes, my lord. I will obey your every command."

"You must find de Brus. I command it!"

He waved a tired arm and I left.

I left the priory and rode directly to my camp and my men. They did not need to know the king's condition. It would only depress their mood. Instead, I gave them their orders. "Begin now. I want the land around Burgh by Sands scouted and cleared of our enemies. When you have reported back I shall send you forth to find de Brus."

"Yes, my lord."

I wanted them to know what was at stake. Three defeats in a row was bad and we needed to have our own victory. "We can afford no more mistakes. Stay hidden and make sure that the enemy scouts and their generals are blind to our intentions."

I did, of course, tell Jack and Hamo about the king. They would understand what was needed. That evening, when I met with the other leaders they asked me what had been said. I did not offend them by telling all but I gave them the outline of the king's plan.

The Earl of Pembroke shook his head, "You have hunted Wallace, Warbow, and know the impossibility of it. If a Scotsman decides to evade then there is nothing that can be done."

I sighed but kept silent. I was going to ask why, when he outnumbered the enemy at Loudon Hill, he had charged uphill in a single column that was doomed to failure. If you outnumbered an enemy then you used your numbers to surround them. I knew that it would be futile and so I gave them a simple answer. "I have my scouts out. The king gave me orders and I will obey them."

The king seemed to rally a little when we met him the next day. Perhaps it was the medicine he was being given or, more likely, the thought of war had stirred the old warhorse. Whatever the reason we moved three days later and headed to the army at Carlisle Castle but it was tortuous going.

When we neared the castle he left his litter. The priests and doctors objected but he would have none of it. "If you think I am going to war on a litter then you are wrong. Fetch me my warhorse."

I had seen courage from King Edward many times, not least when the assassin almost killed him in the Holy Land, but that day I almost wept at the sheer courage and determination that made Longshanks leave his litter and mount his horse. The effort of pulling his long legs over the cantle and hauling his tired body into the saddle seemed to take

The Prince and the Archer

forever. I knew him better than anybody and I saw the pain that was etched on his face but no one else seemed to see it. He rode into the castle to the cheers and shouts of his army. He smiled and waved his arm. He knew how to lead. With King Edward at its head, our army could not fail to win.

He raised his sword and summoned all his strength to point north, "Let us rid our land of this vile man who threatens England. Let us show Robert de Brus that King Edward may be old but he is still a warrior." There were even more resounding cheers. The king wheeled his horse and headed north, back out of the castle. His bodyguards and household knights flanked him as well as the three earls and the Lord Warden of the Northern Marches.

I waved forward my scouts. They had reported no enemies either at Burgh by Sands or across the Solway. They skirted around the king and disappeared north. They would be our eyes and ears. I followed with my men. We were the closest contingent to the king and I was able to watch him as he rode. I knew within a mile of leaving the castle the problems that we faced. A huge army moves slowly but King Edward had to stop every half a mile, it seemed. He was making water and emptying his bowels or having his doctors attend to him. As they were at the rear of the column, with the baggage, then every time they were summoned there was a delay. The six miles we travelled to Burgh by Sands took two days and when we reached the hamlet the king was so exhausted that the Earl of Pembroke took the decision to halt until he was well again. The king was so ill that he did not complain over much and that night, when he summoned us to his tent, he had a Bible next to his bed.

His eyes told me that he could go no further. He was at the end of his strength. He had kept going through sheer willpower. "I wish you all to swear an oath on this Bible." He gave a sad smile as he stroked its leather binding, "It belonged to Queen Eleanor."

We all nodded and assented, "Yes, King Edward."

"I want you all to swear to support my son, Edward of Caernarfon, the Prince of Wales. I know he is weak but you five are the strongest men in the land. You can give him the strength that he will need to rule my land when I am gone. Swear."

We put our hands on the Bible and began to make the oath. It sounded like the mumbling of men making a confession. The king spluttered, "One by one! I want to hear your words as you swear."

The others looked at each other but I took charge and said, loudly, "I swear by Almighty God that I, Sir Gerald Warbow, Baron of

The Prince and the Archer

Yarpole, will do all that I can to support Edward of Caernarfon when he is King of England."

The king smiled, "Stoutly done, Warbow," He looked at the Earl of Pembroke, "Aymer." The Earl of Pembroke swore the oath.

"Sir Robert."

Robert de Clifford followed suit.

"My Lord Warwick."

Guy de Beauchamp, the Earl of Warwick took the oath.

"Earl." The last of us, the Earl of Lincoln swore the oath.

The oath bound us to the prince and, by association, with Piers Gaveston. I prayed that it would not turn out ill but we had been commanded and we were all loyal Englishmen. I do not know about the others but I felt a weight upon me. I had grave doubts about the prince but I had sworn an oath. My fate was tied to his now.

We relaxed but the king said, "I am not yet done. I would also have you swear to prevent that most outrageous of knights, Sir Piers Gaveston, from ever returning to England."

That was an easier oath to swear and this time there was no weight upon my soul. How we would prevent his return was another matter.

The oaths sworn, the king lay back and waved a hand for us to leave. I saw that he still kept one hand on the Bible. Was he swearing an oath too or was he speaking to God?

We went outside and Aymer said, "If we are to support Prince Edward we cannot keep the second part of the oath."

Robert de Clifford said, "Why not?"

The Earl of Pembroke said, "When Edward Caernarfon is king he can rescind the order of banishment."

Their faces were glum, and a sombre silence fell. I said, "There is a way to keep both our oaths."

Guy de Beauchamp said, eagerly, "Then tell us Warbow."

"Simple, we kill Gaveston."

I saw them make the sign of the cross. Unless we could provoke him and I had tried once and failed, then it would be murder. For my part, it did not worry me. It was for England and to me was not a sin.

The Earl of Pembroke shook his head, "Let us pray it does not come to that."

The king sent word that he would leave in the morning come what may and that we should be ready to ride at dawn. His servant said that if he had to he would travel by litter. We rose and armed early. The night guards had kept fires going all night and there was a pot of porridge to fill our stomachs.

The Prince and the Archer

The earls gathered with me at the steaming cauldron of food, "I fear, Warbow, that today we will see little progress. We cannot push the king."

"You are right, my Lord Pembroke. I thought to obey the king's command and scout out the land ahead. I still have my orders and while the army moves slowly we need not. Our slow progress gives the enemy plenty of time to prepare for us. They can ambush and lay traps that will hurt us."

"You are right and we will labour along afterwards."

The wail from the king's tent made every hand go to our swords and we rushed to the tent. The guards were not outside. They had entered.

The king's servants were there and William, the senior servant, was weeping. He shook his head, "The king asked us to help him to his feet and when we raised him…" He shook his head, "The king is dead."

Many people have criticised the Earl of Pembroke but I was not one of them. At that moment he took command, "Not a word of this gets out. Sir Robert, have the camp sealed." He turned to the sentry, "None enters here apart from we five. Back to your post."

"Yes, my lord."

"William, have the king's body wrapped. We will take it to Lanercost Priory. The monks there can prepare his body. I will write a letter to the queen and one to his son." His baleful eyes reflected all our thoughts, "We have a new king. God help us."

I nodded, "And I will seek de Brus."

The others stared at me as though I was mad. The Earl of Warwick said, "It is over. Until Prince Edward arrives and can be sworn in we have no king."

My voice was steeled, "And I cannot sit here doing nothing. I will obey the last command my king gave me. My men know nothing and it will remain that way. I have kept King Edward's secrets my whole life and I am not going to change now. When Prince Edward comes we all know that I will be punished. When Gaveston returns, and return he will, then that punishment may be a final one. I have one last task to do for my king and I shall do it."

None of them dared to stop me. There was no way that they could. I had a cold anger about me. With that, I strode from the tent and marched to my horse. Abel was holding the reins and my men were waiting for the command to mount. I swung my leg over, "Mount, we ride."

Robert asked, "What was that cry we heard, my lord?"

I shrugged, "An animal dying perhaps. We have tarried south of the Solway long enough; we head into Scotland and find the snake.

The Prince and the Archer

Gwillim, I want the scouts to be our eyes and ears. I want no surprises. I am not in the mood."

"Yes, my lord."

Many men have called me hard and uncaring. They do not know me. My eyes were ahead but inside I was weeping and mourning the death of the man I considered the greatest king we had ever had. I knew that men spoke of the second Henry as the greatest king England had ever enjoyed but I had not known him. I had not exaggerated when I said that the arrival of the prince and the return of Gaveston would herald a fall from grace and, probably, the executioner's block. I could not help that but I could try to defeat the king's enemy. De Brus had not meant it but his return had prompted the king to come north and that ride had cost him his life. I swore an oath to myself. I would hunt de Brus until I was ordered or forced to stop.

Chapter 13

North of the Solway Firth July 1307

My scouts ensured that we crossed the Solway unhindered. I knew that we had to make our enemy blind. De Brus' victories were all in this part of the world. This was his heartland. Wallace, too, had enjoyed success here. It was a land of trees, hills and water. Roads twisted and turned, rose and fell affording many places for men to wait. There were few castles but many places where men could be ambushed and Gwillim's archers were determined that Sir Gerald Warbow would not be taken by surprise.

Hamo and Jack flanked me and Robert rode just behind. My silence was uncharacteristic. Normally, when my son and stepson spoke to me I engaged in conversation. On this occasion, I merely grunted my responses. They both knew me too well to risk my wrath. Robert did not.

"My lord, what ails you? You are like a bear woken too early from a winter sleep. I have some tonic in my bag that will enliven your blood and bring back the Sir Gerald who answers polite questions from his family."

I growled, "Peace, Robert. All is well."

He persisted, "If this is well then I would hate to see you when things were not."

My son knew me well and Hamo turned and snapped, "Robert, if you cannot keep silent then ride with Abel and the baggage. My father does not need a chattering French magpie."

My son's harsh words worked and we rode in silence until we reached a remote farm, twenty miles north of the Solway. My scouts had already surrounded it. We were in de Brus land and anyone that we found would be a potential enemy. The farmer and his family tried to keep us outside but Hamo banged his powerful archer's arm on the door and shouted, "Open this door or by God, we shall break it down."

My silence had created a foul mood amongst my men. Hamo was normally more mildly spoken and he rarely used blasphemous words. I resolved to become less taciturn for I risked putting my men into danger.

The door opened and a farmer, middle-aged by his hair, peered out, "What is it? We are peaceful people who mind our own business."

Hamo pushed the door open. He was far stronger than any farmer.

The Prince and the Archer

I smiled and said, "And we will not bother you if you are not an enemy to King Edward. We are seeking King Edward's enemy, Robert de Brus."

"You mean King Robert of Scotland."

That told me all that I needed. This man was a supporter of de Brus. "My king does not recognise the title. We will stay on your farm this night. As you clearly support Robert de Brus I take you for belligerents and enemies to King Edward but I will be lenient. I will not burn down your home and you shall not be hanged." I spoke mildly and I think that made my words more threatening.

His wife must have been hiding for she suddenly appeared and threw her arms around her husband, "My lord, we are good people."

"And that is why I will let you live but none will be allowed to depart and, on the morrow, when we leave, there will be three men to stand watch until noon and ensure that you do not send word to… the man you call king. Keep within your walls and all will be well."

The man was contrite, "Thank you, my lord." He slowly closed the door.

I turned to Hamo, "Set sentries. I spied a barn and cow byre, we will use those as warrior halls."

"Aye, Father."

"Jack, if they have animals in the cow byre, slaughter one and have it butchered for food. I will leave their walls but they are enemies and they can feed us. This will be a chevauchée."

Jack nodded but gave me a curious look. A chevauchée was normally intended to hurt an enemy. He was clever and knew that we were no longer merely scouts, we were raiders.

Abel saw to the horses and Jean Michel made me a bed. I spied Robert skulking at the edge of the barn. I shouted, "Robert, come here."

He came over but looked sulky. It was not like him, "I feared to risk your wrath, my lord, or that of your son."

I sat on a bale of straw, "Robert, you are a good man and I like you but you must know that there are times when I need to be silent. My son and stepson know that. I had things on my mind and I needed to clarify my thoughts. I could not do that when I was assaulted by unnecessary questions. You are right, I am a grumpy bear and it is a fool who continues to prod a bear when he is in that mood. You can read books and have a quick mind. You need to learn to read me and then life will become much easier for you."

He smiled for my tone had been mild, "Yes, my lord."

Gwillim joined us when the old milk cow had been butchered and was cooking. The meat would be tough but there would be enough left

The Prince and the Archer

to keep cooking all night and would be tenderer by morning and feed us all day. We would take the bones and use them as the basis for soup and stew. While we raided we would be living off the land.

"My lord, the scouts have found traces of the enemy. Just a few miles up the road is a small village called Lockerbie. There are armed men there and the manor house is defended."

"De Brus?"

He shook his head, "We think not. There are too few men. The village has just twenty houses. It is smaller than Lucton, my lord."

"You have done well. Eat."

"Yes, my lord."

I turned to Hamo and Jack, "The king wants de Brus to come forth." I hated hiding the king's death from my sons but it was necessary. "This is Annandale and whoever rules this village is de Brus' man. We will raid it and see if that stirs Robert de Brus."

"This is not like you, Sir Gerald. You usually let ordinary people continue their lives."

"Jack, I am following my king's command. King Edward wants a battle to decide who rules this land. If we raid then he may get it."

Hamo nodded, "We are putting our hand into the wasps' nest, Father."

"I know and I am quite happy to withdraw it and flee back to the river but only when we have drawn the sting from de Brus. Leave warriors here tomorrow to watch this farmer and then they can join us at Lockerbie."

We ate and I walked over to Gwillim and Hamo's new vintenar, Peter. "Tomorrow I intend to attack Lockerbie. You and the archers will head to the far end of the village. Use the trees to evade observation and you will wait on the far side. Kill any men who try to leave. I will lead the sergeants to charge through the village."

"Yes, my lord. It shall be done." He spat out a piece of gristle. "How fares the king, my lord?"

I did not like the lies but it was necessary, "I think he is more peaceful now."

"Good, for we need his leadership."

He was right and I dreaded a future ruled by Pince Edward. I would not even countenance giving him the title of king until he was crowned.

I found a quiet corner close to an old hoary apple tree. I think it had been many years since it had borne fruit. I knelt and I prayed. "Almighty God, I pray that my king and friend King Edward is now in your bosom. I would ask you to watch over England for this God-fearing land needs your help more than ever. Amen."

The Prince and the Archer

I sensed a movement behind me and I stood, whipping out my sword as I did so. I relaxed when I saw a fearful-looking Robert, "Sir Gerald, it is me!"

Sheathing my sword I snarled, "How many times have I told you not to sneak up behind a warrior? You are lucky I am old." My eyes narrowed, "How long were you there?"

"I heard 'Amen', my lord."

"Hmn. Don't sneak."

"My lord, I am not a priest and I was not ordained but if you are troubled you can unburden your soul to me and I swear that I will honour the confessional. A man should not hold secrets."

I smiled and put my arm around his shoulders, "Thank you, Robert. You mean well but there are some secrets that are needed because they keep a land safe. You can do nothing to aid me but I take comfort from the fact that you offered. I am sorry I was so short with you earlier on. You are not a warrior and I need to remember that."

There was no need to give instructions to my men. They knew what we were about and they all rose well before dawn. In winter we would still have five hours before the sun came up but this was July when the nights were still brief. The men who had been assigned to watch the farmer were not happy. Jack was firm, "Do your duty and I promise that any loot we take will be shared with you."

The archers silently slipped away. They were like ghosts. We were mailed and helmed. Robert, Abel and the four servants we had brought would stay at the rear with the baggage and the horses. We rode steadily up the road and made no attempt to disguise our approach. Anything which drew the enemy's eyes to us would help my archers get into position. I had gambled that the best men would be with the army of Robert de Brus. I did not know who was the lord of the manor but if he had more than twenty armed men I would be surprised. The clattering of our hooves was loud and half a mile from the village I hefted my shield and couched my spear. Hamo was mailed and he and Jack flanked me. Jean Michel was on the other side of Jack and the rest of the sergeants were in a column of fours behind us. That formation was dictated by the width of the road. The smoke from the homes told me where the village lay although the bend in the road and the trees hid it from us.

When we emerged from the trees I saw that there were men with crossbows and bolts in the road. Behind them were men with spears. Half of the spears were the long ones the Scots had used at Falkirk to keep the horses at bay. Here there were too few for them to be effective.

The Prince and the Archer

Lowering my spear I yelled, "Charge!" I spurred Felix who leapt forward. He was the best horse and he was soon a head's length ahead of the others. It made us into an arrow formation. Those behind Jean Michel and Hamo found space at the side of the road as we entered the village and there were six of us charging the line of men. All six of us were mailed and the Scots were poor archers. Even so, I pulled my shield to cover my face. Felix's shaffron gave him protection from the bolts and arrows. It was fortunate that he was protected for I drew the bulk of the missiles. I was the leader and with the best protected horse, I was deemed to be the best target. The Scots were not using bodkins but hunting and war arrows. I knew that when they struck me. Four arrows hit my shield and mail. None penetrated. A bolt clanked off my helmet and one stuck in my shield. Had these been English archers then another shower of arrows would be heading our way but the eight bowmen were hampered by the six crossbowmen who tried to reload their unwieldy weapons. I rammed my spear into the throat of one crossbowman and a moment later the other five spears found flesh. The bowmen and crossbowmen fled and in their flight stopped the spears of the rest from doing us harm as their flight disordered them. I pulled back my spear and skewered a Scottish spearman in the shoulder. He fell to the ground and one of the horses that was following me crushed his skull with its hoof.

There were screams and shouts from the villagers. Boys swung slings to hurt us with their stones and the women threw anything to hand. The horses that followed us either knocked them to the ground or made them flee inside their homes. The arrows that appeared ahead were not Scottish but English and they tore into the fleeing warriors. I reined in for there was no opposition.

"Gwillim, secure the village. Jack, bring forth the villagers and put them on the green." I turned in my saddle, "Are any hurt?"

James shouted, "Aye, two men were hit by stones."

"Have them tended to and destroy the slings and the crossbows."

I wheeled Felix around. The baggage, with Abel and Robert, was just entering the village. I held the reins for Abel to take and shouted, "Robert, we have injured men."

"Yes, my lord."

The resentful-looking villagers were ejected from their homes. The men were either the youths who had thrown stones or old men who glared in defiance. The exception was the priest who came from the church.

"James and John, organise men to search the houses. We want food and any coins that they have."

The Prince and the Archer

The women wailed at my command and the priest strode up to me, "That is banditry. Are all you Normans warlords?"

I did not like being called a Norman but I kept my voice reasonable. I shouted, "Do you all swear allegiance to King Edward of England and guardian of Scotland?"

An angry silence filled the green.

"Tell me where I can find Robert de Brus and I shall spare your village."

Silence was the response. I turned to the priest, "You are making it very difficult for me, Priest. I am trying to be reasonable but...Can you tell me where I can find Robert de Brus?"

"I do not know where King Robert is to be found but if I did know then I would not tell you."

"Search the homes. I have my answer."

There was another wail and some of the villagers, old men mainly, tried to stop my men. My men were as gentle as they could be but firm.

"Priest, there have been enough deaths today already. If you wish to stop more then exert your influence."

His face showed his dilemma but eventually, he said, "Do not give them the chance to hurt us. God and King Robert will punish them as he did at Loudon Hill."

I pointed to the manor house, "Whose home is that one?"

"That belongs to our lord, Adam de Carlyle."

"And is he within, cowering perhaps?"

The priest became angry, "He is not afraid of Norman dogs of war. He is with the king."

"Good." I saw Edmund Blacksword, "Edmund Blacksword, when all is taken from the manor house, burn it."

The priest pointed a bony finger at me, "I curse you."

I laughed, "Is your faith so shallow, Priest, that you resort to a pagan curse? Tut, tut!"

When he stormed off to console the women I knew I had won. I did not enjoy taking from these people but the last command from a dying king was to be ruthless. I had given them the chance to save themselves and they had rejected it. The Earl of Pembroke's defeat had steeled the Scots.

The village was a prosperous one and we took not only food, ale and supplies but treasure, especially from the manor house. We stayed in the house for it was the most defensible place in the village. As we ate the many fowl we had taken, I held a council of war.

"This time the word will reach de Brus." Our men who had guarded the farm had joined us and told us that they had passed no travellers on the road. My archers had slain as many men as they could but I knew that the locals knew their land better than we did and it was likely that at least one had escaped and would be racing to the Scottish king with the news of the raid.

"And what does that mean, Sir Gerald?"

"It means, Robert, that he has a choice. He can let us prey on his people or try to shift us. Like King Edward, I would prefer the latter. We shall see and use the same method with the next village but proceed with caution. If they do not oppose us then we will not harm them but if they adhere to the Scottish cause then we will take what they have."

Jack said, "This does not feel right."

Jean Michel shrugged, "It is war, Sir John. In France, this happens on a regular basis. That is why we have more castles. Why, Sir Gerald, do the Scots not have many castles?"

"They have them but not as many as we do. Dumfries and Caerlaverock are the two fortresses in the southwest. We will avoid them." The French soldier nodded. I pointed, "There is a castle just a few miles away, Lochmaben. We took it when we hunted Wallace but I fear it is back in Scottish hands. We will avoid that one too."

"Then if we do not go west nor southwest where do we go?" Hamo's was a practical question.

"We head south to the crossroads to the west of Gretna and head northeast to Canonbie. It is a prosperous place and has a priory."

Robert could not contain himself, "My lord, you cannot raid a priory!"

Sighing I explained, "And I have no intention of doing so. The presence of a priory tells me that the place is a rich one."

Hamo had a good memory, "But Gilnockie Castle lies just two miles north of it, Father. I remember from the last campaign."

"And if we surround it and allow one of the garrison to escape then we might draw de Brus to us, eh, Hamo?"

I silenced them. Jack said, "Then we would be bait."

"We would and before anyone says it I know that the main army is still south of the river and will not cross it until we have found de Brus. This way we have our best chance of finding him."

Hamo and Jack came to me as we made up our beds. Hamo said, "Father, it is a bold plan but if you succeed and draw de Brus to you then all of us might die or be taken."

"Hamo, I have no intention of being taken. We are all well mounted and my intention, when de Brus brings his full force to fight us, is to run for the border. I will send a messenger to the Earl of Pembroke and he can bring the army to aid us."

The Prince and the Archer

Jack was quick, "Will the king not lead them?"

"When last I saw the king he was lying on a bed. I believe that the man who will lead the army will be the Earl of Pembroke. If it is the king then all the better." I did not enjoy the lie but sometimes a lie was necessary.

One of the men who had been hit by a stone, Stephen, had suffered a wound that necessitated it being bandaged. I would not risk him in battle but he could be a messenger. The next morning I sent him back to the Earl of Pembroke with our news. I took him apart and said, "I will not commit this to parchment but tell him that I intend to head to Gilnockie Castle."

"Yes, my lord. And I am to rejoin you there when my task is completed?"

"Of course."

We fired the manor house before we left and stayed long enough so that the villagers would not be able to douse the flames. It was a message for this land. If men were loyal to King Robert they would pay the price. I knew that when he had ascended the throne Robert de Brus had burnt the houses of those Scotsmen who supported King Edward. I was being no more ruthless than the man who had murdered his rival in a church. With the horses we had taken and the food, supplies and booty, we were laden as we headed back down the road. The villagers would send the news to their lord and, therefore, Robert de Brus. They would report that we had raided and then headed back to England.

This time we did not leave men behind but I had James and John act as the rearguard. They rode half a mile behind the baggage. Gwillim and the archers rode as the vanguard. When we reached the road that led north to Canonbie I had Hamo and two archers wait for James and John. I wanted our movements hidden as much as possible. We waited a mile beyond the junction until the five of them rode in.

"There was no one in sight. Taking the horses was a good move, Father."

"Was it obvious that we had left the road to Gretna?"

He shook his head, "We swept the droppings from the horses into the ditches. A skilled scout might see it but if they were hastening for vengeance they would carry on to Gretna."

"Good. On to Canonbie."

When we saw the village in the distance I could see that it was larger and more prosperous than Lockerbie. The presence of a priory did that. This time I knew that we had a castle to contend with but that it was a mile and a half north of the village. We had the chance to raid and then be ready to repulse an attack from the garrison. I sent Gwillim and the archers to cut the village off from the castle and then we prepared to attack. This time I did not wear my helmet but let it hang from my cantle.

Jean Michel asked, "The castle, Sir Gerald, is it a strong one?"

I shook my head, "It is old and it is wooden. I do not think it was improved from the time it was built when the Conqueror came north. As I recall there is a wooden wall, an outer bailey and then an inner wall with a mound and a wooden donjon. There are ditches but if they have not maintained them then they will not slow us."

We waited long enough to allow Gwillim to get in place and then we rode, this time in a column of twos, towards the village. We were heard and the sound of our hooves brought men from their homes and the handful of priors from the priory but none had weapons.

I reined in and shouted, "I am Sir Gerald of Yarpole and King Edward has sent me to see if Canonbie opposes or supports him."

There was a buzz as people put their heads together to discuss the matter. Eventually the prior stepped forward. I noticed that his hands had no rings and his raiments were plain. "My lord, we are peaceful people around here. The Lord of Annandale collects the taxes but we have also paid them to the Constable of Carlisle. The people of Canonbie just want to get on with their lives, raise their families and try to eke out a living."

"Then know that you need not pay taxes to the Lord of Annandale. Is there a garrison at Gilnockie Castle?"

There was a slight hesitation. The prior had given me the answer I wanted but he was being economical with the truth. This village supported Robert de Brus but they were wise enough not to risk an attack by my men. "There is a garrison, my lord, but I am a man of God and do not know the numbers."

I nodded but did not believe the lie, "Then I will take my men and discover it for myself. Robert, wait here with the baggage."

He looked up at me with a question in his eyes. I used two fingers of my right hand to point at his eyes and he nodded, "Yes, my lord." He would watch the villagers.

"Forward."

We clattered through the village and, on the other side my archers emerged from the trees. "No opposition, my lord?"

"No, Gwillim, now take your men to the castle and surround it. You do not need to be quiet about it. If we can startle the hare it may flee and join his fellows. That will tell us where they are to be found."

We waited again and then headed to the castle. It had been built in the early days of King William's first foray into Scotland and stood on a

The Prince and the Archer

slightly higher piece of ground guarding a crossing of the Esk. It had been built in a loop of the river which gave just one place where it could be attacked. If it had been important then they would have turned it into one made of stone. The gates were barred and a standard fluttered from the donjon. I did not recognise it.

I rode, with Hamo and Jack to the gates, "I am Sir Gerald of Yarpole. King Edward has sent me to discover the loyalties of the people of this land. Do you support King Edward?"

A mailed man appeared on the fighting platform of the gatehouse. He shouted, defiantly, "I am James Armstrong and I hold this castle for King Robert of Scotland. Leave our lands, Norman. Your Longshanks has lost it now. Content yourself with lands south of the Solway Firth for the north is now Scottish."

I nodded, "Defiant words, James Armstrong, but do you see that I have brought doughty men here? These are the men who caught William Wallace and their arrows felled many brave Scotsmen at Falkirk. If you would leave the castle I will allow you to keep your arms for I can see that you are brave men."

"You can try to take us but we are not bandits. We are of the Clan Armstrong and we are loyal men. If you think these ancient walls are a tasty morsel then try to take them. We will see that you choke."

His men laughed from behind the walls and I nodded, "Then you have this night to make your peace with God for on the morrow you will suffer the wrath of King Edward."

I turned and we headed back to our men. There was the crack of a crossbow and I felt a smack in my back as it struck me.

Jack turned and shouted, "Dishonourable Scot."

Even as he shouted I heard the twang of a bowstring and a moment later there was a scream. Hamo said, "Peter Yew Bow has shown them the price for treachery. Are you hurt, Father?"

I put my hand around my back. The surcoat had been cut but the bolt had not found a way through the mail links. Perhaps the crossbowman had not used a taut enough string on his weapon. "No, I am unhurt but I will have a bruise where it struck." I waved a hand, "Make a camp by the river and fetch the baggage. We will eat first."

Jean Michel asked, "First?"

Hamo smiled as we rode to a piece of flat ground by the Esk. The castle lay to the north of us. As he dismounted he said, "You do not think that Sir Gerald will wait until dawn to attack, did you, Jean Michel? We will eat and then we will attack. When dawn comes it will be our standard that flies from the donjon."

The Prince and the Archer

Just then Gwillim rode in, "One of their men mounted a horse and swam the river as you approached the castle, my lord, and rode to the north."

I smiled, "You let him go?"

"Yes, my lord, as you ordered."

"Then bring your archers here. Let them eat and rest for this night will be a bloody one."

We were in clear sight of the castle which lay just four hundred paces from us and I had Jean Michel take my hauberk from me. The surcoat had a tear where the bolt had struck but it could be repaired. Jack found a hewn log which he pulled towards us so that I could sit. I sat and studied the wooden walls of Gilnockie Castle. When it was dark I would send a couple of the younger archers to check the ditch. I doubted that it would be filled with traps but if we did not check then I knew it would be. The wooden walls did not need ladders for an escalade. It was low enough so that we could boost men over the walls with shields. My archers would be able to clear the walls of any white faces that peered over. If they could hit a mark at a range of more than two hundred paces then a face appearing just twenty feet from them would be child's play.

I turned as Robert and the baggage arrived. The archers had brought down some birds and a couple of squirrels. They would be added to the pot along with some of the food taken from Lockerbie. I asked, "Well?"

Robert smiled, "A man left the village on a horse within a few minutes of your departure. He thought he was quiet but Abel heard the horse and, in any case, I had been alerted when the prior sent one of his men back to the priory."

"Which direction?"

"North."

"Then that is where de Brus is to be found. Two riders will find him, one from the Prior and one from the castle. Good. Let us hope that my message falls on favourable ears and that Stephen brings the earl. That will allow us to trap de Brus between Gilnockie Castle and an English army." I looked around and saw that my men at arms still wore their mail, "Take off your mail. We want the garrison lulled. They will retire early and be ready for a dawn attack. I want us to attack just an hour after sunset. When we have eaten, make beds and lie down as though you sleep."

We ate well. We had plenty of food and the bread was just a day old. The ale and mead we had taken were excellent and there were smiles as well as songs when we had finished. The singing would also

The Prince and the Archer

allay the fears of the defenders. We stopped feeding the fires as soon as the food was cooked. They would die out before we attacked.

When darkness descended we donned mail and left our camp. Abel, Robert and the servants would be the guards for our horses. We filtered towards the castle. It had been built like a triangle. The longest wall was the one we faced, with the gatehouse in the centre. The river naturally narrowed the outer bailey and the inner bailey would be tiny. There had been a time when Gerald Warbow would have strung his bow and his arrow would have been the first to pluck a sentry from the walls. Those days were gone and now I would watch Hamo, Gwillim, Peter Yew Bow and the rest of my archers clear the defenders. Similarly, I would have been, in my heyday, one of the first to clamber onto a shield and be boosted over the walls. Now that would be Jack, Edward Blacksword, James, John and Jean Michel. I would wait until the gates were opened.

The first men at arms had their backs to the walls and the shield ready to boost a warrior when the first defender died. Iago of Ruthin sent the arrow into his head. The only sound we heard was the thud as his body hit the ground. That was enough to bring the other four sentries to the walls. Ten arrows threw them from the walls and my men at arms were boosted to the top of the hedgehog of wood. I went to the gate. Jack and Hamo flanked me along with Edward Blacksword. I had my sword in my hand but I did not use a shield. Instead, I held a long dagger. The sounds of men dying brought the sound of a horn from the donjon. Above me, I heard the clash of steel as my men at arms cleared the handful of sentries from the fighting platform.

The gates opened and the four of us rushed in followed by archers. Each held an arrow loosely nocked.

James Armstrong was a brave warrior but not a wise one. Instead of staying in the inner bailey, he led a charge of his men across the outer bailey. He must have known we outnumbered him but, perhaps, he thought he still had men on the walls who could attack us in the rear. Whatever the reason they charged us. Five were struck by arrows before they had covered twenty paces and by the time James Armstrong and his squire struck their first blows the battle was as good as over. I blocked his blade's blow with my sword and slashed my dagger across the face of the Scottish leader. I made the move to make him retreat but he was foolishly reckless and he did not shirk. My dagger tore across his throat and he fell, gurgling his life away in a pool of blood.

I was angry both with myself and the foolish young knight. I shouted, "Throw down your weapons. We have killed enough men."

The Prince and the Archer

The sight of their lord dying before them and his squire, wounded and swordless, was enough. They threw down their weapons.

"James, John and Edward Blacksword, take men and secure the donjon. Jack, have the prisoners disarmed and take their boots from them. Dai Short Leg, bring our men from the camp."

They chorused, "Aye, my lord."

"Gwillim, make a pyre of the bodies before the castle and when our men are within then raise the drawbridge and close the gates. Gilnockie Castle is English once more."

Chapter 14

Gilnockie Castle July 1307

When dawn broke we burned the bodies of the men we had slain. I had Hamo let the twenty prisoners we had taken, go. They had no weapons and no boots. They might fight us again but I could not kill them and I had not enough men to guard them. We then settled into the castle. It was small. The donjon held just twenty men and the stables were inadequate for the number of horses we possessed. We used the outer bailey as a place where we could let the animals graze. I walked the walls and checked the surrounding land. I saw what I hoped I would see. The river was fordable. The purpose of the castle was to dispute its crossing rather than prevent it. When the time came we could escape across the river and I had my men at arms make a gate in the river wall. We then waited.

There was enough food in the castle to augment the considerable supplies we had already brought. We quickly established order as we waited for the English army to arrive. Even if Robert de Brus arrived first it would not be a disaster. I had been commissioned by the king to discover the whereabouts of Robert de Brus and his arrival would confirm it. I had obeyed his last command. Watches were set and my archers left the castle each day to hunt for both game and signs that the Scots were about.

A week had passed and neither the Scottish army nor Stephen had returned. On the same afternoon that my archers found signs of a Scottish army heading south from Locherbie, a weary Stephen rode through my gates. He hurled himself from his horse and threw himself to the ground, "My lord, the Earl of Pembroke will not stir from Carlisle Castle."

I was not surprised but I was disappointed.

Hamo said, "Then we must leave or we will be trapped here by the Scots."

I shook my head, "My plan was a good one. I will have to change it slightly but we can still follow the king's command."

Stephen rose, "There is more, my lord." There were just six of us in the inner bailey and he looked at me as he said, "The king is dead and his son, Edward of Caernarfon has been named as King of England. I heard that he was on his way north to take charge of the army and his father's body."

Jack, Hamo, Gwillim and Robert could not have looked more shocked but I just nodded.

The Prince and the Archer

Hamo said, accusingly, "You knew."

"Aye, but we were sworn to secrecy until the prince and the queen knew."

"Yes, my lord, I was kept guarded and not allowed to leave the camp. Sir Richard of Craven and Baron Clifford argued. I would still be there had Sir Richard not aided my escape. I pray he is not punished for it."

"Amen to that, Stephen, go and join your fellows."

"All this has been for nothing, Father." Hamo looked as though he had been struck a hard blow to the stomach.

"I obeyed a dying king's commands and have done what he asked. That we cannot bring de Brus to battle is not my fault but that of others." I could see that Hamo felt betrayed by my secrecy. I sighed, "Hamo, I swore an oath and a man must keep the faith or he is nothing. That is in the past. You know the king is dead, now, let us plan our escape. Jack, I want two men at arms to act as guards for Robert, Abel and the servants." I pointed towards the river. "They will cross the river this afternoon and make their way to Carlisle Castle before the Scots arrive. We will bring the rest of the horses here, to the donjon. I intend to make de Brus bleed and then, when he has broken through the outer walls, fire the donjon and cross the river."

Gwillim nodded his approval, "A bold plan and one that might work. When they assault the castle it will be on foot and by the time we are mounted we could have a five-mile start on them."

"It is why I chose this castle and this plan. We are thirteen miles from Carlisle Castle. Even if they catch us it will be close to the Eden."

Robert shook his head, "My lord, our place is with you."

"Your place is where I say it is. What would you do if you were here? Say a prayer or two? I need you and Abel to help the men at arms get the servants and horses to safety. We have gold and silver on those horses. My men need to have some reward for their service to me. Now go." He nodded. "Gwillim, tell the archers my plan."

Left with Hamo and Jack I saw that my son had read the meaning beneath my words. "You think that the new king will punish you."

"If he does not then I will be surprised. This is the last act of Gerald Warbow, the archer who protected a king. I would have one last victory and then, when the king is crowned I will endure his punishment."

By the time the Scottish vanguard was at Canonbie, Robert and the men with him had crossed the river and would be approaching the River Eden. They would be safe. I looked at the sky. There would still be four or more hours for the Scottish to make an attack. My standard fluttered from the donjon and I knew that was the lure that would draw de Brus.

The Prince and the Archer

To ensure that he would be drawn I stood, bareheaded at the gatehouse. Thanks to my capture of Wallace I was known to every Scotsman. We had made our preparations over the last week. The ditch was now seeded with stakes and traps. The edges had been sharpened and the rubbish and detritus of decades removed. As Hamo, John and I stood there my archers were filling the donjon with kindling and four men at arms were moving the horses down to the river. There they would be tethered and guarded. We did not need men at arms on the outer walls but archers. We had all the crossbows from the castle armoury in the inner bailey. My men at arms would use them to provide cover when my archers and I raced back to the donjon where they would cover our retreat from the walls of the outer bailey. I had more beams hammered across the gate. We would not open it. Our escape route was at the rear. They would have to break through the raised drawbridge, the gates and the beams hammered across them. They would not be able to get through them quickly.

De Brus was not with the vanguard but I saw his standard approaching. The villagers of Canonbie showed their true loyalties when they cheered and applauded the new king as he rode triumphantly through the village. It was as though he had already won.

Jack said, "We can see his army now, my lord. There must be two thousand men."

"There may be more, Jack. The ones we see are mounted. If the Earl of Pembroke had more between his legs than his horse we might have trapped and defeated him. This would have been just the place that the king would have chosen."

"But he is dead, my lord, and all hope for England died with him. The men are sad and their spirits as low as I have ever seen."

I turned my head sharply, "I do not want to hear talk like that. While there are Englishmen who are willing to fight for her then there is hope for our country. I am surprised at you, Jack of Malton, I thought I had raised you better."

He flushed, "I am willing to fight, my lord, but…"

The enemy had still to close with the gates and I said, "After Lewes the king and his son were prisoners of de Montfort yet there were men who still fought the rebels. We did not lose hope even though the world seemed a dark and empty place."

Just then a herald blew on a trumpet and shouted, "The King of Scotland would parley with the English invaders."

"Approach." I turned and said, pointedly and loudly, "Archers, only release your arrows on my command."

The Prince and the Archer

They chorused, "Aye, my lord." The whole wall and gatehouse were lined with archers. The only ones with mail were the three of us and Hamo had his bow ready.

Robert de Brus rode up to speak to me. He had a magnificent warhorse and his armour gleamed. I smiled for I knew what he was doing. He was making himself seem like a knight from a romance or a ballad. He could have been Sir Galahad. Wallace had always looked threatening but not noble. De Brus wanted to be seen as heroic. Even before he spoke I knew what he would say.

"Warbow, we meet again."

I nodded, "And here you do not hide and play the part of a loyal knight. I am just pleased that this meeting is not in a church for I would need a double layer of armour to save me from your dagger."

His face looked as though I had slapped him and his knight shouted comments.

"Shame!"

"We will make you eat those insults."

"English bandit!"

De Brus regained his composure and held up his hand for silence. I did not mind the delay for each moment bought time for my men to get to Carlisle and hastened the onset of darkness. We needed the night to effect our escape. "I did what I had to do. You would have done the same for your country." He sounded like a naughty child caught stealing a candle from a church and pleading poverty.

"Murder a man in a church? All the men I killed I faced and they had the chance of life."

"And I give you a chance of life. Lay down your weapons and leave the castle. I will have you escorted to the river and back to England. All that I ask is that you swear not to bear arms against Scotland."

I laughed, "So the fox says to the cockerel, come into my mouth and I will take you across this river. You will be safe."

"I give you my word."

"You gave your word to John Comyn that he would be safe in a church."

His face changed and he snarled, "Then there will be no quarter. We will take my castle back and I will have your heads on my castle at Dumfries. You have had your chance and you have spurned it." He wheeled his horse and headed back to his men. I could not hear his orders but I guessed them.

As I donned my helmet I said, "Archers, ready!"

They all shouted, "Aye, my lord."

The Prince and the Archer

Hamo strung his bow and then chose four arrows. All were bodkins. All of Hamo's arrows were well made but an archer likes to choose the ones he thinks are the best. When he loosed them it would be with more confidence and I could guarantee that he would strike where he aimed. His mail meant he would not be able to send an arrow as far as he normally could but he would still be a better archer than any Scotsman.

The Scots were angry for their king had been insulted but they were not fools. They had fought against Gerald Warbow's archers before and knew the skill they possessed. Men with shields advanced and I knew that behind them were men with crossbows and bows. One change we had made to the defences of the outer walls was to collect all the shields from the armoury and hammer them to the walls. They increased the height of the wall but, more importantly, protected my archers. Crossbows needed a flat trajectory, bows did not.

Hamo spied a knight, helmed and mailed. He was exhorting the men he led to close with the walls. His mistake was that his shield was held loosely and did not cover his body. He was too tempting a target and Hamo pulled back and released a bodkin. His was the only arrow and we all watched it as it arced and then descended. As it was a bodkin it penetrated the mail easily. It tore through the gambeson and into his flesh. I think he was dead before the tip came out of his back.

The effect was astounding. Even those beyond the range of our arrows raised shields. The men who were advancing also lifted their shields. For a handful, it was a mistake. One of those carrying the huge shield did not see the old tree root that had been exposed by falling rain. He tripped and tumbled forward. His back could be clearly seen as were the archer and crossbowman who were hurrying behind him. Six war arrows sped towards the three and all three were hit. It caused a disruption all down the line and in the confusion my archers enjoyed glimpses of targets and they did not hesitate.

The order was given and the archers and crossbowmen were revealed. In those brief moments, it became a race. My archers against crossbowmen and bowmen. Mine won the race and our arrows struck them before they had a chance to send their missiles. The advantage lay with my archers who could see their targets. The Scots had to wait until the shields were lowered before they could aim.

It was Robert de Brus' voice that gave the command, "Charge!" Perhaps he had been counting bows and knew that an attack on the whole wall gave his men the best chance of survival. I looked at the sky. There were still two hours until sunset. I drew my sword. Men fell as they ran but the Scottish king had been right that more of them made the walls than died. The problem they had was that the ditch was now

The Prince and the Archer

deeper and filled with traps. Holding shields above their heads and looking for arrows hurtling towards them meant that at least fifteen men were wounded or injured when they leapt into the ditch. The ones who made the wall suddenly found that, with the shields added, it was too high for them to climb. They would have to use their own shields to climb. We had discovered some darts in the armoury and Jack and I hurled them at the men who sheltered close to the wall. The darts would be lucky to kill but they wounded men who were already demoralised. The horn that ordered them to fall back must have been a release for they all turned and ran.

My men cheered, "Are any wounded?"

"David and Llewellyn both have wounds, my lord."

I heard David snarl, "It is nothing, my lord."

"The two of you go to the inner bailey, we will need you later."

"My lord!"

"Obey me!"

"Yes, my lord."

I saw that the Scottish infantry moved well out of arrow range and the leaders gathered for a council of war. I wondered if de Brus was regretting his decision to attack a castle defended by archers. He could not withdraw now and the best that he could hope for was a victory with fewer losses. To do that he would have to use a different plan. I watched men disappear to the woods that lay close to the village. After half an hour or so they reappeared with bundles of faggots. They were going to use them to negate our stakes. Half an hour later their plan became clear. He had a line of infantry with the larger shields held before them. Behind them, he had mailed men and knights. Following close were the men carrying the faggots.

The horn sounded and the men marched. I smiled. De Brus was not amongst them. He was not risking an arrow. He had seen what Hamo could do and he would not take a chance that I would target him.

Gwillim shouted, as they advanced, "My lord, there are no targets."

"Patience, Gwillim. The sun is getting lower in the sky. Hit what you can but do not waste arrows."

The Scottish soldiers moved slowly and I could see what Gwillim meant. However, such was the skill of my men that they were still able to hit men, mailed ones, with bodkin arrows. The first to make a strike was Peter Yew Bow. I recognised his fletch and his arrow struck the shoulder of a sergeant at arms. It was not a mortal blow but a wounded man does not fight as well as an able-bodied one. Another five men at arms and knights were hit before they reached the ditch. The men with the faggots moved a pace before the men with the shields and then they

The Prince and the Archer

threw their bundles of wood. Three men were hit and, unlike the mailed men, they suffered wounds that would keep them from the fray. Some of the bundles reached the bottom while others were stuck on the slope. When they advanced, and this time it would be with more caution, they could knock the faggots down into the bottom of the ditch.

Jack had sharp eyes and he pointed and said, "Sir Gerald, they have ropes and grappling hooks."

I nodded, "Clever. The walls are old and the hooks might well pull down the walls. Hamo, on my command, I want you to have the archers run for the inner ward. I will not use a horn."

"Aye, Father." He moved down the line giving personal instruction to the archers. The Scottish crossbows and bows were still trying to support the advance but, thanks to our nailed shields, they were largely ineffective. I hurled the last of my darts as the men cautiously slipped down the slope to the faggots. My archers also hit what they could.

When I heard axes striking the wooden walls I said, "Now we leave. I shall be the last."

Jack said, "No!"

"Jack if I move it will hasten their arrival. I want the archers on the walls close to the donjon. My mail and my archers will protect me, now go."

The hammering of the axes drowned out the sound of feet running down the ladders. When the first grappling hook was thrown it was close to me. I lifted my sword and hacked through its rope. The bolt that struck the side of my helmet was too close for comfort and after saluting with my sword, I sheathed it and ran for the stairs. The axes were hacking with greater intensity as they realised what we intended. I saw that most of my men were inside the walls of the inner bailey. Hamo, Peter and Gwillim stood close by with their bows ready.

From the walls, I heard Jack shout, "Faster, Sir Gerald, they have breached the wall."

The worst thing I could do was turn around but when I heard feet pounding behind me I almost relented. My son and the two archers with him sent three arrows and I heard a cry from behind. Then Jack shouted, "Ware behind!"

I was drawing my sword as I turned. Two Scotsmen had closed with me and had used my body to protect themselves from the arrows. I stepped to the side as I swung my sword. Two arrows hit one of the Scotsmen while my sword hacked the other almost in two. There were Scottish warriors just forty paces from me but I was within twenty of the walls. I turned and ran. As I entered the gates were slammed shut and I heard the sound of my archers' bows as they unleashed a rainstorm of arrows. The men at arms on my walls also used the crossbows to add to the missile attack.

The sky was darkening and I shouted, "Men at arms to the horses. Jack, James and John light the fires. Archers, send five last flights and then take to your heels. Men at arms throw the crossbows into the fire."

Robert de Brus would have his castle but the victory would be mine. The evidence lay heaped in the ditch and the outer bailey.

I climbed to the gatehouse and saw that they had torn huge holes in the outer wall and men were pouring through. I saw that there were knights amongst them and took pleasure in that. They were eager to get to me and the closer they were to me the further they were from their horses. I raised my bloody sword in salute as I heard the crackling of the first flames. I descended and saw James and John lighting the bundles they had brought and placed next to the gate. The ancient timber would burn quickly and fiercely.

"Now will you leave, Sir Gerald?"

I smiled, "Aye, Jack."

We went down the slope of the motte and through the hole my men had made in the walls. I saw that my men at arms were already mounted. Jean Michel held the reins of Felix and I mounted. When Gwillim mounted his horse I waved my sword and we forded the narrow river. It was just thirty paces wide and my archers had chosen the best place to cross. I followed Jack into the trees. My archers led and while I could not tell the direction, because of the trees, they could. The horses had been rested for a week and we rode them hard.

By the time dawn broke, we were at the Eden and we crossed the bridge to the castle. We had escaped the fury of the Scots and now we might have to endure the fury of the new king.

Chapter 15

Galloway August 1307

When I saw the royal standard flying from the walls of Carlisle Castle, my heart sank to my boots. The new king was here. Whatever punishment the Earl of Pembroke might heap upon me would be nothing compared with that of the new king.

Robert must have been watching for us for he met us at the barbican, "My lord, King Edward, has been named the new king and he is within these walls." I nodded. "We were questioned by the earl when we returned." I saw four men marching from the donjon and Robert said, "I am guessing, my lord, that you are about to be summoned."

I dismounted, "Hamo, I do not know what will happen now. I leave you to command the men. If I am incarcerated, or worse, do nothing to prevent it. I have cast the die and I will take the consequences of my actions. Do you understand?"

He dismounted and his face showed the pain he felt, "Father, we cannot sit idly by while…"

"Sir Gerald, come with us. The king wishes to speak to you."

"I will come." I turned and snapped, "Do nothing!"

As I walked, flanked by four guards, I hoped that any punishment would be directed to me. Thanks to the king's gift, if I was executed he could not take the title of baron from Hamo. If I were to die then he would be the new Baron of Yarpole. Of course, if the new king and his advisor were in a vengeful mood they could charge Hamo too. As I was marched across the bailey I took comfort from the fact that the king had knighted Hamo and would feel some affiliation with him.

The young king was at breakfast and the earls, as well as Baron Clifford, were with him. His coterie of young knights were also there but I saw that they were seated at another table. Perhaps the new title had changed the prince and he realised that he had to seek advice from older knights.

He looked up as I approached and I bowed, "I am sorry about your father's death, King Edward. He was a great man."

He nodded, "And you think that I will not be."

"I did not say that."

"But you thought it. You are thinking it now."

I sighed, "A man's thoughts are his own, King Edward, but you should know that I am a loyal Englishman who has served the crown his whole life. God willing, I will continue to do so."

The Prince and the Archer

"Yet you left the side of this man you revered and went to the Scots."

"I obeyed the last command your father gave to me. I went north to find de Brus."

I noticed that I had not only the king's interest but that of the earls too. When Stephen had returned he had only been able to tell them of our taking of Gilnockie Castle. De Brus had not arrived when he had left.

The king picked a piece of fat from the ham on his platter and put it into his mouth. After wiping his hands he said, "And did you find him?"

"I did, King Edward. He brought his army to take back the castle. We fled last night after setting fire to the castle."

His demeanour and the faces of the others changed in an instant, "This castle, how far away is it?"

"Fourteen miles or so, King Edward."

He stood, "Then we have him. Muster the men. Sir Gerald, you and your men will lead us there. Perhaps, if we find de Brus it may go some way to mitigating the insults you gave us when we were Prince."

"Yes, my lord."

I did not say that both my men and horses were weary after a night of hard riding. We would have to endure it.

The Earl of Pembroke came over to me, "I would have brought the army, Sir Gerald, and we might have ended this war but when he heard of his father's death we were ordered to guard the body. I dared not risk his wrath."

I said, quietly, "And what would the old king have wished?"

His silence was eloquent.

When I reached Hamo I saw relief on his face. "We are to lead the king to Gilnockie. Have those who were wounded stay here and any whose mounts are too weary."

"But de Brus will run when he sees us crossing the river."

"I know but we now follow orders from a new king." He nodded, "Robert, you, Abel and the servants stay here. Keep Stephen with you, too. I am hoping that the earl forgets his flight."

Robert was going to object but he saw my face and nodded, "Yes, my lord. For what it is worth I think that you did the right thing."

As I mounted Felix I nodded and tapped my heart, "And my heart agrees with you but my mind wonders if the wise move would have been to do nothing and squat like a toad guarding a dead king's body."

The young king shouted, "Sir Gerald, you and your men shall lead us. If there is to be an ambush then you and your men are the ones best placed to thwart it."

"Yes, King Edward."

We were to be bait.

We rode back but the land now looked different in daylight. De Brus' horsemen would have been watching the castle. His knights and men at arms might have struggled to mount their horses and close with us but the border was renowned for its light horsemen. They rode fast horses and wore no armour. They might have even been close enough to watch us crossing the Eden. Within a few miles of crossing the river, I spied the column of smoke from the burnt donjon at Gilnockie. I had decided that we would not ford the river at Gilnockie but use the bridge over the Esk at Longtown.

It was there that the Scots were waiting for us. We were the bait but my men had natural skills and they did not simply gallop across the bridge. They dismounted and scouted it out.

Richard of Lucton rode back with the news, "The Scots are waiting across the river at Longtown, my lord."

"How many?"

"There are a couple of hundred, my lord."

"Hamo, approach the bridge and have the archers prepare. I will inform the king." Without waiting for a reply I wheeled Felix and headed back to the king. "King Edward, there are Scottish warriors at the bridge over the Esk."

"Is Robert de Brus with them?"

I shook my head, "I doubt it, King Edward. They are here to delay us and allow him the chance to escape."

"Then do your duty and clear this obstruction."

"King Edward, there are too many for my small retinue to shift."

He sneered, "I thought the mighty Warbow could do anything. My lord," he turned to Robert de Clifford, "have some of your men give aid to this old warrior."

I took the insult.

Baron Clifford shouted, "Sir Richard of Craven, bring men to support your friend. Perhaps a deed of valour might expunge the shame you bear."

"Yes, my lord," Sir Richard led a hundred knights and men at arms who formed the vanguard and they followed me.

I turned and said, "Thank you for trying to help me, Richard, but I fear it will cost you."

The Prince and the Archer

"Sir Gerald, you taught me well. It is always better to do the right thing for we have but one life and when my life is done I will face God with a clear conscience."

I nodded. There would be time for words later. Now was the time for action. "I will have my archers send a shower of arrows to clear the bridge and then you and I will lead these men at arms across the bridge. We will charge them with vigour. They are here to delay us, that is all."

When we reached the road leading to the bridge I did not dismount but said, "Hamo, take the archers and clear the bridge. After ten flights sound the horn."

"Yes, Father." He took his bow and ran to the watchers who had hidden themselves on the outskirts of the village.

"Jack, you and the men at arms guard the archers' horses and when the bridge is clear bring them. I will lead the charge with Sir Richard." I saw the objection rise in his throat and added, "This is a command, Sir John of Lucton. Now is the time for us all to obey the commands we are given. I need you to clear the road. Sir Richard, you and I will be at the fore. The road is wide enough for six men; we ride in a column of sixes." Jack and my men obeyed and moved from before us leaving me with Sir Richard and his men. I had sent Jack and my men away for they were tired. They had fought at Gilnockie and ridden all night. Sir Richard and his men were fresh.

I drew my sword but left my shield hanging from my cantle where it would protect my left leg. When I heard the horn I spurred Felix and we began to move towards the bridge. This time I held my horse in check. This was not the time to leave the safety of a line of knights. I kept his head level with Sir Richard's horse. We gathered speed as we neared the bridge. Hamo and my archers were still sending arrows over to targets hidden behind buildings. Had the Scots built a barricade across the bridge then they might have hurt us but the king's command to pursue them quickly had caught them unawares. We reached the middle of the bridge and the arrows and bolts, not to mention stones came at us but Hamo and my archers saw the threat and most of the slingers, bowmen and crossbowmen managed, at best to send one missile in our direction. A stone clanked off my shoulder and a bolt hit my shield. It was then that the horsemen, seeing our numbers and our mail, chose to race for their horses. It was a race that they would lose for our horses were now galloping and they had to mount. The men at arms had the hardest task for they had a cantle to contend with. Even the others struggled as the already frightened horses reacted to the thundering hooves and the shouts and din of battle. I swung my sword at the back of a mailed man at arms who was struggling to get his leg over the cantle of his saddle. My archer's arm broke not only mail links but bone and the edge of the sword tore through flesh. He fell. Sir Richard was eager to show the watching king and the Lord Warden of the Northern Marches, that he wished to atone for his mistake. His sword took the head of a light horseman who had a mercifully quick death.

I shouted, "Keep after them." Even though Felix was weary I knew that if we could rid ourselves of this obstruction we had more chance of catching de Brus. He did not want a battle with a large army. He had shown, when he finally came for me at Gilnockie, that he sought easy victories. My dead king had known his enemy and that was why he had sent his hunter to find him. Would the new king do the same?

What the horsemen, trying to flee, did do, was to slow us down. Even though I had given the order to chase them it was hard to do so when the road was filled with milling mounts and dead Scotsmen. By the time we had cleared a path, the road ahead was empty. Six of Sir Richard's men at arms had fallen. Three were dead.

The king and the earls reached us and all that was said was a curt, "Sir Gerald, resume your scouting."

I waved Hamo, Jack and my men forward. Felix was weary and dismounting, I took the reins of a hackney. Its dead owner lay in a pool of blood. I mounted the new horse and when my men at arms arrived, I handed Felix's reins to Jean Michel.

It was the middle of the afternoon when we reached the burnt-out donjon of Gilnockie. We were slowed by three more ambushes. These were attacks from desperate men and they were dealt with quickly. The result, however, was that we were cautious as we approached the castle. We had to ensure that the road was safe for the new king. It was one thing to lose a king but to lose two would be a disaster as the next heir was a boy of less than eight summers.

The king glanced at the burnt-out donjon and said, "We will evict people from their homes and enjoy a roof. Warbow, have your men pick up de Brus' trail."

With that he was gone, followed by his coterie of fawning young knights. I was left with the senior leaders. The Earl of Warwick looked at the castle and said, "You did well to hold off de Brus in that ancient monument."

"It was my archers, my lord." I turned to the Earl of Pembroke, "I do not wish to antagonise the king, my lord, but my men have not slept for almost two days. Weary men make mistakes."

"I know but…"

The Prince and the Archer

Henry Percy said, "I have border horsemen. They have been desperate to show their worth. I will send my men. Yours have done their duty, Warbow, as have you. You have put the rest of us to shame."

"Perhaps you are the wise ones for I am now the focus of the king's ire."

The Earl of Pembroke lowered his voice, "And there is worse news for you, Sir Gerald, the king has recalled Piers Gaveston. He has made him Earl of Cornwall with lands worth £4000 a year."

"Then we have failed in our oath to the king."

Baron Clifford said, "It was a foolish oath for how could we stop a king? King Edward was not thinking at the end."

I shook my head, wearily. I was tired, "And what else could he do? Edward of Caernarfon is the only one who could be king. If Thomas of Brotherton had been named king then Gaveston would have rallied support and we would have had a civil war. We have to live with the two of them."

As we headed to the village the Earl of Warwick said, "The only way to curb their excesses is through Parliament. We have to wait until next April." I was not one who liked politics. Perhaps my time, the time of the archer and man of war, was over. The Earl of Warwick knew how to defeat King Edward and Piers Gaveston, the new Earl of Cornwall. I was just a tired old archer.

There was just one house left vacant by the time we reached the village. I said to the other leaders, "I will camp with my men. I was ordered to find de Brus and I will leave with my men at first light."

My men had food ready by the time I joined them. They were seasoned campaigners. The horses were tethered and we had our own sentries out. Our local knowledge ensured that we had a good site with plenty of grazing and the river was close. There were hovels erected and it looked organised. It was, however, a sombre camp. I think my men shared our opinion of the new king and his close companion.

When we had eaten I said, "We ride early in the morning and we will seek out de Brus."

Just then the border horsemen rode by and their leader, who had been given the orders by both Henry Percy and myself, reined in, "He has vanished, my lord. He must have crossed the Esk. We could not see where he crossed. I will tell Lord Percy."

Hamo asked, "Is he heading for Edinburgh?"

I shook my head, "If he has crossed the Esk then it is to throw us off the scent. When we passed through Edinburgh there was no support for Robert de Brus. I do not think that his few victories will have garnered him more. This is his heartland. We have seen how the people lie for him, even the priests. He will evade battle. If he can avoid a fight before October then the king will either have to keep an army in the field over winter or abandon the campaign."

We were on the road even before the sun had truly risen and we headed for the place where we had been told he had crossed the Esk. It took three hours but we found where they had recrossed. They were heading for the coast. He had used the men of the isles to aid him before and I now had an insight into the man. That was where he was heading.

We rode back and found King Edward on the road to Dumfries. "Well, Warbow, have you found him?"

I had decided that I would be honest with the young king and risk his wrath. "He tried to make us think he was going east, my lord. He recrossed the Esk and his trail leads north and west. He is going to the isles that lie off the Scottish coast. He has support from Ireland and the men of the isles."

"Then you have lost him."

"Yes, King Edward."

He turned to the Earl of Pembroke, "We broke Caerlaverock when my father led us and that means his capital is Dumfries. We will go there and demand I am paid homage." He turned to me, "I want you and your men as a screen to protect us as we travel through these woods. It is what archers do, it is not? You should be able to manage that."

"Yes, King Edward."

I divided my men into two groups and we entered the woods. I suppose it was a wise precaution. King Robert of Scotland might not wish to engage us in battle but his men would seek to hurt us if they could. The problem was that this was August. It was the season of the midges and men and horses were eaten alive by those insidious insects. By the time we reached Dumfries, on the 4th of August, our flesh was covered in the red bites of the insects my men hated more than the Scots. The king, however, was safe.

The huge army that King Edward commanded, allied to the fact that there were no Scottish nobles left in the town, meant that the people appeared to pay homage to King Edward. It flattered him. A feast was thrown in his honour. My men and I were given the duty of guarding the town. I was not bothered but my men were enraged by the insult. I took Hamo, Jack and Gwillim to one side, "I beg you have the men curb their tongues. I would not wish them to endure the wrath of a vengeful and vindictive king. I care not if I am never invited to another feast."

They nodded and went amongst my men.

We had another night without sleep. The next morning I was summoned, along with the other leaders. King Edward said, "King

The Prince and the Archer

Robert has fled and I have taken his town. It is my victory. I will escort my father's body to London for burial and I will consult with my friend the Earl of Cornwall so that we may decide what is best for England in this matter. Warwick, Lincoln and Pembroke, you shall come with me and bring your men. Clifford, you and Percy will disband the muster at Carlisle. There is little point in paying men when we do not need to."

With that command, we were dismissed. I took that I had not been named as a good thing but I was aware of his eyes as he looked at my face for a reaction. I should have been there to escort the king's body. I had been closer to him than any other man. That I was not was deliberate. The king left and as Henry Percy and Baron Clifford had foot soldiers as well as horsemen, we followed their path. The king and those with him reached Lanercost and the dead king's body more than a day before us. When we entered Carlisle Castle, many of the muster were already on the road south.

We ate in the castle. I suspect that the castellan would be glad to see us leave. We had eaten great quantities of his food and devoured much ale.

We ate, largely in silence. The spectre of both my punishment as well as the threat of Robert de Brus hung in the air. There was also the problem of Sir Richard's disobedience of an order. I could not bear the thought that he would suffer through helping me and so I brought up the matter, "I was disappointed, my Lord Clifford, that when my man brought the message from Gilnockie, he was held as though a prisoner."

"That was the earl's doing. He wanted no word to get out."

"And as Stephen would have been bringing the news to me how would that have happened?"

The baron glanced at Sir Richard, "That is in the past, Sir Gerald. The carrot is out of the ground and all is well."

I pursued the matter, "There will be no recriminations? Stephen need not fear further incarceration?"

I knew there would not be but I was trying to get an admission that Sir Richard would not suffer.

"No one will be punished." He emphasised the first words. "The king has been crowned and now has the reins of power. We live with his rule and his decisions."

Satisfied with his answer I said, "I do not envy you your duty, Baron Clifford. The wardenship of the northern marches is a poisoned chalice. The Scots have too many places where they can hide and it is not like Wales where we can ring them with castles."

Henry Percy said, "I intend to make Alnwick a formidable fortress. I had hoped to ask the new king if I could buy Warkworth from him.

The Prince and the Archer

That, combined with Alnwick, would make the eastern side of England safe from the predations of the Scots."

"I do not think that King Edward feels the same about Scotland as his father did."

Baron Clifford asked, "What do you mean, Sir Gerald?"

"If King Edward had been alive do you think he would have given up the chase quite so easily? We had a large army. We were undefeated and we could have taken every Scottish stronghold. We could have won even more support from the Scots for de Brus is not a popular man. The murder of Comyn did not sit well. Balliol's people also dislike him. All that we have done is give de Brus the breathing space to eliminate more enemies and build up an army."

"You sound as though you think that you will not be part of the war against our enemies, Warbow."

"Do you? The new Earl of Cornwall has no love for me."

Baron Clifford snorted, "He has no time for any of us."

"But I was the one who took him to Dover. I was seen as King Edward's gaolor and the one he thought mistreated and insulted him. Do you think that he will forget that? There will be some charges laid and I will be punished."

"You are a baron. Parliament will support you. The new knights are not barons. It is the old king's men who run parliament. I hated Simon de Montfort but he showed that barons can be used to thwart a king. Let us use him as a model."

Baron Clifford was right. If I could last until April without imprisonment then I had a chance, a slim one, but that had always been enough for me before.

The Prince and the Archer

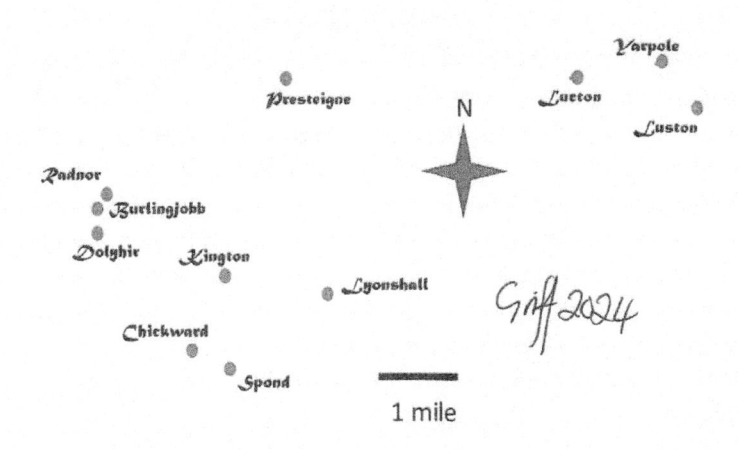

Chapter 16

Yarpole September 1307

Mary was saddened by the news of the king's death. It had nothing to do with the position it placed me in but more to do with the king himself. She had served Queen Eleanor in the Holy Land and she had been there when the king had fought for life following the attempt by the assassin to kill him. Like me, she saw his faults and she also saw the strength that was in the man. Of course, when she had mourned the king we spoke of our lives and our perilous future.

"We could leave England, husband. We have money and an income."

I laughed, "And go where? I am an Englishman and this is my land. Besides, we have the children and grandchildren."

"Who do not wish to see you on the executioner's block."

"It may not come to that. It is not King Edward that concerns me but Piers Galveston. I do not think they would wish a trial but I may have humiliation heaped on me and my family." I knew that a trial would bring up the king's banishment of Piers Gaveston. Both the king and the new Earl of Cornwall would wish that to be forgotten.

She sighed and picking up my hand, kissed the back of it, "And all of this is speculation. We are imagining a terror and that is always worse. When I was taken as a slave and transported to the land of the Mongols I imagined such horrors that I woke up screaming each night. The horrors never came. Life became tolerable and then I found you. Let us take each day as it comes, eh? We go on with our lives and we will take whatever punishment is meted out to us. We have both lived long lives, longer than King Edward and Queen Eleanor enjoyed together. We should be grateful to God for what he has given us."

"You are right and I feel that I am safe until the Parliament. The king and his favourite have a funeral and then a coronation to plan."

We threw ourselves into running Yarpole. There were crops to harvest and animals to be culled for autumn was upon us and winter would soon follow. We heard the news, of course, for Harry's tavern now drew many travellers, and while nobles travelling the road shunned me for fear of punishment by association, merchants happily regaled Harry with news of the world beyond my manor. Harry was never slow to recount what he had heard. He was still my man.

"The new king has dismissed Walter Langton, the Treasurer."

Harry and I were in my Great Hall and as I drank my wine I nodded, "That was to be expected. The bishop was his father's man and

The Prince and the Archer

it was he who carried out the old king's orders. He was the one who wrote out the order for Gaveston's banishment."

Harry nodded. He had learned to appreciate wine and while he drank ale in the tavern, in my home he enjoyed the wine. He sipped and savoured the heavy red wine from southwest France, "There are rumours of two marriages too, my lord. Sir Piers Gaveston is to marry Margaret de Clare." That was a surprise and my eyes widened making Harry smile. "Is the surprise, my lord, because she is a woman?"

I shook my head, "Sir Piers has appetites of all sorts, Harry, no it is the surprise that Margaret's mother is Joan of Acre, King Edward's sister and her father is Gilbert de Clare one of the most powerful Marcher Lords. The king has ensured that his friend is not only rich, thanks to the gift of Cornwall, but that he is also well connected. There may be opposition to Gaveston but it will not come from de Clare."

Harry nodded and took a slice of the cured ham to eat with the wine, "And the king, it is said, is to marry Isabella, the daughter of the King of France."

I frowned. I searched my memory for remembrance of the French royal family. I drew her from the recesses of my mind, "She is a child and barely twelve."

"Nonetheless, my lord, the merchant who gave me this news said that the king would travel to France once his father was buried and Christmas passed. He will negotiate the marriage and dowry personally."

"And when is the funeral to be?"

"He lies at Waltham Abbey and is to be buried on the 27th of October."

I nodded, "I should like to be there and pay my respects."

"Aye, my lord, for he was a good king. You should be there. You were his archer and his rock."

That evening I told my wife all. She smiled, "I remember when Joan was born in the Holy Land. This bodes well for you, my husband. As I recall Joan admired you. She can act as an influence on her brother and son-in-law."

I shook my head, "That is a fantasy, my love. I was never close enough to any of them to expect favours."

"Will you go to the funeral?"

"I should attend but I do not know."

My hopes were dashed when Baron Mortimer of Chirk came to my home a week before the funeral. The Mortimers were no friends of mine and although Baron Mortimer of Wigmore had died a few years earlier, his younger brother still viewed me as an enemy.

The Prince and the Archer

He did not dismount, which by any standard was discourteous but, with his retinue around him and also mounted, spoke to me from the back of his horse. "King Edward has sent a message, Warbow, you are not to attend the funeral of his late father," he paused and smiled, "if you do then you will be imprisoned in the Tower. I should also tell you that you are not to attend his coronation in January."

The man's pleasure was obvious and I wanted to drag him from his horse and strike him but I merely nodded, gave a half bow and said, "Thank you for telling me, Sir Roger."

He grinned and said, as he wheeled his horse, "Oh, it was a pleasure, Warbow, an absolute pleasure."

He rode off and I went inside to tell Mary. She was upset for me, "This is not right. You served the king well and as for not being at the coronation, you are a baron. You should be there."

I shook my head, "Each day I am not dragged off to the Tower means another day of freedom. I view every such day as a gift. I am sad that I will not be there but I spoke with him just before he died and those words give me comfort. I did nothing wrong and should not be punished for I obeyed the king's commands, but right and wrong have nothing in common with royal practice."

Hamo and Jack visited me more frequently than they had before the death of the king. It showed their level of fear. When they came I ensured that they were up to date with all the news. It was Hamo who gave me the latest information.

"King Edward has sired a son. One of the knights from Craven passed through Luston and I gave him a room for the night. I got to know him at Carlisle. He was on his way back from London where the gossip was that the king had taken a woman and she had borne him a son, Adam. His mother is unknown but the rumour is that it was a woman at Rochester Castle where he spent time while visiting Dover and Piers Gaveston."

I frowned, "I do not like gossip."

"The king has acknowledged the boy and he is named Adam Fitzroy."

Jack said, "It proves he is a man, my lord. He is to marry a French princess, you said," I nodded, "if she is but twelve then she is too young to bear children. This way King Edward shows that he can sire children."

My son and stepson were right. King Edward was showing that he knew how to plan. He had inherited those skills from his father. I prayed that he had also inherited his father's martial might but his flight from Dumfries made me doubt it.

The Prince and the Archer

My family all rallied around and even my daughters and their families came to stay for Christmas. It showed me how much they feared for me. Mary and I had become philosophical following the funeral of the king. I had expected dire retribution then but he seemed preoccupied with his impending trip to France. Sir Roger of Chirk was a star on the rise for he was to accompany the king. The result was that Mary and I were happy and cheerful during the Christmas feast and it was my children who looked apprehensive. Our good humour won the day and by the time they left, they were more optimistic.

The visit by Sir Richard of Craven in January brought more news and this was less welcome, "King Edward has appointed Piers Gaveston as Regent while the king is in France negotiating for a bride."

"What! That man rules England?" I found it hard to believe that even the foolish young king would leave such an inexperienced man with his hands on the reins of power. There were many wiser heads that could have kept England safe while the king went to woo a bride. The Anarchy had begun when the heir to the crown had died on passage to France. If anything happened to King Edward during the perilous January crossing of the Channel then there would be civil war. Oaths had been sworn about Piers Gaveston and whilst we could do nothing while King Edward lived, should he die… "How does Baron Clifford view this?"

"As a distraction, Sir Gerald. King Robert of Scotland has eliminated almost all of his enemies and he is now wooing those who were not his supporters. Our spies tell us that he has martial ambitions now that King Edward is dead. When we stopped at Dumfries it gave him a licence to do as he wished. Sir Henry Percy and my lord are on a war footing. We have not raised our men yet but we have border horsemen scouting the crossings."

"You know that my men and I are at the Lord Warden's disposal."

He shook his head, "My lord fears that if he involves you it may risk the wrath of King Edward or Sir Piers." He gave me a sad smile, "I thought to tell you this as soon as I could."

"And you are a good friend, I thank you."

"The Lord Warden hopes that you will keep watch on the Welsh border for many of the Marcher lords are in London in preparation for the coronation and wedding. It is said that London had embraced the young king and his knights. It is a place that is filled with feasts, tournaments and parties. The old king's austerity is gone and King Edward's regent spends coins from his new treasury as though they grew from the ground. The arrangements for the wedding, whilst not going as well as the king might wish, draw to a close. The dates for the coronation and subsequent wedding are set for the last week in February. The king and his bride will marry in Boulogne and then travel to England for an English wedding feast and a coronation."

After Sir Richard had left, he spent three more days with my family, I took my horse and rode alone to Lucton and then Kington which lay on the border. I wanted to be at one with the land and my mind. I needed no distractions and had I taken any of my men then they would have chattered away. I would do as de Clifford had suggested and visit the border. My hunt for Wallace and wars with the Scots had taken me away from the land I had sworn to protect. Abel had saddled for me a newly schooled hackney, Thunder. He was named for the snorting noise he had made when young. This would be a good opportunity for me to get to know him. I left as soon as the sun broke. It was slightly earlier than it had been a week before but the days were still very short and the sun rarely had the chance, if it broke the clouds, to melt the frost and ice left each night. I wore no mail for this was not wartime. I had a padded gambeson and a thick cloak. I needed no furs. My hands were protected by good gauntlets and on my head I wore a beaver skin hat. I headed for the border. I reined in at Lucton which was Jack's manor. He was within his hall, probably enjoying the joys of fatherhood and I would not have stopped at all except that if it was reported to him that Sir Gerald was riding west and alone then he might think there was danger and follow.

I dismounted in his yard and he came to the door with his steward. Jack was wrapped in a fur. "A surprising honour, my lord, I was not expecting a visit."

"I am just riding my new hackney and did not want to alarm you by riding off to the west without letting you know that all was well."

Jack was still young but he had been with me for a long time. I had saved him from my former friend, Sir John of Malton. His eyes narrowed, "West, my lord?"

I smiled, "I know that, of late, Jack, I have ridden in the north but this manor was given to me by King Edward so that I could be a bastion in the west. I go to view lands I have not seen since before I hunted Wallace. If the new king lets me keep my home then I would make it as secure as possible." The warning from de Clifford would not go unheeded.

He nodded, "If you wait I will dress and mount a horse. Come within and enjoy some mulled ale."

I pulled Thunder's head from the icy water trough. He had drunk enough. I shook my head, "The days are short and I would be alone this day. Sir Richard's words, when he visited, have made my mind a

The Prince and the Archer

maelstrom. A ride on this icy morning will help to clear them. When I return I will enjoy a mug of ale with you." I swung my leg over my horse and said, "The new bairn is well?"

He smiled, "Aye, Sir Gerald and has a fine set of lungs."

I laughed. I remembered Hamo and his sisters when they had been babies.

Confident that I would be alone I let Thunder open his legs so that we could go a little faster on the cobbled, but icy road. I did not let him gallop but I enjoyed the faster pace of the canter and the air felt fresh on my face. It was a good morning to be alive and to count my blessings. That was why I had come, to gather thoughts. Despite the spectre of the animosity from the king and his regent that hung over me I had much to be thankful for. I had outlived almost all of my enemies. I had many manors and was far richer than I could have dreamed the day that I became an outlaw, all those long years ago. I had a wife who was my rock and I was as proud of my children as a man could be. I included Jack in that number. I knew that I was well respected, if not by the new king and his coterie of peacocks, but by men like the earls of Pembroke, Warwick and Lincoln who valued my skills, knowledge and opinion. The young Gerald could never have hoped for such an accolade.

I was heading for Kington. Officially there was no border now. The old King Edward, aided by me and other warriors, had subdued the Welsh and now they paid homage to England. I had been born in Wales and I knew the people. They would not be happy to be under the heel of England. They might knuckle their forelocks and appear to be loyal but I had enough Welshmen in my ranks, who were truly loyal, to know that the ones in the old kingdoms of Wales were still seeking a Welshman to lead them. I rode towards the manor of Kington. Kington had been important once. It had been a fortress on the border. Its name meant town of the king for it had been held for the king before the Normans came. Close by were other towns, similarly named, Presteigne meaning Priest's Town and Knighton, the town of the knight. Over the years Kington's defences had been allowed to crumble. It had been abandoned when Lady Maud's father had improved both Wigmore Castle and Ludlow. All that remained of the old castle were the ditches and crumbling walls. I reached it three hours after leaving Jack. I took my time and studied the land as I rode.

The Mortimer family had simply abandoned the manor. Roger Mortimer, 3rd Baron Mortimer of Wigmore, 1st Earl of March, collected taxes but no longer sent men to watch the border. He was influenced much by his older uncle, Sir Roger of Chirk, the man who had taken such great delight in telling me that I was now an isolated man.

I dismounted at the water trough. The ice was now gone but the water would be cold. I took off my gauntlets and looked around. I was known. My archer's frame and grizzled features had been seen, until the hunting of Wallace, in this manor many times. The man who came from the large house, next to the church, was also known to me. It was Hugh of Kington. He had been a man at arms. He had fought alongside me at Falkirk. He was a greybeard. He came over to me and bowed, "My lord, what brings you to this humble place? Is there danger?"

I smiled and clapped him on the shoulder, "Hugh, you and I know that this was once a mighty fortress and bastion against the Welsh. Just because the walls have fallen does not mean that it is not filled with loyal Englishmen. I do not think that there is danger but..."

He stood a little straighter, "True, my lord. Would you do me the honour of coming to my home and enjoying some refreshments?"

I put my arm around his shoulder, "I thought you would never ask."

I led Thunder and when we reached his house he shouted, "Dai, come and tend to his lordship's horse."

A young man appeared from the side of the house. He was skinny and, despite the icy conditions, barefoot. His tunic looked thin but he grinned, "Yes, my lord."

He clearly loved horses for when he had Thunder's reins he stroked his head, "He is a fine horse. Should I unsaddle him and give him a rub down, my lord?"

I nodded and tossed him a copper coin, "That would be kind but my visit is brief."

He caught the coin and said, "He will be ready as soon as you are, my lord."

As we entered the house, I felt the warmth from the fire as soon as I stepped over the threshold, I said, "A fine young man."

He nodded, "Aye, my lord, an orphan. We found him last year, close to death. His family had been murdered." He shrugged, "A local feud that escalated. My wife is a kind woman and as our sons are both dead we took him in."

Just then a woman, wearing an apron and wiping her hands upon it came from the rear of the house, saw me and curtsied, "Hugh, you did not tell me that his lordship was visiting. I am sorry for the state of the house, my lord but..."

I raised my hand, "Peace, Gammer, the warmth of your fire and the hospitality of your roof are all that I need. Do not go to any effort on my account."

The Prince and the Archer

Hugh smiled, "Myfanwy, fetch ale, bread and cheese."

She looked appalled, "Hugh, it is just carter's bread."

I laughed, "Until I was twenty summers old I had eaten nothing else. That will suffice."

Hugh gestured to a chair before the fire. I slipped off the hat and cloak. I would need their warmth when I left. "So, my lord, you did not come all this way on a cold January morning just to eat carter's bread and soft cheese."

I shook my head, "No, Hugh. How stands the border?" He looked up at me and I saw a question on his face. He was unsure if he ought to speak openly. "It is well known that the Mortimers, since Lady Maud's death, do not care for me. Nothing you say will be reported back to them but you know that Lucton, where my stepson is lord of the manor, is just sixteen miles from the border. He is my family and I would not have him or his young family placed in danger. Now that I am back from the Scottish wars and with the Mortimer family in London, I just came to seek information."

His wife brought the bread, cheese, and ale. There was homemade butter and the bread, whilst rustic, was still warm. "A feast, Gammer, thank you for your kindness." I smeared butter on the bread. It melted immediately and I then put some of the soft goat's cheese on it. I saw her watching apprehensively. I bit into it and it was good. The cheese was tangy and I could taste the herbs in which it had been wrapped. I did not have to feign my pleasure and when she saw my smile she curtsied and returned to her kitchen.

Hugh let me swallow the bread and cheese and wash it down with ale before he spoke. He sighed and spread his arms, "You are right about the change in the Mortimers since Evesham and Lady Maud's death, my lord. He has acquired much land. He gained Blaenyllfori and Dinas in north Wales where he is a constable and the family seek to take over Powys. You have been away and you may have forgotten but Owain ap Gruffydd ap Gwenwynwyn was the lord of Powys and he died. His brother is Griffith de la Pole, the same name as his nephew. The baron and Sir Roger, the elder Mortimer, have skirmished and battled these last years with the heir to Powys and the uncle. It has not been more than cross-border raids and the taking of animals but I believe that the death of Dai's family was the result of just such a raid."

"When did the raids start?"

"They have always been a problem but they became worse last summer, about the time the old king died."

I had finished the bread, cheese and ale while he had been talking. "You think it will escalate?"

He nodded, "It is inevitable. The son, the younger Griffith, is headstrong. He has yet to take a wife and has no sons. His sister, Hawise, is also without a family. I would not put it past a lord who had ambitions to rule Powys, to strike first. We heard that King Edward abandoned the chase for de Brus. Now that he is no longer the Prince of Wales he may not see Wales as somewhere worth fighting over. Perhaps it is a good thing that their lordships are in London. That way they cannot light the fires of war. The border would burn if they did so."

I nodded, "You may be right but if what you say is true, then Griffith de la Pole may take matters into his own hands. He may strike first."

He nodded, "I hope you are wrong, my lord, but I fear that you could be right. Still, this icy weather makes an attack at this time of year unlikely and their lordships will be back in a month or so when the celebrations are done." He waved a hand around the room but I knew, from his words, that he was encompassing the land, "The villages that lie close to the border are all loyal and English but we rely on Baron Mortimer to protect us. I keep my sword sharp and the men of Kington train each Sunday but we have few warriors. The other villages that are close by, Radnor, Dolyhir, even Presteigne, just have men who train on Sunday. As far as I know, I am the only man at arms. They rely on his lordship to send one of his sergeants to command the hundreds. None of us have a tower or wall. It is many years since King Edward defeated Llewellyn. Men think that the border is safe."

Hugh was a man not prone to exaggeration and if he was worried then so was I. I stood, "Hugh, if there is danger then send to me or my stepson at Lucton. You might be right and all may be well until the return of his lordship but know that I am ready to come to your aid. The first King Edward charged me with the defence of the border and his death does not change my oath."

He smiled and held out his arm. I grasped it. "You are still King Edward's archer, my lord. All true Englishmen know that and it gives me comfort."

I donned my hat and my cloak and stepped into the cold.

"Dai!"

The young man came out and I saw that Thunder's coat gleamed, "You have done a good job."

"Thank you, my lord. I tend to Master Hugh's horse but yours is a finer animal."

Hugh smiled, "I take no offence, Dai. I was always a warrior who fought with his feet planted on the ground. Sir Gerald was the same."

The Prince and the Archer

I mounted, "I will ride to the border. I shall not stop on the way back for I would get home before dark."

"You are always welcome, my lord."

I rode the few miles to the border. There were Welsh villages in the distance but they were all small. Radnor, Burlingjobb, and Dolyhir were huddles of a few houses and the land around them was crisscrossed by small streams and fens below the rocky crags that rose to the distant mountains. If danger came it would not come from them but from further afield. I stared at the rocky terrain rising beyond the watery land tilled by the villagers. There were few trees and I wondered about trying to have rock quarried. I preferred building in stone. Lucton's manor house was still too close to the border for my liking. It had walls but, in my view, they were too small to be an effective defence. If what Hugh had said was true, then I would have to wait until the dispute between the Mortimers and de la Pole was over. I wheeled Thunder and headed for Lucton. I would identify its weaknesses as I approached from the West. I had to urge Thunder on as the afternoon passed for he was tiring. I had spent longer with Hugh than I had intended.

I spied the village of Lucton and the manor just as a few late beams of light from the setting sun broke through the clouds and illuminated them. The manor was just slightly higher than the rest of the village and an enemy who approached from the west would be soon seen if there was a watch kept. Jack had built a small wooden watch tower. It was, however, not manned. It was too cold and the top was exposed. An enemy who came now, in winter, would be able to use the houses of the village for cover and then rain arrows on the manor. The Welsh archers were good. There was still enough light for me to see when I neared the gate. I was pleased that the gates were closed. I would have been disappointed if they were open and waiting for sunset. The wise thing to do was to close them while there was still light. I banged my gauntleted hand upon the door and shouted, "It is Sir Gerald Warbow."

The gate opened and two embarrassed-looking men at arms said, "Sorry, my lord, we did not know…"

I rode through the gate and dismounted. I smiled, "Had I been able to ride through then I would be angry. You did well."

After tying Thunder to a post I strode towards the light from the opening door. Jack stood there. I took off my hat and cloak and stepped inside. Susanna shouted from the rear of the manor, "I will lay a place for you, my lord."

I shouted back, "I fear I must get home. My visit will be brief but thank you for the offer."

Jack closed the door, "Trouble, my lord?"

The Prince and the Archer

"Perhaps. Hugh of Kington is worried that in the absence of the Mortimers then there may be a raid. Apparently, there is bad blood and there has been an increase in the raids since King Edward died."

Jack nodded, "Aye, he would not have liked the belligerency."

"You are the closest of my manors to the border. I told Hugh to send to you if there was a danger." He nodded, "Your tower needs to be manned every day. You built it to keep a watch but if there is no one there then it is just kindling."

"It is a hard duty, Sir Gerald."

"Then spread it out. You have half a dozen men at arms and half a dozen archers. Give each of them an hour."

"You are being generous to call them men at arms, my lord. They have a helmet, spear and a short sword but that is all."

My voice hardened. I almost rasped the words out, "Jack, you are a lord of the manor. You know how I run Yarpole?" He nodded. "I put any spare coins into my defences and my men. Make the tower better defended against the wind and the rain. Have mail coifs made. Surely you have some we took in the war."

"Yes, Sir Gerald, but not enough for all six."

"Then give them to the best ones and tell the others that when they are of the same standard they shall have that protection."

He said, "I am sorry, that I am letting you down, Sir Gerald."

My voice softened. My fears over my future meant I had been too harsh, "You have not let me down but I would not have your villagers, not to mention you and your family, slaughtered because you were not foresighted." He nodded and smiled. "How many horses do you have?"

The smile left his face for he knew what my next question would be, "Not enough, my lord."

"If you cannot buy them then head for the mountains. There are wild Welsh hill ponies. They can be broken and schooled. Abel has shown skill in that area."

"That takes time and it is winter."

"I do not say now but you must plan for the future." I studied him. He was a good soldier but he was young. Hamo was older and had learned more from me. "I was going to ask you to ride patrols to the west but if you do not have enough horses then it would be a mistake. I will take men to the border the first week in February. We will ride to Radnor. If the de la Pole family see Sir Gerald Warbow riding the border then it may act as a deterrent. We shall see." I donned my cloak and hat.

"I will endeavour to do better."

The Prince and the Archer

"I know you will and my chiding is only to keep you and the ones I love safe."

When I walked through the door to my manor Mary had a frown, "You are late, husband. Is something amiss?"

I shrugged, "It may be and so I must ride the border until the Mortimers return."

My steward, Edgar, had taken my cloak, hat and gauntlets. I unstrapped my sword and handed it to him. Mary linked me, "Come. We have some rabbits cooking that have been hanging since Christmas when the weather was more benign. They will fall from the bone. I have fortified the stew with some old wine."

I smiled, "Good, for the cold has seeped through to my old bones."

She laughed, "You are not old. The white hairs are a disguise as any enemy you face will soon discover."

Chapter 17

Lucton March 1308

The rider from Lucton who galloped in not long after dawn was the man at arms who had apologised to me for delaying my entry. Our gates had just been opened and I was standing in the yard taking deep breaths as I sometimes did. I liked to watch the early morning light over the manor. That light was always a sort of blue and often told me what the day would be like. I had just decided that it presaged well and would be a fair day when I heard the hooves approaching and I turned. His speed and the hour of his arrival made me fearful and my good feelings evaporated, "Gareth, what is amiss?"

"We had a message from Kington, a boy. He said that Welsh raiders descended upon the village in the night. Hugh of Kington, even though mortally wounded, sent the boy to my master."

The sound of the hooves had alerted the single men who slept in my warrior hall. I watched them emerge, "Edmund Blacksword, wake my men at arms and archers." Inside I cursed myself. I had not done that which I had said I would do. I had not patrolled the border and now people had paid the price.

"Aye, my lord."

"Gruffyd of Builth, you are a fast rider, take a horse and ride to my son. Tell him that the border is aflame and I need some of his men at arms and archers. He is to meet me at Lucton with all speed." He began to turn and I added, urgently, "Not all. He must leave men to defend his home."

"Yes, my lord."

Abel had emerged, "Wake the horse master, we need thirty horses. I will ride Thunder."

"Aye, my lord."

Gareth was still mounted. Lucton was not a hard ride away and I said, "Return to Sir John and tell him that we will be with him within the hour. He is not to leave before I get there."

"I will tell him, my lord."

Gareth was a good soldier and had Welsh blood in him. His father had been one of my men at arms who had married a Welsh girl when we had fought in the Welsh Wars. Like Gwillim and my other Welsh speakers, he would be invaluable. "The rest of you eat and then prepare for war. I will choose the men to go with me when we have eaten breakfast." I turned to go within. Edgar was there, "Edgar, I need my war gear."

The Prince and the Archer

"Yes, my lord."

I realised that I needed a squire. Since Jack had been knighted I had done without one. I still felt like an archer but a squire fulfilled a role that I needed. Edgar was a good steward but a squire could be trained to help me arm for war better and quicker. More importantly, a squire ensured that while I was at war I did not need to worry about my horses or war gear.

Mary was already at the table helping the servants to lay out the food. She looked up as I entered. She could not have failed to hear the commotion outside but my wife was the mistress of her emotions. She would not panic, knowing that such a panic would infect the servants. She was placing the freshly baked bread on the wooden platter carefully, as though we were preparing for the visit of a great guest. She looked up and said, calmly, "Trouble, my lord?"

"There could be. Jack sent a rider to me. Welsh raiders are about. I will take some of my men and ride to Lucton. We may be there for a few days until I can ensure that the land is safe."

I saw the eyes of the servants widen. Mary nodded and said, "Go and fetch the rest of the food." They scurried out. "Lucton?"

"Is safe at the moment, but Kington has been attacked and Hugh of Kington slain. That is all that I know. He may be the only casualty."

She took the lid from the butter and shook her head, "You do not think so."

"No, I fear the worst but until I can speak to the messenger he sent I will not have a clear picture. I have asked Hamo for some of his men. The three manors will be defended. This is not a war and I will not allow it to escalate into one. King Edward fought hard to subjugate the Welsh and I will not allow a spark to be fanned into flames."

She left and Robert entered, "Trouble, my lord?"

I nodded, my mouth full already with fresh bread slavered in butter and covered in runny cheese and ham. When my mouth was empty I said, "The Welsh have attacked a village on the border. I will investigate."

"Do you need me, my lord, or will I be baggage?"

I laughed, "Robert, the one thing that you will never be is baggage. Yes, bring your tools and salves for there may be people to be healed. Find a leather jack too. Jean Michel will know where there is one to be found."

He looked surprised, "But I am not a warrior, why do I need a jack?"

I sighed and drank some ale, "The men we face are not an army. They are raiders and they are Welsh. They have some of the finest

The Prince and the Archer

archers you will ever meet and a leather jack will give you some protection."

"Then I will wear one. I have tended men struck by arrows and I do not wish to be the recipient of such a wound."

I ate knowing that while speed was important and I had to get to Lucton as soon as I could, I needed a full belly and it would take Hamo some time to reach me. Premature action could be fatal. I needed the men from three manors and the families of my men to be protected before I acted.

Edgar had my war gear ready for me. I said, "I will not need the hauberk. I will use the gambeson and leather jack."

"Yes, my lord."

He helped me to put them on and fasten them. I sat while he put on my boots. They were comfortable but durable buskins. As he helped me to strap on my sword he said, with concern in his voice, "Will you not need mail, my lord? Should I have it placed in a sack so that you can take it with you?"

I smiled for Edgar was not a warrior and never had been. "We have to move fast, Edgar, and a mail hauberk will slow me down. These are Welsh raiders that we face and they can melt away into the hills as swiftly as fog in the early morn. I will leave men here but I rely upon you to see that all else functions as normal. The life of this manor must go on. Spring will soon be upon us and I would not have us distracted and fail to plan for a good summer."

"I will ensure that all continues as you would wish, Sir Gerald, but," he hesitated and I could see that he was fearful of speaking, "I pray that you take care. You are no longer a young man and the manor needs you hale and hearty."

I was about to become angry but took a deep breath. I knew that I had become a grumpy old man and Edgar meant well. His hesitation showed that. I smiled, "Thank you for your concern, Edgar, but I have no intention of ending my days in a skirmish on the Welsh border. I promise that I will be careful but these Welshmen had made a grave error in judgement. They have forgotten that the man who was King Edward's archer still guards this land. They will pay and that payment will be a dear one."

He nodded and handed me my horn. I would not take my standard for it would get in the way but a horn could be used to signal. When I reached Thunder I hung my shield from the cantle.

I took most of my archers, leaving David in charge of the three younger ones. He was not happy but one look at my face quelled any rebellious answer. Michel and his son would keep most of my men at arms. I took just five, John, James, Walter, Geoffrey of Yarpole and Edmund Blacksword. My farewell to my people was perfunctory. I did not want them alarmed by a tearful parting from my wife. She understood. She would ensure that the manor carried on as normal. That this was a threat to our land was clear. Kington was less than half a day's ride away.

We reached Lucton quickly. Jack had organised his men and they were waiting with their horses. The number he could take was determined by the number of mounts he had. That he would take fewer men than I would did not worry me but I knew that he would take it to heart and realise he had been remiss not to acquire more, either through breeding or purchase. I dismounted and handed my reins to John.

Jack was wearing his hauberk and he strode over. He said, "The boy is in my manor. My wife is comforting him. He was distraught when he arrived."

I went in and saw Jack's wife, Susanna with her arm around Dai, the Welsh boy Hugh had rescued. He had a fur cloak around his shoulders and his face was gaunt and haunted. His wide eyes stared at me like a moon reflected on the surface of a pool. My heart went out to him. To have suffered such an attack once was bad enough but twice, it could destroy a hardened warrior let alone a stripling of a youth.

Jack said, softly, "Dai, tell Sir Gerald what you told me."

"It was in the dark of night, my lord. I had my own room in Master Hugh's house and I heard Betty, my master's horse, whinnying. As I needed to make water I went to the stable. When I was there I saw men in the village. They were armed." He bit his lip and shook his head. "I thought it was my nightmare returned from when my family were taken and this was a dream. When I saw a sword stab into old Geraint as he came to see what noise he had heard I knew that it was not a dream. Geraint's dying scream woke all and I ran back indoors. Master Hugh was already dressing and heading for the door with a sword in hand. He was calm, my lord, and smiled. He said, '*Dai, ride to Lucton. It is east of here. Tell the lord there that Hugh of Kington needs him.*' I nodded and ran to the stable. I took Betty's halter and led her from her stall. Four men broke in and came towards me." He shook his head, "I thought I was dead already but Master Hugh came in and swinging his sword with two hands, sliced one man in twain. He shouted, '*Ride, Dai, ride.*' Even as I mounted the horse I knew that his command had cost him his life for one of the men speared him. He was a tough man, my lord, for he hacked through the neck of the spearman but as I jumped on Betty's back and headed for the door I saw the other two slice and butcher him." Telling me had reopened the raw memory and he burst into tears and buried his head in Susanna's arms.

I put my hand on his head and said, softly, "You have done well and told me all that I need to know. I swear that your master and his people will be avenged and you are now safe. This will not happen again. You have my word."

He looked up and said, "You should not risk your lands for me, my lord, I am cursed."

Susanna was a kind woman and kissed his cheek while she hugged him, "You are not, Dai, and Sir Gerald is not a man to cross. If he says these killers will pay then pay they shall."

I went outside and waved over Gwillim, "Take Gruffyd of Builth, Llewellyn of Rhyl and Dai Short Leg. Get close to Kington and scout it out. Send one back with news. We will wait here for Hamo." He nodded and I wagged a warning finger at him, "Do not alert them to our presence. I want to take as many as I can."

He sighed, "Aye, my lord, and next you will tell me how to string my bow."

"Be off with you, Welshman."

He was right, of course, I had no need to tell him what to do. He was the best scout archer I had ever had.

Hamo rode in at noon. He had brought ten of his best archers and, like me, just four men at arms. While his men watered their horses I told him what we knew.

"A raid or war?"

"From what Hugh told me last month I think it is Griffith de la Pole getting his own back. Kington and the villages close by are soft targets. They are on Mortimer's land but are not defended. The Mortimers are still to return. Piers Gaveston likes tournaments. He will seek to impress the barons and woo them to his cause. The Mortimers are distracted."

"His cause?"

"Aye, Hamo, the aggrandisement of his position and to secure his control of King Edward. You have seen how the king defers to his favourite. The senior lords are all sworn to oppose Gaveston and I cannot believe that since the old king's death men have failed to tell him of the oaths sworn by them at King Edward's deathbed. Gaveston is clever and he will try to subvert as many lords as he can. Baron Mortimer of Wigmore and Baron Mortimer of Chirk will both leap at the chance to be granted favour from the Earl of Cornwall." I waved a hand, "Mount your men. I have Gwillim tracking the raiders. If they have already fled back to Wales then I will pursue them."

The Prince and the Archer

I mounted Thunder and Hamo slipped his leg over his own saddle, "But you think they will not have fled."

"Hugh said that the border was ripe for a plucking. If this is Griffith de la Pole then he would not know that Hugh would send to me. Even if he did then the Welshman might think, that as I was close to the old king, I would be at the coronation. The sheepdogs are away and the wolves can prey on the sheep."

"Then the new king's punishment may actually save the border."

"Fate is funny that way, my son, and I have long ago ceased to worry about such things. Come, we ride."

The only settlement that lay close to Kington on the road from Lucton was Lyonshall. It was six miles from Kington. My archers, passing through, had alerted the men and when I passed through the eight houses their men were armed and gathered in the middle of the hamlet. I pointed a hand to the west, "The Welsh are abroad. I will deal with them but I would have you be vigilant and alert."

Jack of Broxwod, who was the headman, said, "Would you have us with you, my lord? We are happy to fight alongside you."

"A valiant offer but we need to be mounted and I need to have your homes protected in case there are smaller bands that seek to prey on the unwary."

He nodded and looked around as though he expected just such a warband to pounce, "Aye, my lord. We will keep a good watch."

We had travelled barely half a mile when Gruffyd of Builth rode towards us. We slowed and met him at the halt. "The men have ravaged the village, my lord. There is not a man alive but the Welsh left the women and children."

Jack said, "They did not burn the buildings?"

I was annoyed that Jack interrupted the report. He should have known better, "What and alert the border that there was a raid? Listen to Gruffyd and then ask questions."

"Sorry, my lord."

"They have moved south to Chickward and Spond." They were both smaller than Kington and would be easy prey for the Welsh. He pointed due west, "That is the shorter way, my lord. Gwillim and the others are tracking from the north."

I nodded. It was a shorter way but it was across country. For once the frosty ground would help us. Had it been muddy then it would have slowed us. It would be firm without being slippery. I pointed, "Column of twos. Gruffyd, lead on."

My archer rode his tough little pony hard. This was the sort of country for which it was bred. I hoped that Jack was taking notice.

The Prince and the Archer

The two villages were a little over a mile apart as the crow flies and both were so small that the raiders could afford to split their forces. This was a primitive version of a chevauchée. They would take as much as they could from as many places. By picking off smaller communities they could almost guarantee few losses and, if they were undisturbed, animals and what little treasure the locals possessed. Griffith de la Pole would not benefit materially but he would be showing the Mortimer family that he was not a man to be dismissed. If they raided he would too. I knew this was like the feuds along the Tweed. Mordaf had told me of them on my last visit.

The fields gave way to woods. Whilst on the Welsh side the land was riven with streams, fens, bogs and rocks, here on the English side there were tended fields and woods filled with game. One such wood hid the two villages from our sight. I had already decided to head to Chickward first. It was closer to Wales and if they had already been there we could cut off their retreat.

Gruffyd halted and dismounted at the edge of the wood. After peering at the house, he took his bow from its case and was stringing it as he said, "There are men in Chickward, my lord. They appear to have just begun their raid."

"The rest of you wait here. Jack and Hamo, come with me."

We rode to the edge of the trees and looked down at the seven houses that made up Chickward. It was about six hundred paces from us. There were neat fields with low walls and hedgerows between us. As with Lyonshall, there were a couple of farms that lay beyond the village and I could see men there too. Distant cries and screams, as well as the clash of weapons, came to my ears. The movement I saw was familiar. Men were defending their families but, being outnumbered, stood no chance.

"Jack, you have young eyes, look to Spond. What can you see?"

He stood in his stirrups and shaded his eyes against the thin winter sun. "There are men there, too, Sir Gerald."

Being in sole command always suited me for I could make instant decisions and be confident in their outcome. "You two take your men and go to Spond. My men and I will deal with these here. Leave Peter Yew Bow with me."

Both knew me well enough to realise that an argument was futile. They nodded.

"When you have secured the village and killed the raiders, join me."

Jack turned, "Kill the raiders? No prisoners?"

"This is not a battle with men fighting for kings. This is banditry. The men you will kill would be executed for their crimes. Killing them

The Prince and the Archer

is kinder than giving them the hope of a trial that can only have one outcome." I thought of Wallace.

Hamo said, "Come, Jack, we are wasting daylight."

They had only gone forty paces when Gwillim and my other archers rode in. While the others strung their bows Gwillim reported, "They are mainly archers, my lord, but there are four mailed men with them. A fifth mailed man led fifteen or so men to Spond."

"How many are here in total?"

"Twenty or thirty." He shrugged, "There were more than fifty in the warband at Kington and others had attacked isolated farms. It is an estimate."

The estimate was enough. I shaded my eyes and said, "Where are the animals they took from Kington?"

"We left them in a field just south of Kington." He nodded grimly, "The six men sent to take them back to Powys lie dead."

"Good. Take the archers and head for the village. We will ride down the road. The noise of our hooves will draw their eyes. When we approach, unleash a rainstorm of death and show these raiders that we are better men."

As he began to string his bow he said, "It will be a pleasure."

"Robert, stay here and guard their horses. When I blow my horn then come. We shall need your skills."

"Yes, Sir Gerald."

I took out my sword and faced my men at arms while my archers strung their bows, "We will charge down the road. I want their attention on us. There are twenty men there and I want none left alive."

Robert said, "My lord, you have just six men!"

I laughed, "Aye and these five are all mailed and as skilled as any knight. They have just four mailed men. Do not fear Robert, I am confident that Gwillim and my archers will account for the rest of their men."

Gwillim had strung his bow and taken three arrows from his arrow bag, "You are right, my lord. The sight of the weeping women and children in Kington will long live in my memory and haunt my dreams. These men are not Welshmen fighting for their country, they are wolves preying on the weak. Fear not Master Robert, we shall protect our lord and our sergeants. We are brothers in arms."

"Go. We have wasted enough time."

My archers loped off. They would use the cover of the hedgerows and odd trees to make their way unseen to the edge of the village. I pulled up my coif over my arming cap and donned my helmet.

The Prince and the Archer

John, Hamo's brother-in-law, said, "Perhaps, Sir Gerald, you should let my brother and I lead for we wear mail and you do not."

As I pulled up my shield, I took a deep breath. Everyone was too worried about me. They thought I was old. "You two can flank me if you wish but your horses will not go ahead of mine. I want these Welshmen to know that Sir Gerald Warbow is coming for them." I patted my shield where my device was painted for all to see. He nodded contritely, the tone of my voice silencing any further objections. "You others, follow close behind." These two were the least experienced of my men at arms. The others would know what to do.

There were no more arguments and I led them down the slight slope to the road. I saw that the village was less than five hundred paces away. The farm that lay closest to us looked empty. While we completed our formation I deduced that it had been raided first. If there were raiders still there then we would have to deal with them later. While the raiders could not see my archers, knowing where they were moving, I was able to see that they were almost in position. A convenient row of elder bushes and brambles hid them. They were well within range.

Hefting my shield I said, "Keep tightly together." I spurred Thunder and we moved down the road.

John and James had heeded my words and their horses were half a head behind Thunder. I knew that the noise in the village, like the men, would be dying and our hooves would be heard. I saw a pair of mailed men on horses come from a building. I could not hear what they were saying but it was clear, as men took their bows and formed a line that they had been ordered to slay my impudent handful of men. Welshmen were, quite rightly, confident of their archery skills but the archer in me saw that these bows were already strung. Their aim would be good but the arrows less effective than those of my archers who had strung their bows with new strings. Even as the Welshmen drew back I saw the arrows from Gwillim and my men fall amongst them. As I had expected every arrow struck flesh. The odd leather jack did nothing to slow them. The Welsh were standing and we were moving. Even so, despite being attacked with arrows, the Welsh archers still sent their own arrows at us. I was the most vulnerable but I had my shield raised and three arrows hit my shield while a fourth caught me a glancing blow to my helmet. By the time we were close enough to see the faces of the archers, Gwillim and my men had sent three more flights and the Welsh archers were no more. The four mailed men had gathered together and were protected by just eight spearmen. They were in what passed for a green, a piece of common land in the centre of the village. We would

The Prince and the Archer

have to stay in threes until we neared them and that meant John, James and I would be their target. Gwillim and my archers would continue to use war arrows and the spearmen could be ignored. I rode at the one who was clearly a knight. I guessed it was Griffith de la Pole. He had good armour and a full-face helmet. Mine was an open sallet. I liked to be able to see.

The distraction of my archers showed in the position of the Welshmen with spears. They raised their round shields to protect themselves from the arrows coming from their right. It meant they could not protect their horsemen as well. The Welsh knight and men at arms made a classic mistake. They did not counter charge. I was neither a real knight nor a man at arms but I had witnessed enough battles to know that taking a charge at a standstill was fatal. Two of the men at arms did try to move to protect the knight but James and John had spears while the Welshmen had swords. I ignored the two men at arms and concentrated on the knight. He had his shield before him and his sword resting on the shield's rim. He meant to stab at me. My open sallet was just too inviting.

I held my sword at the side. One of the spearmen hurled his spear at me a heartbeat before Peter Yew Bow's red-fletched arrow slammed into his chest. The spear hit my shield. It broke the shafts of two of the arrows there but it was well thrown and hung there for a heartbeat before falling off. Had it struck John's or James' shields then their arms might have dropped. I was an archer and my shield did not move. My two men at arms were the first to strike and they drove their spears like couched lances at the Welsh men at arms. The speed of their horses, their powerful arms and the stationary warriors meant that John's opponent reeled and James' spear drove up under the chin of the second. I swung my sword at the knight's shield as his blade darted towards my face. It took the slightest of adjustments for me to lift my shield and flick the tip away. My archer's arm smashed my sword into the Welsh shield. I had not used the edge but the flat and the knight reeled. He was held in the saddle by his cantle. His horse moved back away from the dubious protection of the other two horses. I knew that Edmund Blacksword and my other men at arms could deal with the other Welshmen and I determined to finish off this knight. He was disorientated and I stood in my stirrups and brought down my sword. He barely blocked it with his shield. I hurt him this time for he screamed. Perhaps I had broken his arm.

From behind his mask, I heard him shout, "I yield! Quarter!"

I raised my sword again knowing exactly where to aim it, "You gave Hugh of Kington no quarter. This is for him!" This time I used the

The Prince and the Archer

edge and hacked down, with all my strength at the neck of the knight. He had mail but no plate. He probably thought he would not need it against villagers. His mail was good but my sword was sharp and my arm puissant. I might have broken bones in the process but his death came when the artery in his neck was severed either by broken mail rings or my sword. His body slipped from his saddle. I looked around and the raiders were dead. I handed my horn to James, "Sound for Robert. It is done."

Chapter 18

Robert had work to do. Some of the men had not yet succumbed to their wounds and while the Welsh dead were stripped and put on wood to be burned, he tended to them.

"My lord, what about the knight's body?"

"Take the armour from it and bind it. We will sling it on his horse and return it to his family. He has a younger sister I believe."

It was late afternoon when Hamo and Jack rode in. One of their men at arms had been slightly wounded but, other than that their battle had been a success. Robert went with two of my men to attend to the wounded at Spond.

"It is too late to do anything more. We will camp here."

Thanks to our timely arrival, they had only begun their attack a short time before we reached the wood, just four of the men and youths had died. The wounds to the others would heal. Robert could have been a doctor. He had gained many skills since joining my familia. Hamo had enjoyed the same success in Spond as we had in Chickward. They had virtually followed the Welshmen into the hamlet and there the villagers had endured just one man's death.

We did not have to use the food from the villagers for the raiders still had supplies raided from Kington. My archers hunted a deer from the woods and we added a few of the dried beans, barley, and greens from the raiders' loot. We shared our frugal stew with the villagers. Robert and my two men arrived back just as we were serving it.

"Well, Father, what now?"

I knew, from my conversation with Hugh, that the de la Pole family lived at Powys Castle. I had already decided to take the body back there. I pointed north, "It is forty-odd miles to Powys Castle. I will go tomorrow to return the knight's body to his family. I will take Robert, Jack and James. The rest of you can return the supplies and animals to Kington and help to put right what was done to them."

"Will the king approve?"

I looked at Robert, "A good question but I hardly think that even if he does disapprove it would change his already low opinion of me. The insults to his friend and the oath I swore to his father are offences enough. I do not regret doing what I did. My only regret was that I did not act sooner and keep a patrol on the border from the moment Hugh spoke to me. Hindsight is always perfect."

After making good the damage at Chickward we all rode together to Kington. It had not been burned but the fresh graves being dug by the

The Prince and the Archer

women and the only man to survive, the priest, were a savage reminder of the vicious feud that had escalated. It had not taken long for the death of a strong king to have an effect. Hugh's house had been damaged. The door hung from its hinges. I paused outside and the priest came over.

He bowed and waved a hand at the animals we had recovered and brought, "Thank you, my lord. The people can start again."

"I am returning the body of the knight who led this raid to Powys. My men have recovered some of the supplies taken. They will stay and help you and your people. The women should not have to dig graves for their husbands." I looked around, "Hugh's wife, I cannot see her."

"Her body lies with the men. She fought the Welsh and paid with her life." He shook his head, "She was a strong woman. We did not find the body of the boy they took in, Dai."

"He is safe and lives with us. He was too late to help you but his message saved Chickward and Spond from this devastation."

He made the sign of the cross, "God be praised."

I turned in the saddle, "Hamo, take charge."

"Farewell, Father, take care."

Robert was badly affected by what we had seen. While my two men at arms rode grimly silent, Robert chattered away like a magpie. I knew my Frenchman well enough to know the reason. He was a clever man who liked to understand all matters both secular and military and he also talked to stop his mind from dwelling on unpleasant matters. I knew to indulge him.

"My lord, how can those people recover? There are no men in the village now and they have lost husbands, sons and fathers. How do they go on?"

"That is the lot of such people. They are the backbone of this land and they are always, if not cared for well, the ones who suffer. When you were in the priory in France you enjoyed a comfortable life in that no one sought your life or home. Here, on the border, that is not true."

"They can start again?"

"Of course. Not everything was taken. They will have a roof and they have each other. There are men who will come through the village and may seek a home. The widows will seek husbands."

"And marry them?"

I nodded, "This is not a romance sung by a jongleur, Robert. This is life. Marriage is not about love, it is about surviving and ensuring that the next generation has it slightly easier than you did. That is all that they can hope for. My manors are filled with old soldiers who are tired of war and married widows. Some, like Harry in Yarpole, do not marry the widows but share a home with them. That is another choice that can

The Prince and the Archer

be made. The death of King Edward was like the dropping of a huge stone into a pond. The ripples have yet to reach some parts but they will. When King Henry, the late King Edward's father died, there was relief for he was not a good king. King Edward was and only time will tell if the new King Edward can take his place."

"You do not think he can."

"The king I served surrounded himself with the best of men. When his cousin, Henry of Almain, was murdered in Italy, he replaced him with others who could give sage advice, like Bishop Langton and men like the Earl of Pembroke. They were like his armour. King Edward's son chooses silks and perfume." Just talking about it had depressed me. "Enough words. We have many miles to go and I would like to be home soon. When King Edward has done with his celebrations he will turn his eye to Yarpole. I wish to spend as long with Mary as I am able."

"You could have sent Hamo to do this, my lord."

"I could but I was the one who killed the knight and I will explain to his family. A knight never shirks from duty and since I was dubbed I have never hidden from that duty."

Powys Castle was a powerful castle and we reached it in the late afternoon. It pre-dated King Edward's reign. Even Wigmore and Ludlow could not compare with it but, as we approached, it looked almost deserted. No standard flew and the handful of old retainers would not have stopped a mob of drunken revellers let alone an army.

We reined in at the gate. The old sergeant at arms had a beard that was more grey than anything and he had the careworn face of one who has tired of battle and seeks a fire and a family. He bowed and recognised my livery for he said, "Welcome, Sir Gerald, what brings you to Powys?"

The kingdom of Powys Wenwynwyn now belonged to England. It had been ceded to England by the father of the man whose body now lay on his horse. "I am bringing back the body of Griffith de la Pole." He nodded and, as he stood aside, I asked, "You know me?"

He smiled and I saw that more than half of his teeth had gone, "I fought against you many a time, my lord. Never as close as this, of course, else I would not be here. If we had enjoyed a leader like you…who knows?"

I nodded, "Yet you survived, soldier, and we have both buried our friends, have we not?"

"That we have, my lord." He seemed to want to say more and I did not force our passage. Men who fight alongside each other have a bond but so do those who fight against. "My lord, I heard that you were born in Wales yet you fought for the English."

The Prince and the Archer

I nodded, "I was born in Wales, in the Clywyd Valley, but I am English. The Welsh blood in my veins made me an archer but my heart is English."

He nodded, "Aye, men always said that you were the finest archer in England."

I had spent enough time talking but I asked, "Who commands the castle now?"

His smile had gone, "Lady Hawise ferch Owain ap Gruffudd ap Gwenwynwyn." He gave her full title. He shook his head, "She is now an orphan. Her mother died when she was young and her father soon followed. Her headstrong brother," he nodded at the body draped over the back of his horse, "he would, at least, have offered her some protection, if he had lived."

I nodded and urged Thunder through the gatehouse and into the outer ward. There were few men around and none in the outer ward. We passed through an unguarded inner gate and found ourselves in the inner bailey. The donjon was a mighty one. I dismounted as a man, presumably the steward, hurried from within.

He bowed and, seeing my spurs, said, "My lord?"

"I am Sir Gerald Warbow and I have come to return the body of the lord of the manor. I would speak with Lady Hawise ferch Owain ap Gruffudd ap Gwenwynwyn." I used the full title.

He nodded, "If your men would wait here, for I shall need their assistance. I will take you and your squire to her ladyship."

Robert smiled at the title. I did not correct the man. I wanted Robert with me for I was not very good at offering sympathy and I doubted that Lady Hawise would view me kindly.

The steward led us into a castle which felt deserted. No doubt her brother had taken the soldiers with him to raid the border. He had chosen a place to raid that was far enough from his home to afford some protection for his sister. That was a point in his favour, I supposed. Lady Hawise was in a small south-facing chamber with a lady in waiting and they were sewing.

She looked up and said, "Visitors, Iago?"

"Sir Gerald Warbow of Yarpole, my lady." He glanced at me and said no more. He did not want to be the one who gave the bad news.

She put down her sewing and stood. Her smile was engaging but she was barely more than a child. I took her to be sixteen or seventeen. She held out her hand for me to kiss its back and I did so. "You are welcome. Will you stay?" Before I could answer she said, "Iago, have rooms prepared." She smiled again, "Goodness knows, since my brother went gallivanting off there are rooms aplenty."

The Prince and the Archer

I could not allow this to go on and I steeled myself to be the bearer of bad news, "My lady, your brother is dead. I have brought his body back."

Her eyes closed and I feared she might faint. Her lady-in-waiting came over. I saw that she was a much older woman. She was well past childbearing. "Sit, my lady."

Shaking her head she opened her eyes, "No, Breffni, I am now the lady of the manor and the heir to Powys Wenwynwyn, although we are no longer a kingdom. How did he die, my lord?"

I took a deep breath. This was harder than I had expected, "He and his men raided some villages in England. He was killed in battle." I paused and held her eyes, "I killed him."

I had expected some vitriol or tears but she nodded, "He wanted glory and he wished for a noble end. Was it noble?"

I did not lie but neither did I give her the whole truth, "He led his men into battle and fought from the back of his horse. He did not shirk combat and his end was quick."

"Good. Then he had his moment of glory but he has left me in a vulnerable position." Her eyes held mine and she gave a sad smile, "You have put me in a place I never wished to be." I saw her staring at me, "Are you not the archer who served the last King of England?"

"I am, my lady."

"My father wished that you served Powys." She used her hands to straighten her dress although there was nothing wrong with it, "Where is my brother's body?"

"Your steward went back for it."

"He will have taken it to the chapel. Would you and your squire come with me?"

"We will, but Robert is not a squire. He is a Frenchman who serves me."

She seemed to see Robert for the first time and she smiled at him. I knew it was a smile forced from politeness. "You are welcome, Monsieur Robert, and I would like to hear your story when we dine this evening."

He bowed, "I am sorry for your loss, my lady, and if I can do anything to ease your pain then just ask." He seemed mesmerised by the beautiful Welsh princess.

She nodded, "I confess that my mind has so much racing around in it that I may well seek counsel from a stranger such as you. If you would follow me, I will lead you to the chapel."

James and John were standing with heads bowed close to the body. Iago was not there. My men at arms looked like honour guards and I

The Prince and the Archer

was pleased that they had done so for I saw it had an effect on the lady. Robert had made the body look as presentable as possible. There was no sign of the wounds. We had found clothes that were unsullied by blood and Robert had dressed him. He lay on a table in the chapel and my men at arms had laid his hands on his sword.

Lady Hawise nodded, "You have good people, my lord. Iago would not have thought to do this. It shows the mark of a warrior. I shall not need the honour guard. Breffni, escort them to the Great Hall while I pay my respects. I will join you there."

We followed the lady in waiting. I said, once we were beyond earshot, "She is a strong lady."

She nodded. I could not see her face for we followed her but she said, over her shoulder, "I was her wet nurse and since her mother's untimely death I have cared for her. She is as dear to me as a daughter. She will weep but not before strangers." She stopped and turned, "I knew this would happen to her brother. He was always a wild child and since his father's death…" She shook her head, "Still we could do without this."

We entered the Great Hall and I saw that Iago had put food and wine out.

"I will return to my lady."

"Of course."

Robert spoke first, "She is a beauty is she not, my lord? I have never seen such strength in one so young. I saw her forcing her body to obey her mind and not her heart."

I nodded and then said, "James and John, that was well done."

John said, "The steward did not seem to know what to do, my lord. It just seemed right."

"And it was."

For one so young Lady Hawise seemed very assured. When she returned from saying her farewell to her brother she insisted that John and James dine with us. She said, "It will be good to have a company who are not aged like Breffni and Iago."

Breffni had not taken offence at the comment and merely sniffed, "Aye, but the food will disappear quickly with these three young men eating us out of house and home."

Lady Hawise put her hand on Breffni's and said, "At least we have food. Those poor people whom my brother, God rest his soul, raided, may not. Let us be grateful for what we have. These men need not have travelled fifty or more miles to be the bearers of such news and I am grateful that I have heard the truth, as unpleasant as it was."

The Prince and the Archer

She did not refer to the death of her brother throughout the meal but, after asking me the story of my life, questioned John and James and especially Robert about their lives. She seemed to be fascinated by Robert's story. The two of them were locked in a conversation that seemed to exclude the rest of us. Without knowing why I knew that this was a good thing. She was an admirable young woman.

We retired relatively early and I rose before Prime. I waited to descend until a servant knocked on our door. "Her ladyship awaits, my lord."

The young woman was still beautiful but she looked as though she had not slept well. She was gracious and smiled as she waved us to our seats. She said, "Robert, would you say Grace please?"

"Of course, my lady."

When he had finished she smiled, "It always seems to make the food taste better when Grace is spoken by a man of God."

"My lady, I was never ordained. I am no priest."

"But you have the heart of one and perhaps, that makes an almost perfect man. You have helped me since you have come and I thank you for bringing a little light into the dark place where I now reside."

He said, "Dark place, my lady? You are the lady of a fine manor and once you have grieved for your brother can begin a life which promises much."

She shook her head sadly, "It promises little. I am an orphan and not yet of an age to inherit the title. I am a ward of King Edward and I have not even met him. Powys Wenwynwyn is not a rocky scrubland but a rich and prosperous land. It is a buffer for England. I will be chosen to marry an English lord and I shall have no say in the matter."

Robert looked at me, appalled, "Sir Gerald, surely the lady is mistaken. This cannot be her fate?"

I said, sadly, "I fear that Lady Hawise is right, Robert. This is not a small manor like Sadberge or Luston. It is a kingdom. It may be ruled by an English king now but it is still a valuable piece in the chess game played by kings and nobles. Lady Hawise will have her husband chosen for her."

The lady smiled and nodding, put her hand on Robert's, "But I thank you, Robert, for I will often think of your exciting story and that of Lord Edward's archer. My life, hitherto, in Powys has been quiet, almost dull. I cannot see that it will change much but now I have the memories of others to share."

As we headed back to Yarpole, it was Robert who was quiet. That night, as we lodged in Stokesay, I was able to speak alone with Robert while my men at arms saw to the animals. "Robert, you have been quiet all day, what ails you?" He looked at me and I could see the indecision in his eyes. "Come, I know that I am a grumpy old man but you know me well enough to realise that I will listen."

"I have lost my heart, my lord. I never thought that I would be so smitten by a maid but I am. I have stepped into a maze and there is no escape. I would be the man in Lady Hawise's life and yet I know it can never be, I wish I had never come with you."

I nodded for I understood him, "And yet, had you not come with me then the Lady Hawise would still have an unhappy future but without the memories of you. I know you have not the eyes to see but your feelings were reciprocated by the lady."

His eyes widened, "Truly?"

"Yes, but she was bred to marry a noble and she knows that. There is no romantic hero for Lady Hawise. There is no knight to sweep her off to a fine castle and a happy future. She is bred for duty and not for love."

"But you have love, Sir Gerald. I see it every day."

"You forget that I was a humble archer and Lady Mary, for all her accomplishments, was still a slave. We had the luxury of making our own choices." John and Jack re-entered, and I added, quietly, "There may be another one out there for you, Robert."

He shook his head, "No, my lord, Lady Hawise is the only one and I must resign myself to her loss."

The rest of the journey home was sad. Robert had lost his heart and a man does not recover easily from such a loss. Even King Edward changed when Queen Eleanor died. I prayed that I would die before Mary. I could not bear a life without her.

The Prince and the Archer

Epilogue

Westminster Palace March 1308

When the haughty knight from King Edward's familia brought me the command to attend him in London I feared the worst. I was given just four days to make the journey and, after the knight had left to stay with Sir Roger Mortimer, now a friend of the new king, I sent for Hamo and Jack. The knight had made it quite clear that he expected me not to return to Yarpole and seemed quite happy about that. While we waited I spoke to Mary and Robert. "This does not bode well. When I have spoken with my son and stepson I will write my will."

Mary smiled and squeezed my hand but Robert said, "Surely that is premature, my lord. I know that the king and his regent are unhappy with you but death seems a heavy price to pay for obeying the orders of the last king."

I smiled, "When I was an archer all that I had to worry about was death in battle. Once you are a lord you have enemies all around and more often than not it is a knife in the back and not an arrow in the chest that will bring death. I will be prepared. I want you to come with me for if my premonition comes true, then I would have my last confession with a friend."

I saw his eyes as I said that and nodding, he said hoarsely, "A friend?"

"Aye, Robert, and a good one."

When they arrived Hamo and Jack both spoke as Robert had done but I would not be swayed. "I will write my will before I leave." I stared at them, "You should know that neither of you will come with me. You are not summoned and I would keep it that way."

They glumly nodded their acceptance of my command.

Mary and I were bright and cheerful as we ate that night but the others were in a gloomy mood. We had the orphan, Dai, with us. He was dressed in better clothes and my wife had bathed and washed him. He sat at the table with us, taking it all in. I had offered him the chance to work with Abel and my horses. He was still in a state of shock but he accepted. My wife was keeping him close until he had regained his confidence. She wanted him to be happy. My son and stepson were spoiling that.

I grew impatient and said, "Look, I have enjoyed a good life. I served a good king and helped to make England safe. If my life is to end then so be it. I leave the protection of this land to two fine young knights. Your mother will need your help and support although I think she will enjoy the peace without me."

For the first time Mary became serious, "No husband, if this is to be the end then I shall mourn you every day for the rest of my life. I cannot erect crosses to your memory as King Edward for Queen Eleanor did but know that I will bear the cross of your death here in my heart. My face will smile but my soul will weep."

When my men heard that I had been summoned they were angry. Gwillim and Harry wanted to come with me. Every man, they said, would follow me and show the young king that he was wrong. I had to use my authority to quell their rebellious words. I sat with them in Harry's tavern and we spoke long into the night. I had to say goodbye to them properly. I owed them that.

I was travelling to court and so we took a sumpter with good changes of clothes. I took my sword but that was my only weapon. It was no longer winter but England, even in the spring was still a cold land. Mary and I had cuddled in bed and said all that needed to be said. She adopted the face, as we left, that would be the one she showed the world. Our eyes spoke our goodbyes. Hamo managed not to unman himself but his choked voice laid bare his feelings. Jack, the boy who had come to me as Jack of Malton, could not handle the moment. He wept.

"My lord, I owe you all and I cannot just stand by while you are punished for nothing."

I had decided to put on a bright face. I would adopt Mary's idea. "It may not be a punishment, Jack. I might just be publicly chastised. There may be a fine. It could be banishment."

"Banishment!"

"Jack, I would be alive, would I not? Wait until I do not return before you shower my hall with tears."

We were not far down the road when Robert said, "You do not expect to return, do you, Sir Gerald?"

"No. I hope that as you are not of my family you will not be punished too."

"That does not matter for if I cannot have Lady Hawise then…"

There were no words I could say to take away the hurt he was feeling so I concentrated, as we rode to London, on saying goodbye to a land that was as familiar to me as anywhere in England; I had travelled the road to London many times. At each place we rested I was welcomed. My enemies were dead and, on the road at least, all that remained were friends.

The Prince and the Archer

I passed into the Palace of Westminster with some trepidation although had it been the Tower then I would have known the worst was about to befall me. London had emptied following the wedding and the coronation but many of the young knights so admired by the king still remained. After leaving our horses with the groom Robert and I entered the palace. He carried my bags. The royal steward was expecting me. I was pleased to see that he had served the old king and knew me. He had been at Burgh by Sands and had been one of those who had been there at the moment of his death.

Edmund greeted me warmly, "Good to see you, Sir Gerald. A good journey from the northwest?"

I smiled, "As good as any journey when you have seen as many summers as I have."

He laughed, "I have your room. I was told to allocate three but..."

I nodded, "One will do. Robert can have a paillasse." I did not want to be alone. I was not afraid but I wanted the company of friends.

"Of course, my lord. Follow me."

The room was well-appointed and faced west. It had shutters on the inside but they were open allowing light and air into the room.

"There is water and cloths to dry yourself, my lord. There is wine, ale and food in the Great Hall. I will fetch you when you are to meet the king." He paused, "It will not be today." He looked at Robert, "Is this your squire, my lord?"

"No, he is my doctor." I saw Robert smile at the deception.

"Then I will ensure that he has a place when we dine."

"I should like him to be close to me."

"Of course." He bowed and left.

"We came on the appointed day, did we not, my lord?"

"We did but this may be a game. Kings often like to play games. The old King Edward did not do so often but his father, King Henry, was a master at it."

When we eventually went down to the Great Hall we were shunned. I say shunned but we were the focus of attention for all those within its magnificent walls. I recognised the other twenty knights as young knights who had been knighted at the Feast of the Swans. That they were talking about me was clear but they were wise enough not to let me hear their comments but I did see their sly, conspiratorial smiles. Did they know something?

The food was as magnificent as I had expected but neither of us enjoyed it with the spectre of a meeting with the king. The minstrels in the gallery played happy tunes but neither of us felt cheery. Robert and I spoke of innocent matters. He looked at the tapestries. The old king

The Prince and the Archer

had ordered them to be made and they reflected his victories at Evesham and Falkirk. He was, as one might expect, shown in a favourable light. Robert asked me about the battles and I used the two tapestries to illustrate the difference between art and reality.

"It is the same when men sing of battles. They were rarely there themselves and reported what the victors said about them. No one ever asked a man at arms how it felt when Simon de Montfort's horsemen, mailed and plated, galloped towards them. Archers were never consulted about having to take cover when light horsemen pursued them. It is all about heavy cavalry charges over ground, that, according to the tapestries and songs, was always flat. The weather was always perfect and there was never a shower to dampen bow strings or a wild, swirling wind to make aiming difficult. Knights always fought well and died nobly." I shrugged, "Perhaps it is better that way. If the truth were known then few men would ever go to battle."

Robert was as bright and clever a man as I had ever met, "Yet you knew the truth and still went into battle."

I laughed, making some of the young knights turn and stare, "Then I must be a bigger fool than even my enemies think."

We were the first to leave. As I stood at the door I turned and smiled, "You gentlemen can now be more open with your comments, eh? The old relic you fear so much is not here to hear them." As the door closed behind us I heard the buzz of conversation rise.

That night I asked Robert to hear my confession. He was reluctant to at first pointing out his lack of qualifications. "Robert, I have heard dying men's confessions. You do not need to be a priest to do so. By confessing I am giving myself a chance of going to heaven. I would like to see Queen Eleanor and King Edward again and to be there when Mary joins me."

I felt better after confession and slept better than I had expected.

The king had not returned by breakfast and Robert and I were the first ones there. Many of the servants recognised me and our breakfast was better than I could have hoped.

William, the servant I had met in the north, came over to ask after our night, "You slept well, my lord?"

"I did. Has the king returned?"

"Not yet, my lord."

The chief steward came over, "Was the food to your liking, my lord?"

"It was. I would like to visit the city." I was going to add, 'one last time' but thought that was tempting Fate a little too much.

The Prince and the Archer

The chief steward shook his head and, leaning in, said quietly, "I would stay within the palace, my lord. It is safer that way. It is quite pleasant by the river. In the summer there is a stink of contagion but in spring the rains sweep it clear and with the blossom on the trees it gives promise of new life. If you are there then I can fetch you when the king arrives. He will not wish to be kept waiting."

The message beneath the words was clear. Stay close to the palace and do not incur further wrath from the new king. "Thank you, Edmund, you are a good man."

"We both served the king and I know just how highly he valued you, Sir Gerald. He thought of you as his rock."

He was right about the blossom and it was pleasant to walk the walls by the river. The sentries moved away when we neared them but I had a smile from each of them. They were soldiers and knew my worth. That was all that was important to me. I cared not about the opinions of peacocks and popinjays.

It was not long before noon and the bell for Sext from the Abbey when Edmund found me. "The king will see you, Sir Gerald," he looked at Robert, "alone."

Robert nodded, "I will wait in our room, my lord. I can pray."

Edmund smiled and chatted as we walked back into the palace. He was trying to put me at my ease and while I appreciated it I wanted silence to compose myself.

I was not taken to the Great Hall, the court where all the knights were waiting. Instead, I was taken up the stairs to a chamber guarded by two men at arms. One recognised me and saluted with his halberd, "Good day, Sir Gerald." The sound of the halberd would alert those within to my presence.

I nodded to him, "Good to see you again."

"I would rather be fighting the Scots, my lord."

I had no chance to reply for an imperious although slightly high-pitched voice from within commanded, "Come."

I shrugged to the sentry and walked in. Edmund did not accompany me but closed the door behind me. Inside the king sat in a richly upholstered chair and behind him, a bejewelled hand upon the king's shoulder, was Piers Gaveston, the Earl of Cornwall. Most of the meetings I had enjoyed with King Edward had enjoyed the presence of a clerk or scribe to provide evidence of what had been said. In his latter years, I had been privileged to have private conversations with King Edward but I did not think this was one such occasion. That we were alone was ominous, for there would be no record of our words.

The Prince and the Archer

The king spoke, "You are a troublesome man, Warbow. You insulted my friend, the Earl of Cornwall and treated him like a common criminal and you showed me little respect. You made him swear an oath which was an unnecessary insult."

He paused and I took the opportunity to reply. If I was going to be damned I would have my say, "King Edward, I obeyed the orders given to me by your father, the late king. I could do no other."

"Those orders were misguided." He put a hand on that of Piers Gaveston.

The earl gave a silky smile, "It is in the past, my liege. I bore the injustice for our friendship and now all is resolved."

"And that shows true nobility. Of course, you were born with it but others," he smiled patronisingly at me, "were dragged up and given titles that they had no right to." I said nothing for there was nothing to say. For the first time in a long time, I was helpless. The fly was in the web and the two spiders were licking their lips in anticipation of devouring their meal. They were toying with me much as a cat does with a mouse.

The king put his fingers together, almost as though he was at prayer and a smile played upon his lips. "What do we do with you? That is the question." I noticed that he said we. "I would be well within my rights to have you carted off to the tower and order a summary execution."

I was about to point out that my rank forbade that. I had to have a trial with a jury of my peers and his new knights were not barons.

Piers Gaveston said, smoothly, "I think that Sir Gerald has done enough for his country to give him a second chance."

When the king spoke I knew that this was all rehearsed, "You are right and his recent actions in Herefordshire were timely. I will give you a licence, Sir Gerald, to continue as a baron, but you are on a short leash. Any further actions which insult either the crown or the friends of the crown will result in punishment."

I was shocked and could not think of an answer. Did I thank him?

Piers Gaveston said before I could blurt out thanks, "There is a price, however. There is a Parliament to be held next month and we would have you stay here, at the Palace, until that time."

The king frowned, "The one in February was most unsatisfactory. You were not there."

I said, somewhat lamely, "I was not invited, King Edward."

"But," said Piers Gaveston, with more force in his voice than before, "you will be at the next one and you will remember that the king needs all the support of loyal barons."

The Prince and the Archer

I was still that fly in the web and I was trapped. If I refused then I would be arrested. I could be held without trial, indefinitely. If I agreed then I would have to support a man, the Earl of Cornwall, that I did not wish to support.

I hedged. "My Lord Cornwall, I have always supported my king." That was true but I had not had to support the new king and my sympathies would be with his enemies.

My words seemed to satisfy them. They smiled and nodded. The king said, "You are a stout fellow for one so common."

The Earl of Cornwall said, "Enjoy Westminster but you must not leave the confines of the palace. That is our express command. Nor will you communicate with any outside the palace." The earl was commanding and not the king.

"But my family."

"Will be told that you are enjoying the hospitality of the king."

King Edward waved a hand, "You are dismissed."

As I left I felt like The Lord Edward after Lewes. He and his cousin had been trapped and taken prisoner. The former king had given his word not to escape. I had not done so but I knew the punishment for disobedience. I had just over a month to work out what to do. As I neared my chamber I smiled. I was alive and while I lived then the man who had helped the first King Edward to win so many times had a chance. I had come to London expecting death. That sentence was not removed but I could not support Sir Piers Gaveston. I did not have long. Robert and I would need to put our heads together and work out a plan.

The End

Glossary

An Còrsa Feàrna - Carsphairn in Galloway
Banneret - the rank of knight below that of earl but above a bachelor knight
Bachelor knight - a knight who had his own banner but fought under the banner of another
Cannons - metal armour for arms
Caparison or trapper - a cloth covering for a horse
Carter's Bread - dark brown or black bread eaten by the poorest people
Chevauchée - a mounted raid
Centenar - commander of one hundred men (archers)
Familia - Household knights of a great lord
Gardyvyan - a bag containing an archer's equipment
Hogbog - a place on a farm occupied by pigs and fowl
Liberty - a unit of men which was independent of the regalian right
Mainward - the main body of an army (vanguard- mainward- rearguard)
Manchet - the best bread made with wheat flour and a little added bran
Mêlée - in battle, a confused fight or a combat between knights at a tourney
Othenesberg - Roseberry Topping, North Yorkshire
Raveled or yeoman's bread - coarse bread made with wholemeal flour with bran
Shaffron - a metal plate to protect a horse's head
Tithe - a tenth
Vintenar - a commander of twenty men (archers)
Wallintun - Warrington
Wapentake - a Saxon term for the fyrd or local muster
Westhalton - Westhoughton (Greater Manchester)

Canonical Hours
- Matins (nighttime)
- Lauds (early morning)
- Prime (first hour of daylight)
- Terce (third hour)
- Sext (noon)
- Nones (ninth hour)
- Vespers (sunset evening)
- Compline (end of the day)

The Prince and the Archer

Classes of hawk

This is the list of the hunting birds and the class of people who could fly them. It is taken from the 15th-century Book of St Albans.
Emperor: eagle, vulture, merlin
King: gyrfalcon
Prince: gentle falcon: a female peregrine falcon
Duke: falcon of the loch
Earl: peregrine falcon
Baron: buzzard
Knight: Saker Falcon
Squire: Lanner Falcon
Lady: merlin
Young man: hobby
Yeoman: goshawk
Knave: kestrel
Poor man: male falcon
Priest: sparrowhawk
Holy water clerk: sparrowhawk

The Prince and the Archer

Historical Note

The incident with the king's tantrum and the tearing of the prince's hair was recorded by the chronicler Walter of Guisborough. The king's words were the ones reported. It was also chronicled about the relationship between the Frenchman and the prince. Prince Edward equipped his friend with horses, luxurious clothes, and £260 of money; a fortune in 1307. I have tried, wherever possible, to use the king's words.

Sir Piers Gaveston was banished from England in February but he did not leave until May. I have fictionalised the journey south. It suited my plot and as Sir Gerald Warbow is a fictional character I had a licence to do so. The prince did lavish gifts on his friend, much to his father's annoyance.

The journey north to Carlisle proved to be too much for the king. His insistence that he travel with the army slowed them down and allowed King Robert to build up support. The news of the king's death was withheld for two weeks on pain of death. The Earl of Pembroke waited to release the news until the heir and the widow had been informed.

The subplot about de la Pole and the Mortimers is based on a feud over the lands of Powys. That subplot will grow in the next book.

Gerald Warbow's story is not over but it is drawing to a close. The journey is unfinished, yet.

Books used in the research:

Edward 1st and the Forging of England- Marc Morris
The Normans- David Nicolle
The Knight in History- Francis Gies
The Norman Achievement- Richard F Cassady
Knights- Constance Brittain Bouchard
Feudal England: Historical Studies on the Eleventh and Twelfth Centuries- J. H. Round
Peveril Castle- English Heritage
Norman Knight AD 950-1204- Christopher Gravett
English Medieval Knight 1200-1300- Christopher Gravett
English Medieval Knight 1300-1400- Christopher Gravett
The Scottish and Welsh Wars 1250-1400- Christopher Rothero
Lewes and Evesham 1264-65- Richard Brooks
Cassini Historical Map 1840-43, Liverpool

The Prince and the Archer

Griff Hosker July 2024

Other books by Griff Hosker

If you enjoyed reading this book, then why not read another one by the author?

Ancient History

The Sword of Cartimandua Series
(Germania and Britannia 50 A.D. – 128 A.D.)
Ulpius Felix- Roman Warrior (prequel)
The Sword of Cartimandua
The Horse Warriors
Invasion Caledonia
Roman Retreat
Revolt of the Red Witch
Druid's Gold
Trajan's Hunters
The Last Frontier
Hero of Rome
Roman Hawk
Roman Treachery
Roman Wall
Roman Courage

The Wolf Warrior series
(Britain in the late 6th Century)
Saxon Dawn
Saxon Revenge
Saxon England
Saxon Blood
Saxon Slayer
Saxon Slaughter
Saxon Bane
Saxon Fall: Rise of the Warlord
Saxon Throne
Saxon Sword

Medieval History

The Dragon Heart Series
Viking Slave *

The Prince and the Archer

Viking Warrior *
Viking Jarl *
Viking Kingdom *
Viking Wolf *
Viking War*
Viking Sword
Viking Wrath
Viking Raid
Viking Legend
Viking Vengeance
Viking Dragon
Viking Treasure
Viking Enemy
Viking Witch
Viking Blood
Viking Weregeld
Viking Storm
Viking Warband
Viking Shadow
Viking Legacy
Viking Clan
Viking Bravery

The Norman Genesis Series
Hrolf the Viking *
Horseman *
The Battle for a Home *
Revenge of the Franks *
The Land of the Northmen
Ragnvald Hrolfsson
Brothers in Blood
Lord of Rouen
Drekar in the Seine
Duke of Normandy
The Duke and the King

Danelaw
(England and Denmark in the 11th Century)
Dragon Sword *
Oathsword *
Bloodsword *
Danish Sword*

The Prince and the Archer

The Sword of Cnut

New World Series
Blood on the Blade *
Across the Seas *
The Savage Wilderness *
The Bear and the Wolf *
Erik The Navigator *
Erik's Clan *
The Last Viking*

The Vengeance Trail *

The Conquest Series
(Normandy and England 1050-1100)
Hastings*
Conquest

The Aelfraed Series
(Britain and Byzantium 1050 A.D. - 1085 A.D.)
Housecarl *
Outlaw *
Varangian *

The Reconquista Chronicles
Castilian Knight *
El Campeador *
The Lord of Valencia *

The Anarchy Series England
(1120-1180)
English Knight *
Knight of the Empress *
Northern Knight *
Baron of the North *
Earl *
King Henry's Champion *
The King is Dead *
Warlord of the North*
Enemy at the Gate*
The Fallen Crown*
Warlord's War

The Prince and the Archer
Kingmaker
Henry II
Crusader
The Welsh Marches
Irish War
Poisonous Plots
The Princes' Revolt
Earl Marshal
The Perfect Knight

Border Knight
(1182-1300)
Sword for Hire *
Return of the Knight *
Baron's War *
Magna Carta *
Welsh Wars *
Henry III *
The Bloody Border *
Baron's Crusade*
Sentinel of the North*
War in the West*
Debt of Honour
The Blood of the Warlord
The Fettered King
de Montfort's Crown
The Ripples of Rebellion

Sir John Hawkwood Series
(France and Italy 1339- 1387)
Crécy: The Age of the Archer *
Man At Arms *
The White Company *
Leader of Men *
Tuscan Warlord *
Condottiere*
Legacy

Lord Edward's Archer
Lord Edward's Archer *
King in Waiting *
An Archer's Crusade *

The Prince and the Archer

Targets of Treachery *
The Great Cause *
Wallace's War *
The Hunt*
The Prince and the Archer

Struggle for a Crown
(1360- 1485)
Blood on the Crown *
To Murder a King *
The Throne *
King Henry IV *
The Road to Agincourt *
St Crispin's Day *
The Battle for France *
The Last Knight *
Queen's Knight *
The Knight's Tale

Tales from the Sword I
(Short stories from the Medieval period)

Tudor Warrior series
(England and Scotland in the late 15th and early 16th century)
Tudor Warrior *
Tudor Spy *
Flodden*

Conquistador
(England and America in the 16th Century)
Conquistador *
The English Adventurer *

English Mercenary
(The 30 Years War and the English Civil War)
Horse and Pistol

Modern History

East India Saga
East Indiaman

The Prince and the Archer

The Napoleonic Horseman Series
Chasseur à Cheval
Napoleon's Guard
British Light Dragoon
Soldier Spy
1808: The Road to Coruña
Talavera
The Lines of Torres Vedras
Bloody Badajoz
The Road to France
Waterloo

The Lucky Jack American Civil War series
Rebel Raiders
Confederate Rangers
The Road to Gettysburg

Soldier of the Queen series
Soldier of the Queen*
Redcoat's Rifle*
Omdurman*
Desert War

The British Ace Series
1914
1915 Fokker Scourge
1916 Angels over the Somme
1917 Eagles Fall
1918 We will remember them
From Arctic Snow to Desert Sand
Wings over Persia

Combined Operations series
(1940-1945)
Commando *
Raider *
Behind Enemy Lines
Dieppe
Toehold in Europe
Sword Beach
Breakout
The Battle for Antwerp

The Prince and the Archer

King Tiger
Beyond the Rhine
Korea
Korean Winter

Tales from the Sword II
(Short stories from the Modern period)

Books marked thus *, are also available in the audio format. For more information on all of the books then please visit the author's website at www.griffhosker.com where there is a link to contact him or visit his Facebook page: Griff Hosker at Sword Books or follow him on Twitter: @HoskerGriff or Sword (@swordbooksltd)
If you wish to be on the mailing list then contact the author through his website.: Griff Hosker at Sword Books

Printed in Great Britain
by Amazon